COLLATERAL
DAMAGE

Books by Lynette Eason

WOMEN OF JUSTICE

Too Close to Home
Don't Look Back
A Killer Among Us

DEADLY REUNIONS

When the Smoke Clears
When a Heart Stops
When a Secret Kills

HIDDEN IDENTITY

No One to Trust
Nowhere to Turn
Nothing to Lose

ELITE GUARDIANS

Always Watching
Without Warning
Moving Target
Chasing Secrets

BLUE JUSTICE

Oath of Honor
Called to Protect
Code of Valor
Vow of Justice

○ ○ ○

Protecting Tanner Hollow

DANGER NEVER SLEEPS

Collateral Damage

DANGER NEVER SLEEPS ①

COLLATERAL DAMAGE

LYNETTE EASON

Revell

a division of Baker Publishing Group
Grand Rapids, Michigan

Published by Revell
a division of Baker Publishing Group
PO Box 6287, Grand Rapids, MI 49516-6287
www.revellbooks.com

Printed in the United States of America

Library of Congress Cataloging-in-Publication Data
Names: Eason, Lynette, author.
Title: Collateral damage / Lynette Eason.
Description: Grand Rapids, MI : Revell, [2019] | Series: Danger never sleeps ; 1
Identifiers: LCCN 2019014909 | ISBN 9780800729349 (pbk.)
Subjects: | GSAFD: Mystery fiction.
Classification: LCC PS3605.A79 C65 2019 | DDC 813/.6—dc23
LC record available at https://lccn.loc.gov/2019014909

ISBN 978-0-8007-3777-1 (casebound)

20   21   22   23   24   25   26   7   6   5   4   3   2   1

collateral damage—Unintentional or incidental injury or damage to persons or objects that would not be lawful military targets in the circumstances ruling at the time.

—DOD definition

○ ○ ○

Even youths grow tired and weary, and young men stumble and fall; but those who hope in the LORD will renew their strength. They will soar on wings like eagles; they will run and not grow weary, they will walk and not be faint.

Isaiah 40:30–31

CHAPTER

ONE

FORWARD OPERATING BASE (FOB) CAMP CHARLIE
AFGHANISTAN
SEPTEMBER

Sergeant First Class Asher James stared at Captain Phillip Newell, sure that he'd heard wrong. "Sir? Isaiah Michaels? He's in sick hall." He let his gaze jump back and forth between his superiors. Asher was surprised to see the task force commander there, along with Mario Ricci and his unit leader, Captain Gomez. Ricci nodded a greeting and went back to his laptop.

"Michaels never showed up to sick hall. One of our interpreters radioed in—he spotted Michaels at The Bistro restaurant in Kabul. You've got your orders, Sergeant James," Captain Newell said. "Bring him in."

Asher hesitated only a fraction of a second before nodding. "Sir, what's he being accused of exactly?"

"Being a traitor and selling information to the jihadists."

Stunned, Asher swallowed his shout of disbelief. "Sir, you know as well as I do that's not true." He was proud of the even tone he managed to keep.

"Not my call. And James?" Newell said. "You're leading this one."

"You're not coming?"

His captain hesitated. "No, I'm needed here. Waiting on a call from home I don't want to miss."

"Forget an anniversary again?" Asher wanted to recall the words as soon as they left his lips. "Sir?" Newell was one of the most private men he'd ever met. All he knew was the man's daughter had been very sick about six months ago, but it wasn't his place to ask.

"No." Newell's eyes met his. "I didn't."

"Good to hear, sir. I'll just mind my own business now."

The man's stance softened a fraction. "You're a good man, James, I'm just a short-tempered son of a gun these days. Getting word about Michaels has made it worse." He glanced at the lieutenant colonel and Captain Gomez. "But we've been presented with proof. I've seen it with my own eyes, because if I hadn't, I'd be reacting just like you are. But this . . . I don't even know where to start explaining, so I'm going to have to let Michaels do that." He waved a hand toward the door. "Now go get him." He turned to Gomez. "I'll be ready for the debrief in five minutes."

Gomez nodded. He looked at Ricci. "Get everyone together in the CMOC. I'll be there shortly."

The Civil Military Operations Center. Why they didn't just call it a conference room was beyond Asher.

"Yes, sir." Ricci stood and grabbed his phone, dust flying from the sleeve of his uniform. With a growl, Ricci swatted at his sleeve, sending another dust plume to the floor.

Whenever Asher decided he was done serving, the one thing he wouldn't miss was the dust. And the death. And the occasional order—like this one—that made him want to revolt.

With a final nod to the men, Asher exited the building. Isaiah Michaels? No way. He didn't believe it for a second. The man was as squared away as they came.

But he'd obey the orders whether he liked them or not. He walked across the dusty yard to the twenty-two-ton MRAP and settled into the vehicle commander's seat with a grimace. The monster machine's air conditioner hadn't yet had a chance to penetrate the suffocating interior heat. The other MRAP, with vehicle commander Sergeant B. J. King, the squad's fire team leader, would also participate in this mission.

Private Jasper Owens sat in the driver's seat next, frowning at Asher. "What's wrong, Sergeant?"

"You got the target, sir?" The shouted question came from Staff Sergeant Mark Dobbs before Asher could answer Owens. Dobbs was their squad medic and was seated in the far back, finishing off an apple cinnamon ranger bar from his MRE.

"I got it," Asher said, turning to face the guys in the back. They sat along the walls of the vehicle, facing each other with their eyes on him while he struggled to push the words past his lips.

The guys exchanged glances. "You going to fill us in?" Owens asked.

Asher shook his head and lifted the radio to his mouth. "King, this is James. How copy? Over."

"James, this is King. That's a good copy. Just waiting for our orders. Over."

"Ash?" This prompt came from Sergeant Mitch Sampson, their gunner and resident artist—also known as Michelangelo—who was seated behind Owens.

"I . . . yeah. It's . . ."

"What, man?" Owens said. "Spit it out." A pause. "Sergeant."

Asher met each one of his unit members' eyes before locking gazes with the engineering sergeant of the team—and Asher's best friend—Gavin Black. Raking a hand over his buzz cut, Asher finally said into the radio so King could hear as well, "It's Michaels. They're saying he's a traitor—selling off information to jihadists—and we're to bring him in for questioning. Over."

Protests erupted in the vehicle and over the radio. Asher let them vent before raising a hand. "I agree, but Captain said there's evidence and he's seen it."

Silence fell. The only noise came from the rumbling engine.

Finally, Dobbs blew out a breath, and Asher narrowed his eyes. "I don't believe it either, but these are the orders."

"Then let's go do what we've got to do," King said. "Over."

"I'm not doing it," Owens said.

The others stayed silent. Owens was the youngest of the group and gave the appearance of being unconcerned about the consequences of disobeying a direct order.

Asher knew differently and lasered him with a hard glare. "I get it, Owens. I feel the same way you do, but let's at least be the ones to find him and ask him what's going on." Owens finally nodded and Asher studied the outraged men. "Because if we don't do it, someone else will."

Heads bobbed in agreement. Owens set his jaw and cranked the engine, then lifted his radio. "King, this is Owens. You take the lead. We'll be right behind you. Over."

"That's a good copy, Owens. Stepping off in two mikes." King acknowledged the plan, and two minutes later the MRAP in front of them started to move.

Fifteen minutes later, the dust beat against the ballistic glass windows as they rolled along at five miles per hour in the Baraki Barak District in Logar Province, Afghanistan. Asher gripped his Colt M4 rifle. The MP4 at his feet would be for close-quarter fighting and the Beretta pistol for even closer. He hoped he wouldn't have to use any of them. His nerves twitched as he strained to see through the plumed cloud ahead of him.

Owens drove with tense fingers wrapped around the wheel. They rode slowly through the wide-open expanse of land that had become known as a death trap, thanks to the improvised explosive devices that were often planted along the route. Asher would have recommended taking a different way; however, this was the fastest course into Kabul and they could speed up shortly.

"Hey, what's that?" Sampson shouted over the engine noise and pointed. "You see that? A vehicle just went behind that hill. White SUV."

Asher squinted, trying to see what his buddy had managed to spot out the side window through the dust cloud. "Hill? What hill?"

The tension in the vehicle grew to mammoth proportions, and while the air conditioner had finally cooled the interior, sweat started to flow again.

"King, this is James. Did you or your unit notice a civilian vehicle? White SUV. Over."

"Negative. Over."

"I don't see anything." Asher looked back at his friend. "You sure you saw something?"

Sampson rubbed his eyes, then shook his head. "Yeah, but I don't see anything now. I'm sorry, I've been at this too long. It's not good for my blood pressure. Time for me to get out of this business and go home."

"I know what you mean."

The MRAP in front of them began moving once again and Owens followed. Asher rotated his head, trying to loosen his locked muscles. The thought of home beckoned, and for the first time in a long while, he allowed himself to envision it, allowed the longing to see his family to sweep through. Even though they didn't understand him, they loved him—except maybe his brother. Definitely no love lost there, but Asher wished things were different.

The explosion came out of nowhere, hitting the MRAP in front of them, lifting it into the air and shoving it over on its side, then the top. Owens hit the brakes as the wave from the blast sent them rolling backward. They rocked from side to side, and for a moment, Asher thought they'd roll over as well, but they finally came to a shuddering halt right side up.

"King!" Asher shouted into the radio. "Give me a report! Over!"

Silence. Owens slid out of the driver's seat to the floor.

Asher radioed a 9-Line Medevac request for help, while Sampson pushed Owens aside. "What are you doing, man? Get your weapon." Sampson scrambled for the passage that would take him to the top of the vehicle where he could man the mounted assault rifle.

"They're coming from everywhere!" Sampson's warning came just as Asher caught sight of the Taliban fighters spilling in behind them. "They've got some kind of grenade launcher," Sampson yelled. "Sir, if that thing hits us, we're done for!"

"Air cover is on the way. Three mikes out!" Asher yelled. They didn't have three seconds, much less three minutes, before they'd be hit.

"Then start shooting!" Sampson said. "Aim for the third vehicle in that row coming toward us. See it?"

Asher saw it. Sampson opened fire. The line scattered, but the third vehicle continued to bear down on them. The weapon mounted on the bars of the Jeep fired.

"Get out! Get out!"

Asher and his men rolled from the vehicle and found cover behind a hill as the first grenade hit. Then the second and a third. They all continued to return fire, but there was nothing from the occupants of the MRAP in front of them. Asher pushed down the sick knowledge that every man was dead.

And they were next.

Sampson let loose another volley of bullets while Asher and the others fired back. Bullets pelted all around him and overhead.

"Where are those birds?" Sampson cried. His voice carried over the radio, along with the spat of the 240 he fired.

"One mike out!"

"They're getting ready to hit us again with that RPG!" Sampson continued to man the assault weapon while Asher joined him in trying to take out the Jeep holding the weapon that would sign their death warrants.

The man behind the rocket launcher fell, hit the dirt road, and didn't move.

For the next sixty seconds, they defended their position as the enemy pushed closer.

Then the sound of the helicopters roaring overhead penetrated the chaos. Sampson fired off another spate of bullets and the choppers joined in. At the launch of the first rocket dropping from the sky, the attackers turned and ran. The birds followed and would make sure they didn't return.

Asher bolted to his feet and ran to the smoldering MRAP thirty yards away.

He could hear his captain's voice over his radio checking in. The others were right behind him, heading to find their buddies. Asher stopped to answer his captain as sweat dripped down his face, dust caked the inside of his nose and lungs, and his heart pounded with grief for the lives he knew were lost. "Captain Newell, this is James. It was an ambush, sir," he said, doing his best to keep the tears out of his words. "They knew we were coming. They hit King's MRAP. He's dead. They're all dead. Over." He gritted his teeth and let his gaze sweep the area. He could grieve later.

Curses blistered the airwaves and Asher listened as the man ranted. "All right," the captain finally said, "I've got this covered. Abort the mission and get back here."

"They knew we were coming, sir. Someone told them. And if Michaels had anything to do with it, I want to find him." But Michaels couldn't have known anything about it. Their friend was in trouble. "We're going to get him, sir. Over."

The captain didn't protest. None of the others did either. They were with him.

Asher closed his eyes, blanked everything from his mind except

the orders he and the others would follow before they could process what had just happened. "We're on our way."

Sampson stood next to him. "Michaels?"

"Michaels."

"I'm getting a couple of souvenirs from that IED, then I'll be
there."

Asher frowned. His friend's affinity for collecting pieces of any
bomb that didn't kill him was weird, but whatever. He had more
pressing matters to worry about. Like bringing in a buddy accused
of treason.

○ ○ ○

Military Psychiatrist Captain Brooke Adams was ready to go
home in spite of the fact that she'd come to appreciate the Afghan
people, their country, and their determination to survive—and
thrive. She'd been in Kabul for the past six months, doing her best
to help the men and women in the United States Army serving on
the front lines, and she was tired.

No . . . *drained.*

No, that wasn't it either.

She was . . . empty.

Done.

And tired of having a male escort every time she went off base.
Three more weeks and she could go home. She almost felt guilty
about the way she just couldn't seem to adapt; then again, she was
aware of her limitations and she'd reached them. It was better to
leave before . . . well, just *before.*

But first, she'd promised to meet her friends. The ladies she
now considered family in this war-torn land. Sarah Denning and
Heather Fontaine would already be at the café waiting for her,
along with Kat Patterson, the combat photographer they'd come
to love and appreciate. Rarely did any of them venture away from
the base—other than Kat—but things had been quiet, and they

all needed something other than military rations and Kentucky Fried Chicken. Okay, the food wasn't that bad, but The Bistro fare was amazing. The café, set on one of the busiest streets in Kabul, offered a variety of French-Afghan deliciousness that had her mouth watering just thinking about it.

Brooke pulled her hijab a little tighter at the neck and stepped through the door. Her escort headed to the men's side of the restaurant where he'd wait until she was finished.

"Brooke." Sarah waved. "Over here."

The three ladies sat toward the back, away from the windows in the section reserved for women only. On the positive side, things were already changing for the better for this country. She just hoped that would continue.

The red walls boasted lovely paintings of desert landscapes— probably done by a family member of the owner. The wood-burning stove in the middle of the room definitely wouldn't be necessary today. Brooke ducked between the stove and the nearest table to wind her way to the corner table.

She dropped into the one empty chair and let her breath out slowly. "Whoo."

"Everything okay?" Kat asked.

"Sure."

"Liar," Heather said.

Brooke hesitated. "Okay, so no," she finally said, helping herself to one of the cinnamon rolls from the bread basket someone had so thoughtfully placed at her seat. "Everything's not okay." She waved the roll. "But this helps."

Heather raised a brow. She'd changed from her surgical scrubs and wore a simple pair of khaki pants and a blue long-sleeved collared knit shirt. The hijab wrapped around her head held matching colors and brought out her eyes. Which probably wasn't a good thing in this area.

"Wanna share?" Heather asked. Her eyes held compassion—

and a keen intelligence that a lot of people missed when they focused on the woman's outward beauty. Built like a runway model, Heather had chosen medicine over the modeling career that had funded her first two years of medical school.

The Army had paid for the rest of it, and now Heather devoted herself to helping put the wounded back together. She took care of the physical brokenness, and Brooke tried to help with the mental. Being a military psychiatrist wasn't for the weak or the easily wearied. "It was a hard morning. I had to recommend a soldier be sent home for suicidal reasons." And just like that, she'd managed to suck any levity right out of the atmosphere. "Sorry. Forget I said that. Let's not talk shop." She lifted her glass of water. "So, who's excited about going home? What's the first thing you plan to do when you get there?"

"I'm going to walk down the street and not worry about getting blown up," Sarah said.

Kat rolled her eyes. "I'm from the worst part of Chicago. I can't walk down the street without worrying about getting shot or something. So"—she drew in a deep breath—"I'm going to find different streets to walk down, I think."

"Come walk down my street," Brooke said with a grin. "I just bought a house."

"What?" Kat gaped. "When?"

"Yesterday. Well, the offer was accepted, and all that's left is to do the paperwork. My lawyer has been granted power of attorney and is taking care of all of that for me."

After a round of congratulations and cheers, Sarah grimaced. "But that's going to have to wait for me."

Kat frowned. "What do you mean?"

"I'm here for at least another year."

"What!" Brooke and Kat said together.

Sarah shrugged. "I don't have anything I need to rush home to and I love my job. Besides"—she glanced around the restaurant and lowered her voice—"I'm working on something and I'm not going to have it wrapped up by the time I'd have to leave. So . . . I requested to stay in for a while longer."

"What are you working on?" Brooke asked.

"Something big. Something that's going to make a lot of people unhappy—and probably put some people in prison." She paused. "In prison and unhappy. Kind of goes together, doesn't it?"

Brooke leaned in. "Sarah, what are you doing?"

"Well, originally, I was doing whatever was necessary to get a spot with a major newspaper that would lead me to Morning Star Orphanage, where I was going to do a story on some of the kids there. Instead, I wound up in a part-time volunteer position that has led to—" She stopped and met each friend's gaze. "Never mind. Suffice it to say that this is serious and it's going to blow up a few careers if my source is being truthful with me. And I think she is."

"What source?" Kat asked. Her eyes narrowed. "What's going on at the orphanage?"

Sarah shook her head. "So far, my evidence is circumstantial. But I know—" She held up a hand. "Never mind. My turn to change the subject." A pause while everyone stared silently. "But if something happens to me, it's probably because of this story."

"What?" Heather narrowed her eyes. "I thought you were coming to the hospital to see me. Are you saying you've been coming for other reasons?"

Brooke snorted. "Of course she is." Sarah was always investigating. She was a good reporter and didn't generally overreact to things. The intensity of her words and facial expressions made Brooke wonder if this time she might be getting in over her head. "Your life's not worth a story, Sarah," she said.

"Normally, I'd agree with you, but this . . ." Sarah looked away, blinking back tears. "Just pray I'm wrong."

Kat and Heather continued to press Sarah for details, but Brooke tuned them out, having a hard time focusing on her friends' words.

Not that she didn't care, but her heart was heavy, her mind on the fact that she'd ruined a man's career this morning. That he was from her hometown of Greenville, South Carolina, just made him all the more special—and her responsibility all the more heartbreaking.

Heather's hand clasped hers under the table and she looked up to find the three ladies staring at her. "Sorry, I did it again, didn't I?" She stood. "I'm afraid I'm not going to be very good company today. I think I'll take off." Amidst the protests of her friends, she turned to go.

The little bell over the door jangled as it opened to admit two soldiers dressed in Army Combat Uniforms. Out of the corner of her eye, she saw Isaiah Michaels at the bar, turning toward the newcomers. His eyes caught hers and he nodded as his friends settled into the two seats next to him. They both glanced back at her but didn't acknowledge her. The fact that Isaiah did was more than if he'd shouted her name.

Brooke returned the slight nod and sat back down. "Or maybe I'll order my food and enjoy myself."

"That's the spirit," Kat said. She moved her ever-present camera to the side of her plate and held up her water. "A toast. To home."

"To home!"

"And to Brooke's new place. May we eventually spend many a hot summer's day gathered around her pool."

Brooke gaped. "I didn't say anything about a pool."

Heather laughed. "Are you kidding? I'm surprised you're not in the Navy the way you can't live without water. You have a pool, don't you?"

"Well . . . yes, but still . . ."

The others cracked up, and Brooke couldn't help the smile that curved her lips, even as she shot another glance at Michaels sitting with his friends at the bar. He caught her gaze, held it for a brief second, then looked away. He wanted to talk. She almost snorted, her ire rising. Well, he could wait on her this time.

18

"What's he doing here?" Sarah asked.

"Who?"

"Isaiah Michaels."

"You know him?" Brooke asked.

"Mm. Yes. Met him on the base a couple times, then ran into him at the hospital when I was there covering something for a story, then again at the orphanage."

"What was he doing at the hospital and the orphanage?"

"That's not important." Sarah's eyes bounced between Michaels and Brooke. "How do you know him?"

"That's not important," she mimicked and ignored the eye roll from Sarah.

"He keeps looking this way," Sarah said. "At you. Like he's waiting on you or trying to get your attention."

"Well, he can keep waiting on me." He was a client and he'd called to schedule an appointment, which had shocked her socks off. She'd always been the one to schedule the appointments and then had to practically drag him to them—or threaten to report his absence. Then he'd failed to show up. Which hadn't shocked her nearly as much.

They ordered their food and, for the next forty-five minutes, talked and caught up before duty called Heather and Sarah away, leaving Brooke alone at the table with Kat. "You really think Heather will decide to leave the Army and go work in a hospital?" Kat asked.

Brooke lifted her hands, palms up. "Sounded like she wants to."

"She'll be bored."

"She's a trauma surgeon. I doubt *bored* is in her vocabulary," Brooke said with a wry smile.

"Seriously, I'm a combat photographer. You think I could just go home and start taking headshots?"

"It'd be a lot safer."

"Brooooke . . ."

"I know. What am I thinking? You never have been one to play it safe. I have a theory about that, you know."

"Hmm, so, who's the guy?" Kat asked.

"Which one?" Brooke had no trouble following her friend's deliberate change of topic.

Kat smirked. "The one you locked eyes and exchanged nods with. The one who's still sitting over there with his friends pretending he's not waiting on you. I mean, I know his name, thanks to Sarah, but anything else I need to know?"

"Nothing much gets by you, does it?"

"Not if I want to stay alive."

"I can't say who he is," Brooke said.

"Ah. That means he's a client."

Brooke smiled and took a sip of the hot tea the server had brought.

"And by that look he gave you when he came in, he has something he wants to talk to you about." She sighed. "Which means, I need to say goodbye."

"I don't know what he wants," Brooke said, her voice low. "I have a lot of clients who are ordered to see me and sit there in silence for an hour. Not saying he's one of those, but I do have a lot."

"I know."

"So you know what I do?"

Kat raised a brow.

"I talk," Brooke said. "And I talk some more. The whole time. About PTSD and coping strategies. I talk about faith and God, saying things like, 'I don't know if you even believe in God at this point, but if you do . . .' and so on." She swallowed. "I don't know if it makes a difference or not and I'm tired of trying. Tired of being treated like I'm an intruder who can't understand what they're going through—much less isn't able to help." She shook her head. "Nope. It's time for me to leave." She stood.

"Aren't you going to see what he wants?"

"If he wanted to talk, he should have shown up two hours ago for his appointment." Brooke heard the brittle hostility in her tone and took a deep breath. "And now I'm breaking the rules in even saying that."

Kat stood, too, and placed money on the table. "You're doing good, Brooke. I know you can't see it, but you are."

Brooke let her gaze linger on the soldier who refused to look her way but was clearly waiting on her, as noticed by Kat. She closed her eyes and let the words wash over her. "Thank you," she whispered.

"No problem. I'm going to scram. Let me get out the door before you leave so he won't think we're together anymore. Then your escort will follow you, the guy who wants to meet with you will follow him, and his friends will . . ." At Brooke's scowl, Kat gave her a sheepish smile. "Well, you get the idea."

A single man and single woman didn't meet together in a public place. It would be fine to walk and talk with her within a group, and his friends would make sure that's what it looked like.

"I think I know how it works at this point," Brooke said.

Kat grabbed her camera and looped it around her neck. "See ya."

"Stay safe, friend."

"Always. You too."

"Always."

Kat left and Brooke waited a few seconds before following in her friend's footsteps. Just as Kat predicted, the moment she passed the man at the bar, he turned and followed her. And his friends did the same.

The window next to the section where she'd been seated exploded and she went to her knees. A hard body hit hers, covering her as debris rained down.

She managed to gasp in one breath and then another explosion rocked the building.

TWO

The MRAP shuddered from the blast wave of the second explosion. "Back up! Back it up!"

Asher grabbed his rifle while Owens slammed on the brakes and reversed the big machine. Asher looked out the window, his field of vision consisting of one big wall of dust.

"That came from The Bistro," Owens said.

Dobbs wore his medic bag over his body armor. The gas mask was strapped to his thigh. Asher pushed the door open and climbed out, his weapon held ready, mask over his face. Dobbs was right behind him, followed by Owens and Sampson.

People and smoke streamed from the restaurant. Dobbs stopped long enough to pull on his mask before he headed into the smoking, burning building. Sirens in the distance signaled emergency crews would be here soon. Even in Afghanistan, they responded pretty fast. Asher barked orders while he grabbed another extinguisher.

Following the path Dobbs had blazed, Asher continued shooting the flames with the extinguisher, looking for any victims—and his target. While all he heard was the roar of the blaze farther in, the rest of his squad would be bringing up the rear. He stopped to help an elderly man stand. "That way!" Asher said the words in Dari and again in Pashto. The man held a hand to his bleeding head and Asher wished he could help him further, but once the man was out on the street, help would be steps away. Flames spurted from the back of the restaurant, but while the smoke was thick, he could still see. That wouldn't last long. "Talk to me, Dobbs! Where is he? Where's Michaels?"

"Straight back from the front door and to the left! I think I see him. I'm trying to get to him. He's on the floor." Dobbs's voice came through the radio and Asher hurried to follow the directions, but he was stumbling blind—and praying another explosion wasn't just waiting to happen.

o o o

Brooke coughed, gagged. Pain sizzled across her shoulders and back. Smoke and fire billowed through the restaurant.

Flames leapt from her sleeve.

Panic flaring, she scrambled out from under the heavy weight of the body that had slammed into her and threw herself backward. She rolled, beating her body and arms against the tiled floor.

Screams from wounded patrons and workers registered. She wanted to add her own to the chaos, but she needed to breathe. Only all the oxygen had been sucked from the area.

Brooke wrapped the edge of the hijab around her mouth and nose, ignoring the razor-sharp pain racing through her arms, her back, her shoulders.

A hard hand clasped hers. She looked down and gasped. Specialist Isaiah Michaels lay next to her, and with a sob, she realized he'd been the one to throw himself over her, covering her, protecting her. "Hold on, Michaels, hold on."

A good portion of the left side of his face was gone, from the cheek to his hairline. Her stomach lurched, but he was trying to tell her something. She scuttled closer, clutching his trembling fingers. "Shh . . . don't try to talk," she croaked. "I'll get you some help. I'm so sorry. So sorry." It was her fault he was here. Guilt hammered her.

His hand squeezed hers and she realized he wanted her even closer. And he was trying to get her to take something. She squinted. A bracelet? Automatically, she wrapped her fingers around it. "Keep . . . it . . . safe . . . ," he rasped.

"Who does it belong to? Who do you want me to give it to?"

"Miranda . . . tell Miranda . . . love her . . . didn't know."

He wasn't making any sense. "You want me to give the bracelet to Miranda?"

"Brooke! Brooke! Where are you?"

Kat? "Back here!" A coughing spasm seized her and stars danced in front of her vision.

And still the man wouldn't loosen his grip. "I didn't know . . . I didn't know what they were doing . . . Tell her I didn't know."

He had to be delirious with pain—or in such shock he wasn't feeling it. The fact that he was even conscious was nothing short of miraculous. "Know what? What didn't you know, Michaels?" Miranda, his wife. He'd mentioned her once during their final session, saying how he had to talk to her, mumbling about needing her forgiveness and saying he didn't know.

Now he whispered something else. She leaned farther in, trying to ignore the pain, smoke, and blackness fighting to claim her consciousness. A small pocket of air allowed her to pull in a breath before the smoke rolled back over her.

Still holding his hand and the bracelet, she put her ear to his lips.

". . . traitor," he whispered. "Tell . . . Miranda . . ."

"What?"

"Not. A. Traitor," he wheezed. "Don't . . . let them . . . say . . . I am." He went still, his eyes fixed on a spot behind her left shoulder.

"No," she cried, coughed, gagged, refusing to let him go. "No, don't you die on me! Not you too! I'm sorry!" She shoved the bracelet into her pocket, then wrapped her arms around his shoulders and buried her face in his chest.

Then hands were pulling her away. She fought to bring him with her, but the blackness pressed in. She turned to see storm-cloud gray eyes behind a mask.

"Save him. Please save him," she whispered with no hope of the man hearing her as the flames crept closer.

This time she couldn't fight the blackness that stole her vision and then her breath.

THREE

FOUR MONTHS LATER
JANUARY
GREENVILLE, SC

FBI Special Agent Caden Denning checked his watch just as SLED Agent Kyle Deveraux turned off the main street and into the wide-open expanse of field. The man steered the black Chevy Tahoe to the edge of the yellow crime scene tape and stopped. He climbed out, then pulled on a pair of blue gloves and shoe coverings.

Caden and his partner, Zane Pierce, were already dressed in their crime scene gear, ready to walk Deveraux through the scene as soon as he joined them and Sheriff Mickey Daniels, who stood to Caden's left.

The South Carolina Law Enforcement Division, FBI, and local authorities would band together to figure out how the mass grave site came to be. This was the sheriff's jurisdiction. Caden and Zane were only there because Mickey had asked them to be.

"I think we've got a serial killer on our hands. I'm not exactly out of my depth here, Cade," Mickey had said on the phone earlier that morning, "but I think I'd like another set of eyes on this. We're probably going to need your resources too."

Now that he was here, Caden could see why.

It didn't take Deveraux long to duck under the tape, sign the crime scene log, and walk over to them. "Thanks for calling and letting us in on this," he said.

"No problem," Caden said. "Mickey wants every available resource on this, and I don't blame him. Several coroners and medical examiners got here about an hour ago."

Deveraux's gaze roamed the open expanse of land. Caden did the same, seeing the scene through the newcomer's eyes. Twelve possible graves. Maybe more, maybe less. It was hard to tell at the moment.

"A hiker found this?" Deveraux asked.

"Not the entire thing, but yeah. His dog started digging and found the first body. Our hiker is an MD and realized what his dog had discovered pretty quickly and called it in. We brought in cadaver dogs to see if it was the only one."

"Obviously it wasn't. How many?"

"He alerted to twelve possible. Most of them are shallow, just deep enough to cover a body. Others are deeper and undisturbed." Caden blew out a breath. "The first was definitely an infant. And we know that because the hiker is a pediatrician and knows what a kid's bone looks like. Said it was a femur belonging to an infant around six to seven months old."

Deveraux winced. "Any signs as to cause of death for the ones you can see?"

"No, not yet," Caden said. "We've got another ME on the way and a forensic anthropologist coming from the hospital. One of the bodies is in advanced decomp, one was just a skeleton, suggesting they were buried at different times. It's going to take a while to get them all dug up and transported."

"At first, I wanted to say it was a serial killer," Mickey said, his voice flat, jaw tight. "But now I'm backing off of that idea."

"Why's that?" Zane asked.

"Just talked to that ME. He said the victims vary in age."

27

"Okay," Caden said, "that does kind of change things, doesn't it? Serial killers usually go after similar victims. A variety of ages would suggest something else."

Mickey rubbed his chin. "So, could this be some kind of illness that swept through a family or something? Some kind of cult thing?"

"We'll have to examine both possibilities to rule out—or confirm." Caden scanned the scene once more. "Whatever the case, some of the graves look like they've been here for a while. Others look fairly recent—which matches with the different stages of decomp in the victims I saw."

"I know it's all speculation," Deveraux said, "but still . . . right now it looks like whoever killed these people has been killing for a while and we've just now discovered it."

"Which means we need to stop this killer before he—or she— claims the next victim," Caden said.

Because there *would* be another.

o o o

Brooke dropped the newspaper onto her kitchen table and tried to blink away the picture—and her sense of betrayal—just like she'd done every day for the past five days. "How could you, Kat?"

The photos brought it all back. The explosions, the flames, the fear, the pain. Isaiah dying in her arms.

If only she'd left the café when Isaiah had wanted to talk to her. Instead, because she'd been in a snit and letting her emotions control her, he'd died.

Her fault. The ever-present sobs rose, and it took everything in her to push them back down to focus on the photos.

Kat had taken them that day at the café right after the second explosion. Snapped milliseconds apart, they were a progression of Brooke's last few moments with the man as she knelt at his side, smoke and flames billowing behind her, around her. But there had been the small pocket of air near the floor and she'd found it as Isaiah whispered his last words and breathed his final breath.

"*Not a traitor. Don't let them say I am.*"

His words echoed. Blood flowed freely from the left side of his face. Smoke choked her. She covered her face with her hands, but the flames grew hotter, the screams echoed louder.

Brooke jumped up from the table and covered her ears. Then punched the air. "Stop. It's not real. It's just a memory. Brooke, *stop now*!" Jab, jab, duck, jab.

At the sound of her voice and the physical movement, the worst faded. Except the pictures on the table. Calling herself a glutton for punishment, she looked at them once again. One by one. In the first, Brooke had just dropped to her knees beside him. The second showed Isaiah gripping her hand with the bracelet dangling from his fingers. The third showed her weeping even as she absently shoved the bracelet in her pocket. Kat had caught the moment just as a tear dropped from her chin, to be held in midair for all eternity, along with Brooke's agony.

And the last one. The picture that cut a swath of grief through her heart. Isaiah's blank eyes stared upward while Brooke's face was buried against his chest. In spite of the smoky haze, Kat had managed to capture each moment in clear detail before someone had yanked her out of the building. That was all Brooke remembered before waking in the hospital in Germany, where she learned that Asher James had carried her out and Gavin Black had scooped up Isaiah.

Kat had shown her the last photo two months ago, just before Brooke had been released from the burn unit in Atlanta, Georgia. "You made a difference, Brooke, don't ever think you didn't. You were there and he didn't die alone because of that."

Brooke swiped tears and waved a hand. "Get it away from me. I never want to see it again."

Kat hesitated. "My editor wants to run it. The whole series. He thinks this could be Pulitzer material."

"No." Brooke stared at her friend, horrified. "No!"

Kat swallowed and nodded. "Okay. I understand. It's too soon, too raw."

And she'd promised not to use any of them. And yet there they were. Front-page news. So why did Brooke keep torturing herself by looking at them every morning? It was like the proverbial train wreck. She simply couldn't look away. She fingered the bracelet in her pocket. Isaiah had entrusted it to her that day and she'd been lax in carrying through with a dead man's last wish. Why? Because she was a coward. Facing Isaiah's wife was almost more than she could bear. Avoidance. Excuses. Maybe even a little denial had kept her from going to see Miranda Michaels. And then there was that deep-seated need to have that piece of jewelry with her wherever she went.

It had been four months since that day in Kabul. Months that had brought healing and change—and nightmares she doubted she'd ever be rid of. And guilt. Oh, the guilt.

"Suck it up, Brooke Baby," she muttered, mimicking her father. "Life goes on. Wallowing in self-pity never changed the course of life. Do what you've got to do and do it well. No complaining, no whining, no crying." She pulled out the bracelet and looked at it before stuffing it back into her coat pocket. "Do what you're supposed to do," she whispered. She swiped the tears from her cheeks. As much as she hated the whole stiff-upper-lip mentality, she had to admit it was getting her through the days—and allowing her to survive the nights.

For now.

But Kat . . . how could she?

Brooke's phone rang, and just like she'd done every time Kat had called for the past five days, she pressed the little red End button. Her punching bag in the basement called, but it was time to go to work. Asher James was coming to see her today. He'd actually called and made an appointment.

The thought of seeing him almost had her calling in sick. She'd taken a counseling position, joining a friend in private practice. One that didn't see veterans so she didn't have to talk about war and dying. She glanced at his name again. Still there. How was it she'd managed to avoid just about anything that would remind her of Afghanistan for the past four months—other than her healing injuries—and in one week, all of her progress had come to a screeching halt?

All because of a few photos and Asher James. He shouldn't be on her appointment book. But he was.

She stood. "Fine. I'll talk to you, Asher, then you can be on your way so I can get back to forgetting." She grabbed her purse, laptop case, and other work essentials and walked to the door. She comforted herself with the fact that her name hadn't been mentioned in the article and no one would recognize the polished professional as the same bloody, smoky, agonized woman in the picture.

Her phone rang again.

She stopped and snagged it from her blazer pocket. Kat. Again. She needed to set up a ringtone for Kat so she didn't have to waste her time looking at the screen.

Once more disconnecting the call, she continued out the door, down the porch steps, and climbed into her ten-year-old Jeep Wrangler.

A helicopter whirled above her and she ducked before remembering she didn't have to do that anymore.

Sweat broke across her forehead and she sucked in a quick breath. "Stop." Twisting the key in the ignition, Brooke started the Jeep and backed out of her drive.

And once again the phone rang. "Oh, for the love of . . ." She braked at the stop sign and grabbed the phone, barely catching herself in time before hanging up. She pressed the green button and the phone connected to her car's Bluetooth system. "Hi, Heather."

"Hey, Kat said you won't speak to her."

"I'm fine, thanks, how are you?"

"Sorry, I'm running ragged already this morning. I'm heading to surgery and just wanted to call and say talk to Kat. She wants to apologize for those pictures, and she's been trying to get you since they came out."

"I don't care." The words left her lips, but in truth, she did care. Very much. "I can't believe she did that."

"She didn't know about it."

She snorted. "Right."

Silence. "This isn't like you, Brooke. You always listen to the other person, weigh the facts, and make your decisions logically. You're letting your emotions rule you."

Like they did the day Isaiah died. "Says the surgeon who cries over every lost patient."

More silence.

"Sorry," Brooke muttered, ashamed of herself, "that was low, but come on, Heather, do you blame me?"

"Yes, because this is Kat."

Brooke fought another sudden surge of tears. Man, she was a mess. "I . . . know. I'm sorry. I'm just—"

"This is not Kat's doing. Her editor went behind her back and published them. She was livid. She said she left you several voice messages explaining what happened but figured you were too mad to listen to them."

"Oh man," Brooke breathed. "She's right." She drove on autopilot, thinking how it was a blessing and a curse to have friends who knew her so well. She would not let her anger win and separate her from someone who meant so much to her. Not again. "She really didn't know?"

"She really didn't. Talk to her."

"Okay."

A pause. "At least he didn't print your name."

"At least."

"Gotta go," Heather said. "Talk to her, my friend."

"I will, I will." And she would. After she met with her first client of the day.

CHAPTER

FOUR

Asher found a parking spot outside the medical building and shut off the engine. He closed his eyes and leaned back against the headrest, doing his best to resist the temptation to flee.

But he needed help, and after seeing the picture in the newspaper of Brooke Adams hovering over the body of his buddy, Isaiah Michaels, he figured she was the one psychiatrist who might actually understand what he was going through.

Maybe.

Before he could change his mind, he climbed out of the vehicle and slammed the door with a little more force than necessary. *Get it together, James.*

The parking lot was almost full even this early in the morning, and he dodged several people as he made his way inside. As he'd been instructed when he called to make the appointment yesterday, he took the first elevator he came to and punched the button for the fifth floor.

When the doors opened, he stepped into a hallway and turned right, following the signs that said HEALING PATHWAYS, INC. to a wooden door. He pressed the handle and entered the lobby.

For a moment he stood still, taking in the details. Comfortable, but not luxurious by any stretch. Magazines sat on the coffee table in front of the tan leather couch. Three more cozy-looking chairs on the other side of the coffee table invited conversation and relaxation—something he doubted happened very often, but the illusion was nice. A water cooler and a Keurig in the corner beckoned. As did the candy bars in a small basket. Interesting. He helped himself to one and munched on it while he waited. Maybe the receptionist was running late. Sharon? Shelly? He couldn't remember.

He'd been so stressed during the conversation when she said, "You're in luck. We've had a cancellation and can get you in tomorrow," that he hadn't caught her name. He thought he'd have more time to prepare himself for the appointment.

Not sure he'd call that luck.

But he was here, so . . .

He glanced at his phone. 8:02. They opened at 8:00. And the door had been unlocked when he entered five minutes ago. Which meant someone had been here early.

Frowning, he approached the desk. The nameplate read SHARON HARDY. Okay, then, Sharon it was. "So, where are you, Sharon?" he murmured.

Asher stepped behind the desk to note a brown purse tucked into the foot space next to the chair. Steam rose from the coffee mug on the coaster beside the keyboard.

So, she was here somewhere and she hadn't been gone too long from the desk. Bathroom? Getting paperwork ready for him to fill out? No, she'd have that at the desk. His appointment was at 8:30, but he'd always been a stickler for being early. This morning, nerves had just about gotten the best of him, so he'd bolted from his home and driven straight to the office.

So he'd wait. And pace.

Four steps into his trek across the width of the lobby, his phone rang. He grabbed it, grateful for the distraction. "Hello?"

"Hi, son."

"Hey, Mum."

"I'm just calling to check on you. When you left yesterday, you seemed . . . well . . . out of sorts."

"Because Nicholas was being a brat?"

She sighed. "Yes, he was, wasn't he?"

Asher stopped his pacing, his sudden halt almost sending him off balance. "What?" She always took Nicholas's side. He was the son who could do no wrong.

"I heard what he said when you two were in the kitchen and he didn't think anyone was listening."

"I saw you there but didn't realize you'd heard what he said. So . . . what? You were spying on us?" He was almost amused at the thought of his prim, proper, upper-crust British, never-do-anything-wrong mother standing outside the kitchen door eavesdropping.

"Asher. Really? Spying? I should think not."

"Of course not. Sorry."

"I simply heard the tension in your voices and stopped because I didn't want to interrupt. And I heard him say that you were an embarrassment to the family."

"I see." He closed his eyes. His parents' wealth and status in their community had been a sore spot for him, and he'd always felt like an outsider. Mostly thanks to Nicholas and his constant pestering.

It was one of the reasons he'd stayed away and didn't taint their gated neighborhood or dinner parties with his presence, but his sister, Lyric, had begged. And she was his weakness. So, in honor of her twenty-first birthday, he'd dressed in his best khakis, long-sleeved white-collared shirt, and blue blazer and shown up.

He'd gotten a few looks—probably thanks to the tattoo on his neck that he couldn't completely hide even with the starchiest shirt in his closet—but for the most part, the guests had been cordial.

Lyric had been thrilled to see him. Her flirtatious friends even more so. He grimaced. They were sweet, but he wasn't the least bit interested in getting to know them, other than as his sister's buddies.

"Asher? Are you there?"

"Yes, Mum, sorry."

Another heavy sigh. "I just want you to know I set him straight. We may not understand why you chose the path you did, but you are *not* an embarrassment to the family."

"Thanks. I'm glad to know that."

"Asher . . ." She paused. "Are you getting help for your PTSD?"

"What PTSD?"

Another long pause. "I see."

He figured she probably did.

One of the guests had popped the cork on a bottle of champagne and he'd had one of his *moments*. It had made things uncomfortable for those around him—including his snotty, stuck-up older brother, who'd been standing beside him and witnessed the episode.

"Get some help, you freak," Nicholas had hissed after cornering Asher in the kitchen. "You have the whole world available to you, thanks to Dad and his position in the community. And you choose to behave like a miscreant. Who cares about those people thousands of miles away? You're an American. Why don't you start acting like it? And while you're at it, get some control. Freaking out over a stupid popped cork? Honestly, you're such an embarrassment."

Asher looked into his brother's eyes. "You have no idea how much control I'm exerting right now." When he turned to leave before doing something he'd regret, his sister and mother were standing in the doorway.

"Shut up, Nicholas, and quit being such a jerk," Lyric said, her tone mild, but it was the sadness in her eyes that had finally driven him to actually consider that he might need help.

The pictures of Brooke had made him think she could give it. And so here he was.

"I've got to go, Mum. I'll talk to you later." Where was the receptionist?

"Do you believe that I meant what I said?" she pressed. "That we don't consider you an embarrassment?"

Did he? "I'm not sure, to be honest, but thank you for saying so. Seriously, I need to go."

"All right. Goodbye then."

"Bye."

He hung up and stuffed his phone in the back pocket of his jeans.

It was time to get this over with before he changed his mind and chickened out. Off the lobby was another door that led to the back. He opened it and stuck his head around the corner.

Restrooms on either side, but no lights on in them, according to the dark cracks at the bottom. Two doors at the end of the hallway. The one on the left was closed, the one on the right, open. Asher walked toward it.

"Hello? Anyone here? Sharon? Ms. Hardy? Brooke?" He stepped just inside the doorway to the office and stopped to take in the destruction. "Whoa."

The overturned file cabinets caught his attention first, followed by the desk drawers on the floor. The bookshelves were empty, their contents scattered across the hardwoods.

A foot sticking out from behind the desk snagged his gaze, and he rushed to find a woman sprawled facedown, a bullet hole in the back of her head.

Careful not to disturb the scene any more than he already had, Asher shut off his initial horror and knelt to press two fingers to the side of her neck.

Nothing. He grabbed his phone and punched in 911.

"911, what's your emergency?"

"I'm at—"

A flicker of movement to his left. He jerked his head toward it just as a small pop sounded and a bullet whizzed past his left ear. Instinct kicked in even as flashes of his last gunfight in Afghanistan surged to the front of his memory. Asher threw himself behind the desk next to the dead woman. Another bullet shattered the small reading lamp in the corner.

"Hey! Shots fired!" Miracle of miracles, Asher still held the phone. He rattled off the address. "Who are you? What do you want?"

Footsteps entered the room and Asher realized this guy wasn't leaving until he'd put a bullet in Asher's brain just like the woman on the floor.

Heart pounding, Asher army-crawled to the edge of the desk and peered around it. Booted feet greeted him. It was act or die. He snaked a hand out, grabbed the calf, and yanked just as the guy pulled the trigger. Fully expecting to feel the burn of the bullet entering his body, Asher tightened his grip on the man's leg.

Curses rang through the office as they fought. Asher clung, but the guy just wouldn't go down.

Then a scream from the open doorway.

The attacker froze for a split second. Long enough to give Asher the moment he needed to throw a punch into the man's knee. The guy shouted, dropped his weapon as he crumpled to the floor. Asher swept a foot out, snagged the gun with his heel, and sent it sliding under the desk. The killer rolled, kicking out and catching Asher in the side of the head.

Stars spun and his vision wavered. His slight hesitation gave the guy enough time to gain his feet and dart toward the woman standing in the doorway, gaping, holding a cup of coffee in one hand and a briefcase in the other.

He briefly registered that it was Brooke Adams. Her moment of paralysis must have lifted, because she moved fast, flinging her coffee at the face of the man.

A harsh scream carried every ounce of his rage as he swiped at his eyes and stumbled through the door. Asher leapt to his feet and snatched his phone from the floor. Without a word to Brooke, he raced past her in time to see the attacker push through the exit door just beyond Sharon's desk.

Stairs.

He slapped the device to his ear. "You still there?"

"Sir? Officers are on the way. What's going on?"

"A woman's been shot. Fatally. I'm in pursuit of the killer." Quickly, he calculated where the stairs would come out if the guy went all the way down. Then decided he wouldn't. He'd get off on one of the floors and find another way out.

"Sir? Sir? Don't chase him. Let him go."

"Not on my watch."

"Are you law enforcement?"

"No. Former special ops." Asher drew to a stop in the stairwell and listened.

Silence.

No footsteps. No doors opening and closing. "But it doesn't matter," he said. "I lost him."

And now he had to go check on the woman he'd come to see—and wished with all his heart he could avoid.

○ ○ ○

Brooke knelt next to Sharon and knew she was dead. The wound in the back of her head offered no hope. Tears gathered and pooled. Who'd done this? And why? She'd thought she left the killing and the dying thousands of miles away in a country she did her best to forget existed.

And now this.

Footsteps hurried toward her and she looked up to see Asher James step back into the room. "He got away, but the police should be here any second."

As though speaking the words had summoned them, two uniformed officers appeared in the doorway behind him. The first one pushed into the room, her hand resting on the weapon strapped to her hip. "What's happening here?"

Brooke met the gaze of the officer who'd spoken. She looked young. Too young to be dealing with life and death on a daily basis. "Sharon's dead." Rough and thick with emotion, her voice didn't even sound like hers. "The guy ran."

"I chased him," Asher said, "but he got away."

The first officer hurried to drop to her knees next to Sharon and placed her fingers on her neck. "No pulse."

Brooke caught a glance of the officer's name tag. Johnson. Officer Johnson radioed her position along with the need for the medical examiner. When she finished rattling off her information, she turned to Brooke and Asher. "Tell us what happened."

All Brooke could do was stare at her friend on the floor. Then nausea hit and sent her stumbling backward, aiming for the door.

"Ma'am? Where are you going?"

"I'm going to be sick." She made it to the trash can in the bathroom. Once she'd lost her breakfast and her first two cups of coffee, she rinsed her mouth and drew in a deep breath, trying to get a handle on her stomach and emotions.

"You okay?" a voice asked from the doorway.

Asher.

She turned. "No."

"I'm sorry you had to see her like that."

Tears flooded her eyes and he moved swiftly to take her in his arms. Sobs threatened to break through and she bit them back. *Crying doesn't change anything, Brooke. Quit being a baby.* She sniffed and swiped away the tears as though she could wipe away the sign of weakness at the same time but couldn't quite bring herself to pull her forehead away from his chest. The comfort she felt just standing there—in basically a complete stranger's arms—and letting him hold her floored her. Finally, she pulled back. "Sorry. I didn't mean to cry."

He lifted a brow. "No need to apologize. I'd think crying might be called for in this situation."

"No. I need to be strong and deal with this. She has a husband and two small children." More tears surfaced and Brooke had to clamp down hard on her lip to hold them back.

"Hi, everything okay in here?"

Brooke looked around Asher to see a man dressed in khaki pants and a blue long-sleeved knit shirt. The badge on his belt said he was law enforcement. She shook her head. "Just trying to get myself together."

"I'm Detective Lonnie Arnold." He motioned to the woman to his left. "This is my partner, Detective Zoey Fisher. We're going to secure the scene while Officer Johnson waits here with you two," he said, pulling on a pair of gloves, followed by blue booties. "We'll be back shortly."

"We can sit in the lobby if you want," Johnson said.

Brooke took a seat on the couch and Asher settled next to her. Officer Johnson took up a guarded stance next to the elevators while keeping Asher and Brooke in her line of sight through the open office door.

Sharon's empty desk seemed to dominate the area, and Brooke did her best to avoid looking at it. She pulled out her cell phone. "I need to call Marcus."

"Who's that?"

"Marcus Lehman. This is his practice. He hired me when I left the Army and needed a job a couple of months ago."

"He's not here today?" Asher asked.

"No, he had an appointment at the bank first thing, then he was coming in."

"Anybody else work here?"

"No. It was just the three of us." She pressed fingers to her eyelids, then released them. "What now?" she asked.

Before he had a chance to answer, Detective Arnold returned. "I'll need to get a statement from both of you."

"Sure."

"Separately, if you don't mind."

Brooke hesitated, then stood. "Of course. We can use the conference room."

Once Brooke was seated with Detective Arnold, he pulled out a small notebook. "Could you give us a run-through of how you found Mrs. Hardy?"

Brooke described in detail how she'd come to the office door and was greeted with the chaos. "I could see Sharon's feet from the door, but what had my attention were Asher and the killer. They were fighting and the guy ran."

"Anything else? A description?"

She shook her head. "He had on a black ski mask. I . . . I'm sorry. It happened so fast. It's all just a blur. Asher could probably help you with the description. He was a lot closer to the guy than I was."

"Of course."

Detective Arnold tilted his head. "What was Mrs. Hardy doing in your office?"

"She often fixed my coffee for me and left it sitting on my desk."

"Everything out here looks fine, but your office is pretty torn up. Any thoughts on that?"

Brooke frowned. "No. I don't keep anything of worth in there. I take my laptop home with me, so I have no idea why someone would do this."

The detective made a few notes, then looked up. "Did Mrs. Hardy have any enemies that you know of?"

"No," Brooke said. "I can't imagine it. She's a wonderful woman. Or . . . was." She pressed fingers against her lips to still their tremble.

42

"What about her marriage? Any trouble there?"

Brooke flinched. "You don't think—"

"I don't know, ma'am, but whatever you can tell us will help figure it out."

"Yes, she and her husband were having trouble."

"Another woman?"

"No, it wasn't that—at least she didn't think it was. It was his job. He's an engineer and his boss is making him work crazy hours. Sharon wanted him to look for something else so he could be home more. She said they were arguing a lot, but I sure don't think it's something he would kill her over."

The detective shook his head. "You'd be surprised."

"Maybe," Brooke said, "but why do it here? I would think that would happen at home in the heat of the moment or something. Not following her to her office."

"Possibly. Anything else you can think of?"

"No," Brooke said. "I don't believe for a minute that he would do this. They may have had some issues to work out, but they loved each other—which is why they were working on the issues."

Detective Arnold grunted. "Okay, let's go over this one more time."

Brooke stifled a groan.

FIVE

For the next hour, Asher tried to still his impatience as they went over everything several times until the detectives were satisfied there was nothing more to be learned. He'd accounted for his own location that morning, his relationship to the deceased—which was he'd spoken to her on the phone exactly once—and given the description of the attacker as best he could. "He was about six feet tall, maybe a hundred ninety pounds," Asher said, "but he had on a black ski mask and black gloves, so I'm not sure about race or skin tone. He had on jeans and a black sweatshirt." He paused. "He never said a word, so I can't tell you whether he had an accent or not. Other than that, I can't help you."

Marcus Lehman had arrived and promised to take care of everything else—including telling Sharon's husband. He left and the detectives seemed to be satisfied their stories lined up with each other and dismissed them before returning to Brooke's office to talk to the ME who'd finally arrived.

Asher turned to Brooke. "Let me follow you home."

"Why?"

He let out a short huff of laughter that didn't hold an ounce of humor. "You've just had a shock. I suppose I just want to make sure you get there safely."

"Oh. Thank you. That's very kind of you, but I'll be fine."

He gave her a tight smile. "You might be fine, but I'm not sure I will be unless I see you safely home." He paused. "Aw, heck, I don't know if it's even appropriate to ask this due to the situation, but would you be willing to go somewhere and have a cup of coffee with me?"

"Coffee?"

"Yeah, that black stuff people can't seem to live without. Surely you've heard of it."

She flushed. "Of course, I know what coffee is." Her eyes sparked with a hint of indignation at his taunting, and he was glad to see the sign of life there. "Excuse me if I'm just a little scattered. Coffee would be lovely, thanks," she said. She paused. "I hate to admit it, but the thought of going home and being alone makes me shudder."

"No roommate?"

"No." Her expression blanked. "I don't like roommates."

And just like that, the initial connection he felt with her when he'd seen the photograph was back. He didn't like roommates either. He wasn't exactly fond of his little studio apartment, but at least he could afford it and he could be alone when he needed to be. "I understand."

Her lips twitched as though she wanted to argue with him, but she didn't. Instead, she glanced at Sharon's desk and winced. "But first, I've got phone calls to make and appointments to cancel."

"Do you want to do that from here?"

"I'll have to get the information from Sharon's computer."

"You'll have to get permission from the detectives. They'll want to watch what you access."

"Of course."

"I'll wait on you."

45

She nodded. "Thanks."

He waved his phone. "I need to call one of my partners and let him know I'm going to be out for the rest of the day."

"Partner?"

He shrugged. "After that last mission, Gavin Black and I had the opportunity to get out, so we did. Travis Walker, a buddy from high school, opened his own security business a couple of years ago. He'd been nagging me about joining him ever since. I've been a silent partner for about a year. Now . . . I'm not so silent. Same with Gavin."

"I didn't realize . . . I mean, I guess I thought you were just on leave or in between missions or something."

"Nope, I'm out for good. It was time."

"Oh. I'm . . . sorry?" She frowned. "Or am I happy for you?"

"The jury's still out on that."

"Right." She pointed to the desk. "I'm just going to go find a detective and cancel those appointments."

"I'll be ready when you are."

◘ ◘ ◘

Kristin Welsh, assistant director of the Morning Star Orphanage in Kabul, waited as Dr. Ali Madad checked his phone one more time. "There's no Wi-Fi again today," he muttered.

"No. Not yet. We're hoping soon." She exchanged glances with Hesther, the older woman who stood in the doorway to ensure Kristin and the doctor were not left alone in the room.

Dr. Madad worked at the local hospital, and once a week he made his "house call" to check on the children who needed medical attention but weren't bad enough to require hospitalization. The children adored him and Kristin appreciated that he didn't seem to mind her presence even though she was a woman.

Right now four-year-old Jabroot lay in his bed uninterested in anything going on around him.

"How is he?" she asked.

"About the same as when you brought him to see me at the hospital yesterday," he said without looking up.

For some reason, today his lack of eye contact made her want to grab his chin and force him to look at her, but this was Kabul. It was his way. "What can I do to help him?" she asked. "Does he need to be transported back to the hospital?" His gaze actually flicked up to meet hers for a brief second before he looked away. Surprise raised her left brow, but instead of saying anything about it—brief as it was—she stuck to business. "I'll do whatever's necessary."

"No, not yet. Continue to give him the medication I prescribed last night and monitor him. He does have some cold symptoms, like the congestion in his chest, but he doesn't have a fever. However, I've drawn some blood and will run a few tests just to rule anything else out. I'll let you know the results as soon as I get them back."

"Thank you." Most doctors weren't so conscientious. Not here. And certainly not for a "mere orphan." She used to respect that—now she couldn't help but find it suspect. And that made her very sad and very wary. But also, strangely hopeful—if her friend was right about him. She cleared her throat.

"What's his story?" Dr. Madad asked as he packed his supplies in his old-fashioned medical bag.

"His story?"

"Yes. How did he come to be at the orphanage and how long has he been here?"

"His mother dropped him off about two months ago, saying she couldn't feed him but she would be back to get him as soon as she could find work. She comes every so often to see him, and it breaks his heart when she leaves him." Broke hers too, but that was the way it went here.

Still keeping his gaze averted, Dr. Madad made a notation on his phone. "I think I'd like to ask that all of the children's files be updated with as much information about the parents as possible."

"What?" She stared at him, and his eyes flicked to her once more before dropping back to the child. "That's not even possible, you know that."

"It will be difficult, yes, but as you well know, the more history I have, the better I'll be able to treat the children." He sighed. "Just do the ones you can."

He had a point, but . . . "I'll speak to the director and make your wishes known." Because she could think of a dozen other reasons he could want that information—none of which she was comfortable with. Maybe Mr. Yusufi would be able to help her out. Not that she would hold her breath on that one. The director cared nothing for the children and didn't make any secret of the fact. Mostly because he didn't have to.

"Thank you," Dr. Madad said.

"Of course."

He might not like looking at her when he talked to her, but he needed her. And like it or not, she needed him. But what if she was wrong about her suspicions? Only one way to find out. "Doctor, I wanted to talk to you about something, if you—"

Running footsteps caught her attention, and she turned to see Paksima dart around Hesther's grasping hands. The six-year-old launched herself at Kristin, and she caught the child up in a hug, inhaling the little-girl scent. "What are you doing?" she asked in the Pashto language. "You're supposed to be in school."

"I wanted to see you. I missed you." She settled her head next to Kristin's, and emotion swept over her. This little orphan had wormed her way into Kristin's heart with very little effort. In a world that had given her nothing but pain, she offered joy, smiles, and love in return. "You need to get back to class before Teacher realizes you're missing. I'll come find you soon, okay? We'll have a snack later before you go to bed and I'll tuck you in."

"And say prayers?"

Kristin cut her eyes to the doctor, who didn't seem to be paying attention, but she wouldn't assume anything. "Of course. We always say our prayers. I'll make sure the prayer mats are in the room." Even though the prayer mats were the same as those used by the other Muslim children and adults to pray, she and Paksima prayed to a different God. The one true God who could work miracles.

Like the one she needed to discuss with Dr. Madad.

"Okay." Paksima skipped off, down the hall, back toward the classroom she shared with forty other children.

"If the doctor is finished," Hesther said to Kristin, "I'll make sure Paksima gets back to class."

"He's finished," Kristin said.

Hesther left, hurrying to catch up with the little girl.

"You've become attached." Dr. Madad grabbed his bag from the table, stepped past her, and walked toward the door.

He didn't approve. Of course he didn't. "Dr. Madad, please wait."

He stopped but didn't turn. "Yes?"

"I want her to come live with me." The words left her in a rush.

He remained silent for a moment. "She already does," he finally said. "You live here and so does she." He spoke to the open doorway.

"No, I mean . . ." She had to be careful. "I mean if I were to leave the orphanage for whatever reason, then I'd want the . . . ability . . . to take her with me."

He laughed. "Impossible."

"But I heard you could help me," she said. "That you've made it possible for other Americans."

He set his bag down and spun, his eyes narrowed but finally locked on hers. "What do you mean?"

"You know what I mean."

"No, I don't."

"What I mean is, you do good work. You care about these children and they know that."

His wary gaze never wavered. "I have to earn their trust in order for them to let me help them."

"I know. And I want to help Paksima. No matter what it costs."

His eyes slid from hers once more. "You are helping her. By doing what you're doing. There is nothing else you can do."

Frustration swamped her. "I know, but it's a shame Americans can't adopt these kids—the ones with no family. Like Paksima." There. She'd said it.

"You are not Muslim, therefore it is not possible and you shouldn't bring it up again if you value your head."

A fission of fear spiked up her spine. She'd misspoken, misstepped. A move that could be deadly for her. "I'm sorry. I see that I'm mistaken. I must have . . . misunderstood."

"You must have. I would never risk my career—my life—ever. Do you understand?"

"Yes, yes."

"You will not start rumors of what you have just insinuated."

"No, oh, no, I wouldn't, I promise. Like I said, it's my mistake and I'm very sorry. In my desperation, I blundered. I meant no insult."

"Who did you hear this from?"

"No one. It was just an observation. Obviously, it was . . . inaccurate."

He stayed silent, fingers curling into fists at his sides.

"Is there anything else I can do for you?" she asked, her stomach tumbling into a tight knot. She'd said too much. Risked and lost. Would he find a way to send her home—or worse, make her—or Paksima—disappear?

"No." He picked up his bag and strode down the hall. "I'll be back next week," he said without turning. "You have my number if he worsens."

"Of course." He left without another word and Kristin frowned at his retreating back. She'd been so sure he could help her. She texted her friend and part-time orphanage volunteer.

> Dr. Madad refused to help me. He was very angry at my insinuation that he was involved in black market adoptions—not that I used those exact words, but close enough.

She thought, then typed,

> Maybe I was wrong.

The return text came through in under five seconds.

> He's probably worried about trusting the wrong person.

She replied, her fingers flying over the letters.

> Yeah, I sure understand that.

> And from what I've found, I don't think you're— we're—wrong, but don't be too overt. Do things to gain his trust.

> I'm afraid it may be too late for that.

> We'll figure it out. My shift starts in a couple of hours. We'll talk then.

> Okay.

> Maybe I was wrong. Maybe he's not involved.

But she was inclined to believe her instincts.

> The patterns say we're not wrong and that he's driven by greed. I really thought he'd go for it.

Especially when you told him you were willing
to do whatever it took, no matter the cost.

> I thought the same. I was telling myself that
> all I wanted to know is that the children were
> safe, but in truth, I was hoping he would say he
> would help me.

Because if he had said it, she would have done it—found a way to
pay him whatever he wanted in order to call Paksima her daughter.

We'll figure it out. Don't give up hope.

> Of course. Thank you, Sarah.

SIX

Brooke pushed her coffee cup to the side and leaned forward. Folding her arms, she studied the man opposite her. "Okay, Asher, we've made small talk for the past thirty minutes. Will you tell me why you wanted to see me this morning?"

He rubbed his eyes. "Straight to the point, huh?"

"Well, not really, but I think you'll feel better if you get off your chest what you need to say." A pause. "Even if it's not what you necessarily *want* to say."

He looked away from her with a shake of his head. "I'm . . . wow." His eyes connected with hers again. "I thought I'd developed a pretty good poker face at this point. How'd you read me that fast and easy?"

"I don't know. I didn't think of it as reading you. But . . ." Brooke tilted her head. "Maybe it's because deep down you recognize that I'm not really a threat to you. Regardless, I'm here to listen."

He stared at his half-finished cup of coffee. After another sip, he linked his fingers on the table and leaned forward. "I realize that we only met a few times in passing while we were in Afghanistan, but that day of the bombing . . ."

"You pulled me out of there," she said, her voice low.

"I did." He cleared his throat. "Frankly, I wasn't sure you were going to make it. Your burns looked pretty bad, but I was more concerned about your smoke inhalation."

Brooke bit her lip, fighting the images that immediately bounded into the forefront of her mind. "The burns were mostly second-degree. A few spots were third on my arms and back and across my shoulders. I won't be wearing a bathing suit anytime soon." She rolled her sleeve up and showed him the still-healing areas on her forearms. "It's been four months and I'm just now feeling up to resuming normal day-to-day operations—or life, I guess I should say, since I'm not serving in the Army anymore." She rubbed a hand over her eyes as though she could scrub away the memories. It didn't work. "I tried to get in touch with you. To thank you and your team for getting me out of there. If you hadn't arrived when you did . . ." She looked away. It was still so very hard to talk about.

"I know." In a slow move, he slid his hand across the table to grip her fingers. "I'm glad we were there. I got the message—your thank-yous—eventually."

She frowned even as she took comfort in his touch. "How did you get there so fast? Was it just dumb luck that you guys were in the area and saw what happened?"

"No, we were headed there for a reason."

"What reason?"

He shook his head. "It doesn't matter. It no longer exists."

She studied him for a brief moment. "You were going there to see Sergeant Michaels, weren't you?"

His hand tightened around hers for a fraction of a second, but his only other response was to raise a brow. "What makes you say that?"

"A feeling." When he said nothing, she closed her eyes. "I still see his face sometimes . . . and hear his voice."

She lifted her lids to see Asher sitting a little straighter, his eyes narrowed. "He spoke to you in the café?"

"Well, not when he first walked in, but later, yes, briefly. As he was dying." Her throat tightened.

"What did he say?"

"That he wasn't a traitor and not to let them say he was."

He jerked like she'd punched him. "He said that? That he wasn't a traitor?"

"Yes." Asher's reaction intrigued her. "He also said that he didn't know."

"Didn't know what?"

"He never got that far. Just that he didn't know." They fell silent and Brooke finally said, "It's my fault, you know."

"What is?"

"That he was killed."

Asher let out a disbelieving laugh. "What? How is that possible? Why would you think that? A terrorist killed him with a bomb planted in the restaurant. A bomb that almost killed you."

"He came looking for me," she said, thinking back to her impressions of that day. "He seemed to know I was going to be at the café and he came to find me."

"How would he know that?"

"It was no secret my friends and I met regularly at that particular café—or as regularly as possible with our crazy schedules."

"You think he followed you?"

"Yes." She hesitated. Frowned. "Actually, I know how he knew where to find me."

"How?"

"I . . . can't say."

"He was a client."

She groaned. "I can't say."

"Yeah, you can because he told me himself that he was seeing you."

"He did?"

"Yes. He didn't say much, just that listening to you talk was . . . soothing."

"Soothing?"

"His word, not mine." He gave her a half smile. "Apparently, you were the only chatty female who didn't make him crazy."

"Good grief." She looked away, the guilt building within her.

"So how would he know where to find you?" Asher asked.

Ugh. Brooke rubbed her eyes. "Sarah called to set up the day and time of our next get-together."

"The café."

"Yes. I'm pretty sure Isaiah overheard me and later remembered. Or something."

Asher shook his head. "But that doesn't make sense. He had your undivided, confidential attention in your sessions. Why track you down at the bar?"

Brooke paused. How could she put it without violating Isaiah's right to confidentiality? "Okay, look. A lot of clients ordered to attend the sessions thought coming to see me was a waste of time, so they would sit there until the clock ticked down to the last minute and then leave."

"Isaiah did that?"

"Yes. And sometimes clients wouldn't show up at all. Don't get me wrong, sometimes it was a legitimate excuse, but most of the time, it wasn't. We had an appointment the day he died—not his regular appointment time, but one he scheduled. I had hoped . . ." She waved a hand. "But, surprise, surprise, he never showed."

"He skipped it?"

"Yes, and I had just seen him that morning on the base and reminded him of the appointment. He said he'd be there. It wasn't the first time he ghosted me, or even the second. I wrote it off and figured he got sent out on a mission or something. Then I saw him in the café." She pinched the bridge of her nose, then dropped her hand. "Which is why I was so mad at him. I thought he had a lot of nerve. I mean, he couldn't meet me when he was supposed to but wanted me to give up my lunch date with my friends to speak to him? Well, that wasn't happening." She rubbed her eyes. "I was so selfish," she whispered. "But I was also so empty. I had given everything and . . ." A tear dripped from her bottom lashes and she swiped it away. "There was just nothing left to give."

"I understand," he said, his voice low.

"Do you? Do you really?"

"Yeah. I do."

She sniffed and drew in a breath. "Do you know what Isaiah meant when he said not to let them say he was a traitor?"

He slid out of the booth in a smooth move and stood. "I can't talk about it." He dropped a five-dollar bill on the table. "Come on and I'll follow you home, then I've got to go."

"Please, sit back down," she said. If he walked out the door, she just might have to chase him down, because she had more questions that needed answers.

Asher hesitated and pressed his fingers to his lids. When he finally opened his eyes, she gasped at the exposed torment there. Torment he masked so quickly, she wondered if she'd been seeing things. "Why?" he asked.

"Because you still haven't told me why you wanted to see me this morning."

"It doesn't matter."

"Of course it matters."

He backed toward the door.

"Um . . . Asher?"

"What?"

"You're kind of making a scene." Other patrons were watching them. Some using their peripheral vision, others outright staring.

Asher pulled in a deep breath, then calmly walked back and

dropped into the seat. "This was a mistake. I never should have come today."

"A mistake? Not from where I'm sitting. Your presence this morning makes twice that you've saved my life. I'm beginning to think I need to keep you around."

He gave her a small smile at her attempt to lighten the atmosphere. The smile lasted all of two seconds before sliding into a frown. "I saw the pictures in the paper and I—"

"Wait a minute, you recognized me?"

"Of course. I mean, if someone hadn't seen you like I did right after the bombing and then later saw the picture, they wouldn't know who you were. But I did. And . . ."

"And?"

"And . . . I started thinking." He clasped his hands. "You were there. You know what it was like. And . . . I need feedback from someone like that."

She frowned. "I wasn't in combat or anything. What about your buddies who were in your squad?"

His jaw tightened. "I talk to Gavin sometimes—when he'll talk about it."

"I see."

"Anyway, the day of the bombing, as we were heading to the café, there was an attack. Wiped out half our unit. We had to leave them there. Couldn't even—" He closed his eyes and swallowed. "Of those who are left, they're scattered. Some are still serving, one's turned into an alcoholic and is living a life of denial, and I just . . ." He spread his hands before clasping them once more. "You were there. You know. And you have the skills—" He blew out a breath. "Wow, I didn't know trying to ask for help would be this hard."

She *had* been there. She *did* know. "What is it you need help with?" God help her, she felt like a fraud. She couldn't deal with her own issues. What made her think she could help him? Instead of blurting out the truth, she swallowed the confession.

"I can't stop thinking about that day. About Isaiah and—you."

"Me?"

He nodded.

"Oh," she said. "Why me?"

He gave her a gentle smile. "Probably because I carried you out of there and I wanted to make sure you were truly okay."

Brooke studied him. "Uh-huh."

"What?"

"And?"

"And . . . I thought maybe you could help me deal with some . . . stuff. From that day."

o o o

There. He'd said it. He'd admitted he needed help, and while he was tempted to get up and run out the door, she hadn't even blinked. Instead, she continued to study him with those unwavering green eyes that had him convinced she could see straight into the deepest, darkest areas of his soul.

"What exactly do you think I can help you with?" she asked.

He cleared his throat as though that would somehow help him release the words. More words. "I have—I mean, some nights I have . . . It's not so bad when—"

"Nightmares," she said.

"Yes." The word was clipped. "Nightmares. I'm okay during the day. As long as I stay pretty busy, I don't have too many issues. Unless a car backfires or there's an unexpected scream on the television or someone pulls up next to me at a stoplight or—"

"Or a helicopter flies too low overhead?" she asked.

"Exactly." His heart rate slowed a notch. She got it.

"But the nights are different."

It wasn't a question and this time he didn't look away. Her low voice was a balm to his agitation. Her presence soothing, comforting. She really got it.

Hope rose its slumbering head. "Very different."

"So, what do you do when the nightmares hit?"

"If it's during the day, I deal. If it's at night and I can't sleep, I run. What do you do?" He switched from his coffee to the water and lifted the glass to his lips.

"I scream at myself that it's not real. And . . . I have a punching bag in my basement."

He sputtered on the water. Coughed and cleared his throat. "A what?"

Amusement glittered in her eyes, and a dimple appeared in her left cheek. The sight warmed him. She gave a small laugh. "Breathe, Asher."

"I'm breathing," he gasped. "Barely."

"Why that reaction? You okay?"

"Yes, but . . . a punching bag? I'm sorry. You're so . . . calm and gentle and . . . serene. I guess I'm just having a hard time seeing you going at it with a bag."

"Interesting description of me. Hmm. But I do. Go at it with a bag, that is. Quite frequently actually. My dad taught me to box. Or at least attempted to. I'm afraid I was a huge disappointment to him because I was never very good at it." She grimaced. "But one night about a month ago, when I couldn't sleep, I decided to see if punching on the bag helped. I found I liked doing it when I didn't have someone screaming at me about form and such. It gives me a great workout and allows me to process my feelings and emotions in a very physical way."

"That's what running does for me." He paused. "I may have to try boxing one day."

"I'll be glad to give you a lesson." The dimple briefly appeared again.

"I'd like that. Would you want to go running with me?"

"Only if you have an oxygen tank handy."

He let out a surprised snort. "Come on. If you work out with a punching bag, going on a run shouldn't scare you."

She grimaced. "I haven't been working out that long, but the truth is, I hate to run."

He held up a finger. "Ah, but you've never run with me."

"Why would that make a difference? Running is still running."

"You'll have to let me prove you wrong. Come running with me."

"What? When?"

"Tomorrow morning."

She hesitated. "I don't know, Asher, I need to wait and see how everything's going to play out at work."

He stilled. "Of course. I'm not thinking. I'm sorry."

"Don't be sorry. You're doing the same thing I'm doing. Compartmentalizing. Trying not to think about Sharon."

"Or Isaiah."

"Yes."

Brooke looked like she wanted to say something. He leaned forward. "What is it?"

"Okay . . . so . . . speaking of running . . . would you like to run an errand with me?" she finally asked.

"What kind of errand?"

"I need to make a delivery and while I've not exactly been putting it off—okay, that's not true. I *have* been putting it off and telling myself I just haven't found the right time to do it, but now I'm just sliding into being irresponsible."

"Seems to me like you've been pretty busy healing," he said.

"Yes. In the beginning. And I used that as an excuse. When I was in the hospital for so long and then getting transitioned back into civilian life and my job . . ." She shifted, looked away, then back at him. "The truth is, I just don't want to do this errand alone, but I wasn't sure who to ask to go with me."

"I'll go." He paused. "Where are we going?"

"To see Isaiah Michaels's widow."

Asher went still. "You want to go see Miranda?"

"I have something I need to give her."

"What?"

She opened her purse and pulled out a piece of jewelry. "Before Isaiah died, he slipped this bracelet into my hand. He told me to keep it safe, then said to make sure I told her he wasn't a traitor." She took another sip of the coffee the waitress had just topped off. "It's time for me to do that."

"I saw the bracelet in the pictures," Asher said.

Brooke pinched the bridge of her nose. "Those pictures, ugh. I don't want to think about them."

He wanted to argue with her about how truly amazing they were—not just the pictures themselves, but what they revealed about her personality, her character. But it was too soon, and she wasn't ready to hear that all those pictures showed was an incredibly brave woman. He'd save that for another time. "Have you talked to Miranda?"

"I called her the day I left the burn unit. I've left voice messages asking her to call me back, but she hasn't. As the days passed and she didn't return my calls, I kind of let it go. But . . . I think I owe Isaiah to honor his last request."

"She's grieving. Maybe she's not checking her messages."

"And not answering numbers she doesn't recognize. I think it might be best just to drop by and see her. She lives in Columbia, though."

"That's an hour-and-a-half drive. Are you sure you want to take a chance on her not being there?"

Brooke shrugged. "It's not too far and I did a little research. I know she works as a waitress at a local diner and she's off on Tuesdays and Wednesdays and every other Saturday. And she doesn't live on the base."

"How'd you find that out?"

"She's not in Columbia but in a small town adjacent to the city. I knew the name of the church she and Isaiah went to, and when I called and explained to the secretary who I was and that I had something from Isaiah to give to Miranda, she was more than willing to share information." She sighed. "But I don't want to bother her at work. Showing up unannounced there seems like a bad idea."

"Yeah, home is better. She can cry there and not worry she's making a scene or something."

"Well, there is that, I suppose."

"All right. Tomorrow's Wednesday. I'll be happy to go with you. You want to drive or you want me to?"

"Um . . . you can, I guess." She paused. "But I have a question before we go any further."

"What?"

"When you scheduled the appointment for this morning, were you wanting a long-term counseling thing or were you just coming to see me because you saw my picture in the paper?"

"I don't know," he said. "To be honest, I hadn't thought much beyond today. Why?"

"Because I don't work with vets," she said. "That was one of my stipulations with Marcus. I'd come work with him if he wouldn't assign me any vets."

Asher's heart plunged. "I see." He frowned. "Then how did I get this appointment for this morning with you?"

"Did you ask for me?"

"Yes."

"And did you mention to Sharon that you were a vet?"

"No. I just told her that you and I had some history and that I'd like to see you. I didn't mention it was from the Army, and she didn't ask where I knew you from."

"Patient assignments are decided strictly by what's on the paperwork—or if the client mentions it on the phone."

"Ah," he said. "Well, I hadn't filled out any paperwork yet."

"Because you were a work-in."

"Right." His mind spun. She didn't work with vets. Fine. "Well, looks like I won't be a client then." He stood. "You ready to go home?"

With only a slight hesitation that hinted at her uncertainty, she nodded. "Sure."

Asher led the way to the parking lot. "So, how'd you meet this guy, Marcus Lehman?" he asked when they reached their vehicles.

"I've known him all my life." She gestured to his truck. "It doesn't bother you to drive?"

He shot her a quick glance. "What do you mean?"

"A lot of clients have trouble driving once they're home and trying to adapt to civilian life."

His jaw tightened. He knew what she was referring to. "It's okay most of the time. Other times, it makes me sweat." Because in Afghanistan, when someone pulled up beside you, it meant they were going to kill you. Or at least try to. "I know no one here is going to pull up beside me and start shooting. Or throw an explosive at me. I know that."

"I know you do. Just like I know the ceiling fan in my bedroom isn't a helicopter, but it doesn't stop me from thinking about tearing the thing out."

He barked a short laugh. "Yeah." They fell silent before he cleared his throat. "Climb in for a few more minutes. I want you to finish telling me about you and Marcus, and it's cold out here."

She did as he asked and her gaze landed on the opened bag of trail mix in the cupholder. "Oh, I love that stuff."

"Help yourself."

"Thanks." She tossed back a handful and crunched it while he settled himself behind the wheel.

"So . . . Marcus?" he asked.

After a short pause during which she scarfed more of his trail mix, she finally let out a low breath. "Our fathers served in the

Army together and are best friends," she said. "Marcus and I were born two days apart, so even though we moved a lot when I was a kid, Marcus and I ended up in the same high school graduating class. Then we both wound up at the Medical University of South Carolina and hung out a lot, had all-night study sessions with a couple of other military brats, and were just good friends."

"Nothing more?"

She shook her head. "He's been in love with Christine Blake since eighth grade and married her four years ago. But he always had it in his head we'd open a practice and be partners. However, at the time, I wasn't interested."

"Why not?"

"I wanted to join the Army."

"And he didn't?"

"No way. He was all about working for himself and not taking orders from anyone."

"Dictator Dad syndrome?"

"Yeah."

"Yours wasn't?"

"He was. Still is." She shot him a wry smile. "But I have a different personality than Marcus. I just let it roll off. Most of the time anyway."

He cut her a sideways glance. "He tells you what to do, you smile and nod, then do your own thing?"

"Pretty much." Her lips twitched and she ate another handful of his trail mix. "This stuff is so addictive."

"No kidding."

It wasn't long before she'd finished off the bag. With a guilty glance at him, she crumpled the plastic and shoved it into a small garbage bag she saw in the door pocket. "Guess I need to stop at a grocery store on the way home and replenish your stash."

"Don't worry. I buy it in bulk."

CHAPTER
SEVEN

Caden had watched as three more bodies were transported to waiting ambulances. The ambulances would carry their cargo to the morgue.

He had studied each victim, taking notes in his little black notebook. He'd worked along with the crime scene photographer, hoping the information would be helpful as the investigation progressed. Just digging everything up and making sure they hadn't missed anything was going to take days.

Caden watched the third ambulance disappear around the curve and rubbed a hand over his weary face. He was no expert, but of the last three bodies he'd examined, two had looked like kids to him. The third had looked older, like an adult. She'd been buried deeper, and once the dog had alerted for the second time in that area, the dig team had gone to work and unearthed her. Blue jeans and a short-sleeved pink T-shirt had still covered her, and Caden had a feeling she'd been one of the first. Someone had taken more time with her. As though they cared?

His stomach rumbled loud enough to be heard by those in close proximity. The four stale peanut butter crackers he'd found in his coat pocket and scarfed down three hours ago were long gone.

Mickey and Deveraux looked at him. "Need to stop and get something for that grumpy stomach?" Deveraux asked.

"If you guys have time. It'll be a while before we get the first bits of information on the ones in the morgue, and I need to keep my strength up."

"Don't we all?" Mickey said. "Let's head to that little meat and three place on Congaree Road. We can eat and discuss how we're going to handle finding who those victims are."

It didn't take long to round up Zane and head out. Soon, they were seated at a table and the food was brought by a skinny waitress with dishwater blonde hair and pretty blue eyes.

Only Caden found himself suddenly without an appetite. For a moment, he simply stared at the full plate in front of him and wondered about the children in the graves. What had their last meals been? Were there more children?

"Cade?"

Mickey's voice pulled him from his thoughts. "Yeah?"

"You okay?"

Caden forced a tight smile. "Sure." He wasn't a green agent. He'd been at this for several years now and had seen more of the darker side of life than he cared to think about, but when it came to the kids . . . yeah. The children got to him. He knew he wouldn't be able to rest until he figured this out—and arrested those responsible for the deaths of those kids. And if for some reason it miraculously turned out that they had died from natural causes—he mentally scoffed but allowed the possibility to register—then he'd find the person responsible for tossing them out like yesterday's trash.

"Bothers me too," Deveraux said.

Caden looked up and met the man's eyes. "Yeah." And in spite of his churning gut, he ate the food.

"So," Mickey said, "let's think about this. Twelve shallow graves. Twelve bodies. Some are kids. We won't know ages or time of death until Clarissa and her team finish with them, but it looks like there are various ages and dates of death." He paused. "I'm not buying that they all died from some mysterious disease."

"Come on," Caden said, "no speculation. We won't be able to say that until Clarissa gets back to us. They'll start with the most recent death and work backward, I would think."

"Sounds about right to me," Deveraux said. "But just because one died a certain way doesn't mean they all did."

"I know that."

"Of course you do," Mickey said, "but I'm thinking if we can identify one of the bodies, there will be a connection to the others and everything will fall into place."

"Maybe." Caden had a funny feeling about this case. "Clarissa said she couldn't see an immediate cause of death. Meaning no gunshot wounds, stabbings, et cetera. I realize that some of the bodies have been scavenged, so she may find something like that after the autopsies, but what else could have caused this? Deaths over an extended period of time? Say it was murder or some kind of Jim Jones thing."

"A cult?" Mickey asked.

"Why not? Drugs? Poison? Or even a human trafficking ring?"

Deveraux nodded. "Could definitely be a cult. But if it's human trafficking, why kill them? It sounds cold, but aren't you hurting your profit margin if you kill your inventory?"

It did sound cold and Caden didn't like the way the man worded it, but it was accurate. "Maybe the ring didn't want kids, just the parents," he said.

Mickey shook his head. "We could sit here all day and come up with a hundred different scenarios and reasons for the bodies in those graves. Until we know more, I say let's move on to another part of the investigation."

"I'm good with that," Deveraux said. He took a sip of his tea. "Let's talk location. Whoever picked that spot for the graves did so for a reason. There's no security footage in that area. It's remote and no one really goes up there much. The killer could have some kind of personal, historic connection to the place and feels comfortable here. Taking the time to bury numerous bodies at various times says he's not too concerned about being discovered."

"And probably wouldn't have been if not for the doctor and his dog," Caden said. "Did he say why he was taking that route this morning? I'm assuming it's not his usual one."

"Said he was bored and simply decided to go a different way," Mickey said. "I noticed the tracker on his wrist. We'll get a warrant for the information from it and see if it matches up with what he told us. We've got a call in to the owner of the land and will do a full workup on him as well."

"Good." Caden finished the meal and pushed his plate to the side. "Let's head to the morgue. I can't handle this sitting around and waiting stuff."

"Clarissa will just kick you out," Mickey said.

"Well, maybe she'll talk a little while she's kicking."

○ ○ ○

Asher pulled to a stop in the drive of a small cottage-style house painted a light blue with white trim. Brooke had a two-car garage straight ahead, and to his right was a short walkway that led to a covered front porch. "This is nice," he said.

"Thanks, I love it. I've only lived here two months. I found the house online while I was in Kabul and put in an offer. After a bit of haggling, it was finally accepted." She shot him a glance. "The day before the bombing. I gave my real estate agent power of attorney so I didn't have to be at the closing. After the bombing, the owners graciously waited until I was conscious and lucid enough to decide whether or not I wanted to proceed."

"They were going to let you out of the contract?"

"Yes. They have a son in Iraq, and when they were told what

happened, they . . ." A fond smile curved her lips. "They were very kind. They even came to see me in the burn center in Atlanta."

"Wow, that's above and beyond."

"I know. I've seen them several times since I've moved in. They're lovely people." A small sigh slipped from her.

"What?" he asked.

She waved a hand. "It's silly."

"Silly is good. The world is filled with way too much seriousness."

"Well, that's true enough. I . . . it's kind of embarrassing, but sometimes I fantasize that they're my real parents who just discovered I'm the daughter they gave up for adoption thirty-six years ago and are trying to get to know me before they decide whether or not to break the news." She said it in a rush of words. "I know, I'm pitiful. I have no idea why I shared that with you."

Asher's heart hurt for her and he gripped her fingers. "You've got a long way to go before you reach pitiful."

"Ha. Well, thanks, I think."

The flowers amidst the shrubs snagged his attention. "You have red flowers blooming in the middle of January? How in the world did you manage that?"

She shot him a tired smile. "They're amaryllis. They only bloom in the winter and I love coming home to them." She opened the door and stepped out, pulling her keys from her purse. Her phone rang. Once. Twice.

"Aren't you going to get that?" he asked.

She glanced at the screen. "It's coming up as a private call, so no."

"It could be one of the detectives needing to talk to you about this morning."

"If it's important, they'll call back or leave a message." She stuffed the phone in the pocket of her coat. "I just can't deal with anything else at the moment."

He could understand that.

"Although I do need to call Kat at some point."

"Kat took the pictures. I remember her well. She was on the base always snapping something."

"Yes." She unlocked the front door, stepped inside, and punched in the code to disarm the alarm system.

"Are you going to be all right?" he asked, shutting the door behind him.

For a moment, she just stood there in the foyer, back to him, head lowered. He noted the dining room to the left and a room set up as an office to his right. Straight ahead, the foyer opened into the great room.

Finally, after several seconds, she turned. "I don't know. Walking into my house feels so normal, it's hard to believe that Sharon's really dead. That the next time I go in to work, she won't be there. I think I'm still in shock—or denial. Or both." She pinched the bridge of her nose and drew in a slow breath.

Asher let his hands rest on her shoulders. "I'm not the psychiatrist here, but I'd say that's probably an accurate diagnosis."

"I didn't know her long," she said, "and before I accepted the job, Marcus said how much I'd like working with her. He talked about how she was kind to everyone around her and had a gentle spirit and good-natured humor. I got to see evidence of that in the past couple of months, and I was enjoying getting to know her."

A low thud from the back of her house stilled Asher. Brooke didn't seem to notice. His hands fell from her shoulders, and his right hand went to the weapon in the shoulder holster. "Brooke?" he said softly.

She frowned. "What?"

"Do you have any pets?"

"No, why?"

When he pulled his weapon, her eyes went wide. "What is it? What are you doing?" For a split second, he could see the flash of mingled doubt and fear that she'd misjudged him.

He let that roll off as he held a finger up to his lips. "I heard something. Stay behind me." Without question, she let him step ahead of her. "Tell me the rest of the layout," he whispered.

"Um . . . straight ahead is the great room and kitchen that overlooks the pool and the backyard. To the right off the great room is my guest bedroom. To the left of the kitchen and eating area is my master bedroom."

Her hushed voice barely reached him, but he heard her—along with the fear his sudden caution had generated. His ears strained. No other noises reached him other than the faint pant of her quickened breathing—and the thundering of his own heartbeat. And then that faded and his senses focused, homed in on whatever threat was in front of them. "You have your phone?"

"Yes."

"Call 911, then place your hand on my shoulder and stay with me." He could feel her moving to comply. When her hand settled on his left shoulder, he tilted his head. "Who's there?" he called out. Holding his weapon in ready position, he aimed it toward the back of the house and started walking.

CHAPTER
EIGHT

Brooke's heart thundered. Had he really heard something or was this something his mind had conjured up? She hesitated, not wanting to automatically assume he was having an . . . episode, but—

Thud.

She gave a low gasp. Okay, she heard that. Her fingers flexed on his shoulder, the muscle beneath her palm a solid block of concrete.

He slowed at the corner of the entrance to the great room and the end of the foyer. To the right was the guest bedroom she'd mentioned. He glanced in. "Clear," he whispered. He stepped inside and pulled her after him. While she stood with her back to the wall and next to the door, Asher checked the room, the closet, the connected bathroom. He returned to her side. "It's all clear. Stay here while I check the rest of the house."

He didn't give her a chance to argue but slipped out of the room and left her hugging the doorframe. Just as he stepped into the great room, a figure dashed from her master bedroom and shoved the patio door open.

She bit down on a scream.

"Hey! Stop!" Asher darted after him.

"Oh no, he's not getting away," Brooke muttered. Without thinking, she bolted for the French doors off the guest bedroom, threw them open, and rushed out onto the deck. The man slammed into her, knocking her off the deck and onto the cement next to the pool. Brooke landed hard, her elbow banging against the rough surface. Pain snaked through her arm and up into her neck.

"Brooke!"

Asher's cry warned her. She jerked and rolled. The man's hard fist grazed her cheek, and between her roll and her desperate attempt to dodge his bone-crunching blow, she tumbled into the pool.

The heated water closed over her head. *Don't panic, don't panic. Get out and help Asher.* The instant her feet touched the bottom, she pushed off and shot upward.

When she broke through the surface, Brooke gulped air and her eyes landed on the two men fighting for control of a weapon. Asher had his hands wrapped around the man's wrist, his strength the only thing between him and a bullet. Strength that seemed to be equally matched by the man trying to kill him.

What had Asher done with his gun? Dropped it when he tackled the guy? She hauled herself out of the water, shivering when the cold air whipped across her soaked body.

Asher grunted and rolled. The attacker managed to move the weapon closer to Asher's face. Brooke raked the water off her face, frantically searching for a way to help.

The skimmer. She grabbed the long pole and swung it.

The netting slipped over the man's head, and while that hadn't been her original intention, it would work.

She yanked.

He screamed.

Asher swung and his fist slammed against the man's nose. Another scream ripped from him as blood flowed. His grip loosened and the gun tumbled to the concrete.

Brooke dove for it, but he was quicker. His shoulder caught her on the chin and she fell back, twisting, fighting gravity and losing. Once again, she hit the concrete hard. Only to look up and see Asher running toward him. With no time to aim and fire, the man swung out, catching Asher across the jaw with the barrel. Blood spurted. Asher went down with a harsh yell, and she found herself staring down the barrel into a pair of narrowed blue eyes.

"Police! Drop the weapon."

The man's finger twitched.

Brooke rolled and covered her head.

Two shots sounded.

She froze, eyes shut, expecting to feel a burst of pain as the bullet blazed a path through her. A millisecond passed and she felt nothing.

She registered the sirens, the running feet, hands picking her up. *The smoke choked her. The fire swept across her, burning her. Isaiah called her name and pressed the bracelet into her palm. His eyes connected with hers. She coughed. Couldn't breathe.*

"Brooke? Brooke! Look at me."

She blinked. The man with the weapon lay facedown on the concrete. The officer who'd fired the shots exited her guest bedroom—the same way she'd come—and hurried toward the fallen man. Other officers swarmed the area.

A hand tilted her chin, pulling her gaze from the body. "Brooke. Right here. Focus on me."

Asher. Blood dripped from his chin, but he didn't seem to notice it. Her gaze jumped from one thing to the next. Deck chairs, the wrought-iron table with the etched-glass top and umbrella. She was at home in her backyard near the pool, not in the burning café in Kabul with the dying Isaiah in her lap.

She gasped.

Brooke locked on Asher's gaze, and the knowing there shook her harder than the tremors from the cold.

"Are you all right?" A young cop with aged gray eyes stooped next to her.

"Y-yes. I think so." She didn't have any bullet holes or anything else, so she figured she was all right. A mammoth shiver racked her. "J-just really c-cold." She thought about getting back in the water just to warm up.

A blanket settled around her shoulders. She grasped the edges and pulled them together in front of her.

Asher pulled her to her feet. "Come on, let's get inside so you can change."

"Sorry," the officer said. "That's a crime scene now. We'll have to find something for you that's not in there." He handed Asher a piece of gauze and Asher pressed it to his bleeding chin. "Paramedic said to give you that."

"Thanks."

Brooke pointed to the open French doors connected to the guest room. "I h-have some clothes in the closet in that room. He wasn't in there, j-just the master." The thought turned her stomach.

The officer hesitated, then stepped to the side. "All right."

Brooke darted into the bedroom, where she grabbed jeans, a long-sleeved T-shirt, and a heavy fleece. "It's freezing in here," she muttered. Or maybe it was just her. She walked into the bathroom, quickly changed clothes, and pulled her wet hair into a ponytail.

The shivers had mostly stopped as she walked back into the guest bedroom to find Asher waiting for her. Someone had butterflied the cut on his chin, but that didn't soften the grim set to his jaw. "What is it?" she asked.

"The man who broke into your house is on his way to the hospital, but they're not holding out much hope he'll make it through surgery."

She swallowed and nodded. "Okay."

"And . . . I know him."

"Know who?" The brain fog wouldn't lift.

"The guy who broke into your home."

o o o

Her eyes widened a fraction. "You do? How?"

Asher was surprised at how steady he managed to keep his voice, since he was still dealing with the terror he'd felt when he realized Brooke was going to die and there was nothing he could do about it—that moment when the intruder had knocked him hard enough to see stars and turned his weapon on her.

With effort, he pushed the image away and focused on the fact that she was standing in front of him. Alive and in one piece—with a look on her face that said she was waiting for him to answer. "He was in Afghanistan with us. I didn't know him well, but enough to recognize him. His name was Mario Ricci. He was part of another unit." He paused. "He was good friends with Isaiah and he was there the day of the bombing at the café."

She shook her head. "I'm confused. Why would he break into my house?"

"I have no idea, but he was determined not to get caught."

"He was willing to kill, wasn't he?" she asked.

"Yes. This wasn't some random break-in, Brooke. And now I'm thinking that wasn't some random thing at your office this morning. The guy from this morning wore a ski mask and so did Mario. The guy from the office and Mario are the same build, and those ski masks looked exactly the same. Same jeans, same black sweatshirt. It's not a far stretch to think it's possible he was the one who killed Sharon."

"But why?" She shivered again, and Asher didn't think it had anything to do with the cold. "What's going on?"

A knock on the door took his attention from her before he could tell her he was as confused as she was. Another officer stood in the entrance. "Could you come take a look at your bedroom?"

"Yes, of course."

Asher followed her through the living area, bypassing the kitchen and eating area, and into the small hallway that led to the entrance of her bedroom.

"What's—oh." At the door she stopped so fast he nearly ran into her. It looked a lot like the office had this morning. Drawers pulled out and dumped on the floor. Anything that could be opened and emptied had been. The television had been smashed and now lay on its side underneath the window.

She stood still as a statue in front of Asher, so he couldn't see her face. "Brooke?" He rested a hand on her left bicep. "Why don't you—"

"I'm okay," she said, her voice low. Tight. Controlled. She shrugged off his hand in a subtle move that was almost as polite as she'd been earlier. He let his hand drop. "It looks like he was just getting started," she said, "since this is the only room that's been trashed."

"He came in that window," the officer said, pointing to the one opposite her bed—the one the television had sat in front of. "Cut the glass, unlatched it, and climbed in."

"Destroying my television in the process."

"Yeah. It would have been in the way, so he just gave it a shove."

"It's a good television," she said. "He could have gotten a lot of money for it."

"So he wasn't looking for stuff to fence," Asher murmured. More to himself than to be heard, but Brooke glanced back at him.

"I have an alarm system," she said. "The doors are wired, but not the windows."

"Which explains why it didn't go off," Asher muttered. "We'll rectify that immediately."

She turned and raised a brow but didn't dispute him. She let her gaze scan the room, then started forward.

The officer stopped her with an upraised hand. "Ma'am, please don't come in. If we want to keep it as pristine as possible for the crime scene unit, then I'll need you to stay out."

"Right, but you've already been in there."

"To check and make sure no one else was here."

"Then could you check the drawer that's on the other side of the bed? I had about six hundred dollars in cash there. It's wrapped with a rubber band."

He stepped away to look.

"That's a lot of cash to keep in your bedside drawer," Asher said.

"I sold a laptop and hadn't gotten a chance to get to the bank yet."

"It's here," the officer said. He leaned over and with a gloved hand picked up the wad of cash.

"So not a burglary or a junkie looking for his next hit."

"I know the guy who did this and he's not a junkie—at least not that I remember. And besides, a junkie would have taken the money and the stuff to sell. He would have been a lot more careful with the television."

"He's not one of my clients," Brooke murmured.

"Do you have someone you can stay with tonight?" the officer asked.

"Um . . . yeah. I can call my friend Heather."

"Heather?" Asher asked.

"Heather Fontaine." She rubbed her forehead. "You should remember her. She was in Afghanistan the same time we were. She and I actually left on the same day and flew home together."

"She lives here in Greenville?"

Brooke shot him a tight smile. "She does now. We decided we wanted to live in close proximity, and since she doesn't have very many ties to her hometown in New Mexico, she got a job here. We hang out as much as we can work into our schedules."

"She's your person."

"Definitely."

"Gavin Black is mine." He studied her. "You didn't call Heather to tell her about this morning, did you?"

Brooke frowned. "No, I knew she was busy at work and I didn't want to worry her." Her eyes locked on his. "It helped that you were there. If you hadn't been . . ." She looked away and shuddered. "Let's just say I'm glad you were."

He took her hand. "I'm glad I was too."

NINE

"He's still alive," Victor said. "He's in surgery and will be in ICU if he survives. Cops are all around him."

The man glared at Victor. Video calls weren't usually the way he liked to do things, but today he needed to see Victor's face. He pressed on the right AirPod to settle it in his ear. "Did he find the bracelet?"

A slight grimace crossed Victor's face. Not a good sign. "Are you even sure that bracelet has anything to do with what Michaels took?"

"Of course I'm not sure, but Michaels got the files shortly before the explosion. It's obvious in those pictures that he passed that bracelet to the shrink for a reason. We've searched everything belonging to him and come up empty. The bracelet is the only possible way he could have passed them off."

Victor hesitated. "If he passed them off." He sighed. "And if that's the case, then it's very likely she has no idea what Michaels gave her."

"Michaels wouldn't have had a chance to hide those files anywhere between the time he stole them and the time he arrived at the restaurant. The only reason we even know about them is because he was seen by one of our guys leaving Madad's office."

"I know."

"I thought we had this under control. There's no way he was going to take them to his grave—or let us get our hands on them if he could help it. Brooke Adams was right there."

"It makes sense," Victor said.

"So . . . back to my original question. Did Ricci find it?"

"He texted that he'd just finished searching her bedroom when he heard them come in," Victor said, "so I don't think so."

"You don't think so. Is there any way to find out for sure?" He kept his voice even. The desire to scream at the man was nearly overwhelming, but that would just draw attention to himself. With his back to the wall, he tilted the phone so he had a better view of the screen—and to ensure no one else could see.

"I'm working on that," Victor said. "I have to wait until things settle down before I can get close to him."

"Where were you when all this was going down at her house? Why didn't you step in and help Ricci?"

"I was too far away. By the time I realized something was wrong, I didn't have time to help. If I'd gone in, we both would have been caught. I didn't see that helping our mission any. And you know what you always say about sacrifice."

"Right." A slight pause. "I don't suppose I need to reiterate how bad things will be if that information falls into the wrong hands."

His cohort scowled. "It's already in the wrong hands. That's why Ricci and I are here, right?"

"Don't get smart with me," he hissed, keeping the smile on his face. "Just do what I hired you to do. We both have a lot of money on the line, but more importantly, people are depending on us."

Was that a slight roll of the eyes?

"I got this," Victor said. "Now chill. I'm headed to the hospital to see what I need to do about Ricci." He hesitated a fraction of a second. "You don't think he'll talk to the authorities, do you? I mean, if he's even awake?"

The man's eyes narrowed. "He'd better not." A pause. "You need to be there when he wakes up."

"I plan to be."

"And, Victor?"

"Yeah?"

"Can you do what needs to be done if it needs doing?"

A split-second widening of Victor's eyes said he knew exactly what that meant. Then a deep frown creased his whole face. Again, not a good sign. "It won't come to that."

"But can you do it?"

"I'm a lot of things," Victor said quietly, "and as you well know, I've done some illegal things, but I'm no killer. That's Ricci's gig."

What a baby. A muscle twitched in his jaw, attesting to the self-control he was exerting. "Look, I didn't arrange to get you and Ricci discharged and sent home—instead of prison, if I may remind you—for this to blow up in our faces. You're there to take care of this. If Ricci talks, we're done. Everything will shut down—everything. Not to mention that little thing called prison—"

"I know, I know." Victor was getting antsy, irritated. He could hear it in his voice—and his attempt to hide it.

"All right," he soothed, keeping his expression neutral while on the inside he couldn't help the surge of disgust for the man. If he hadn't needed Victor—but he did. "You just threw my words about sacrifice back at me. Well, now would be a good time to repeat that to yourself. As much as we may hate it, in this business, sometimes you have to make sacrifices—like sacrificing the one for the good of the many."

Silence greeted him, and he could see the man's mind working, taking in his words, processing. Finally, Victor gave a short nod. "I know. I've got this."

"Once again, can you do what needs to be done with Ricci if it comes down to it?"

"I can do it." Victor looked away for a moment.

"What is it? What are you thinking?"

"I think we need to replace Ricci. He's down for the count and I'm going to need help."

Of course he did. Why had he thought this man should be a part of this highly sensitive mission? "You'll receive a call within two hours."

"Good. I'll be ready."

"We're counting on you. All of us." He hung up and considered whether he could actually trust Victor to get it done.

If not, he'd have to take things into his own hands and he needed to figure out what that might look like. He dialed another number and waited.

The screen opened up and his wife's face appeared. "Hey, kids, come see who's calling!" She turned back to the screen and smiled. "Hi there, handsome. How's it going?"

"Hey, it's going okay. How are the kids?"

"They miss you."

"I miss them."

His children gathered around the iPad and he cherished the few moments with them before he had to figure out a way to clean up the mess Isaiah Michaels had made.

○ ○ ○

The lights flickered as Kristin stood just outside the door of her boss's office, trying to hear what he and Dr. Madad were saying. Unfortunately, even though the door was cracked, their voices were too low. She thought she caught the word "Tajikistan" but couldn't be sure. Frustration clamped down on her. Then Mr. Yusufi's voice rose. ". . . his family comes back to claim him? What do I tell them? No, it must be . . ." His voice faded again.

Again, the lights flickered and she had hope that the power would soon be restored.

Footsteps in the hallway sent her pulse skyrocketing, and she spun to see the line of children walking down the hall past the offices. Paksima was at the end. When the little girl spotted her, her whole face lit up, and Kristin's heart clenched.

How she loved that child and desired to give her the home she deserved. But for now, she'd settle for seeing her every day at the orphanage—and keep searching for a way to adopt her. She hurried over for a quick hug, then Paksima skipped along behind her classmates, a contented smile on her innocent little face.

Some people would just tell her to convert to the Muslim faith, but she couldn't do that. Not even for her love of the little girl.

When she turned, she caught Hesther watching. She gave the woman a small smile. It seemed like every time she turned around, the older woman was there. Spying on her. Watching her. Chills danced up her arms and she shivered.

The bounce of a dark hijab captured her attention and Kristin hurried after Sarah, her friend and newest hire. It had been five months since Sarah arrived in a part-time volunteer position, and Kristin had been delighted to hire the woman for several reasons—the first being that her last volunteer had disappeared with no warning or word of where she was going. Kristin worried that she'd met an ill-fated end simply because when she asked about her, she'd been shut down and warned to mind her own business. But this woman was different. Like Kristin, she was an American with a desire to do her part to help rescue the children. Unlike Kristin, she had the necessary resources to do so.

Kristin suspected that the woman was a missionary in disguise, but of course, she'd not admit it. Instead, she called herself a humanitarian worker who loved children and let it be known that she'd do anything, *anything*, to see that the kids had whatever they needed to survive the craziness and horror they'd been born into—or help them get out of it. At least that was her cover story. Kristin often wondered if there was more to her story due to the way she talked and acted.

Whatever the case, she was quite sure it had been God who had orchestrated their meeting that day in the park. It hadn't taken long to convince Sarah that she would be a perfect fit to help with the orphanage. In the past three months, they'd become close friends. At least on Kristin's end. Mostly because the other woman had figured out her deepest secret—her desire to adopt Paksima—and had offered to do whatever she could to help make that happen.

Kristin often wondered if trusting her had been a wrong move, but if Sarah was going to betray her, she would have done it when Kristin finally admitted to Sarah that she had guessed her secret.

She caught up with the woman and found her writing something in a small notebook. "Sarah, hi."

Sarah looked up, startled. She snapped the pages shut and smiled. "Hi."

"Everything all right?"

"Of course." She waved the notebook. "Just making notes and observations. I think the children could . . . um . . . use a playground."

"A playground?" Kristin gave her friend a confused smile. "They have the area out back with the swings."

"I know, but what if we actually had a jungle-gym-type thing built for them?"

Kristin worried her bottom lip. "I don't mean to knock down your ideas," she finally said, "but think about it. Out of all the things these kids need, do you really think it's wise to spend money on a playground? It's all we can do to keep the money out of the wrong pockets and food on the table. We need beds and linens and school supplies, not a playground."

"What if I got it donated for free?"

She offered a sad smile. "The director won't go for it."

"Why? Because he will think it will somehow keep money out of his pocket?" Sarah snapped her lips shut and clapped a hand over her mouth. "Sorry. I shouldn't have said anything." She sighed. "You're right. In addition to everything that you listed, what these kids need are homes."

"Exactly."

"But if you're not Muslim, you can't adopt them."

"Trust me, I know."

Sarah gave her a sympathetic look. "I know you do. So no more progress on that end?"

"No. None."

"I don't understand. According to the pattern, it works." Sarah frowned. "Don't do anything else until I do some more digging. We don't want to set off any alarm bells if we can help it."

"What kind of alarm bells?"

"The kind that got Isaiah Michaels killed."

Kristin studied her friend. "Who are you really?" she asked softly.

"What do you mean?"

"You talk about doing more digging and setting off alarm bells and Isaiah Michaels—and you found the pattern that suggests Dr. Madad is arranging black market adoptions—and using American soldiers to transport them to their new homes." She narrowed her eyes and decided it was worth the risk in pressing ahead. "And the more I think about it, the more I think you may be right, even though he wouldn't admit it to me. So again, I ask, who are you? Because while it's obvious you care about the children and truly love working with them, I don't think you're just a volunteer."

The other woman hesitated. "Let's say I have connections and I have the best interests of the children at heart. Is that enough?"

For some reason, Kristin believed her. "I suppose. If you won't tell me anything else."

Sarah pursed her lips. "Tell me something," she said.

"Sure."

"This is a privately funded orphanage, right?"

"Yes."

"Do you have access to the books? The finances?"

"No, I don't. Just Mr. Yusufi." She sighed. "Haven't you figured it out yet? I'm just a reluctant necessity at the orphanage in the form of caregiver—or organizer of caregivers. I'm a woman and they need women to look after the children, but the men handle everything else."

Sarah grimaced. "That was my impression."

"Why?"

"I'd just like to see where all the money is going, because it's sure not going to the kids. They barely have enough to eat and their clothes are threadbare." Sarah squeezed her hand. "I'll talk to you in a little bit. I'm going to see if anyone needs some help."

Kristin watched her go with a frown and decided she would just take it one day at a time.

"Paksima loves you very much," a quiet voice said from behind her.

Kristin turned to see Hesther. She never could tell if the woman liked her or not. "I love her," Kristin admitted. "She makes it easy."

Hesther gave her a small smile. "Maybe your God will find a way to allow the two of you to be together one day."

Her words speared Kristin's heart. "I'm not Muslim," she said, not saying anything about her God, unsure what the woman was after.

"I know. I also know the family of little Paksima."

Kristin gaped, then frowned. "She has no family."

"That's what her mother said when she brought her here, but I recognized her. Paksima's a child with a price on her head. Her family's enemies would do anything to get their hands on her. For revenge."

"So she's hiding here?" Kristin whispered.

"Yes. I tell you this in case one day you need to know."

The mysterious words reverberated and left Kristin's mind spinning. "But . . ."

"Her mother is dead, now they look for her."

"What's her last name?"

"Shahid."

Kristin studied the woman. "Why are you really telling me this?"

"Like I said, you may need to know that one day." Hesther gave her that Mona Lisa smile once more, then slipped down the hall toward the classrooms.

○ ○ ○

Caden hung up the phone with Joan Banks, one of the medical examiners assigned to the bodies being brought in from the scene. Clarissa had been too busy to talk to him. Joan had been happy to help. Okay, maybe not *happy* exactly, but at least she'd been willing after he'd promised to use his connections to get her box seats at the next South Carolina–Clemson game.

Unfortunately, that was the least of his worries.

He pressed his fingers to his eyes and knew that if he didn't get some sleep, he was going to pass out. He'd go home and crash soon, but first things first. Seated at his temporary desk in the sheriff's office, he opened the case file Joan had sent to him.

Working with the forensic anthropologist, Joan had completed and documented two autopsies. The first victim had been the bones of the infant found by the doctor's dog. After laying them out, Joan's report stated she'd found no obvious signs of trauma. DNA had been extracted from some of the remaining marrow, and they'd run it through the database, but nothing was in the system. Not that he'd expected there would be. The victim had been approximately eight months old, and given the condition of the body, the weather, the heat, the shallow grave, Joan guessed the child had been dead for about five months.

The second victim had been a young man between sixteen and eighteen, but his body had been scavenged. Basically, torn apart and missing too much to piece together what might have happened to him.

But again, Joan had stated that his skull was intact with no obvious trauma in that area that would explain how or why he'd died. And while most of the chest cavity had been missing, she'd not found a reason for his death in the part she'd been able to examine. "Knives or bullets can often leave chips or fractures in bones, but there's none of that here." Enough tissue was left in his pelvic area to do a tox screen, and she was waiting for that to come back.

It was something, but not much. But he hadn't expected much. It was time for him to head home and get some sleep. His phone rang just as he stood. He grabbed it with a glance at the screen, didn't recognize the number, but swiped to answer. "Caden Denning."

"Caden! Finally! I've been trying to reach you for days."

He sat forward, frowning. "Sarah? I've been right here and I haven't seen any calls from you come in."

"I know. It's not on your end. We've been without power a lot of the time. One of the grids was destroyed in a blast a few days ago. I've been able to call and text locally, but we just now got Wi-Fi back."

The tension threading his sister's voice spiked the hair on the back of his neck. "What's going on?"

"I'm investigating a story, Cade, and . . . it's turning into a real doozy."

"The same one you've been on for the past six months?"

"Yes."

"And?"

"And . . ." She blew out a sigh. "You know how much it pains me to admit this, but I may be in over my head."

"Then back off."

"I can't. For various reasons."

He tapped the little picture of the video camera that would turn the audio call into a face-to-face one. She accepted his request and her sweet face filled his screen. Or it would have been sweet if it hadn't been creased with worry and . . . fear? "Sarah, what exactly are you investigating?" She'd been vague when he asked before, and he'd let it go. Now he wanted every detail.

"A lot of different things. At first they didn't seem to be connected, but the more I dig, the more I'm finding."

Another vague answer. "Are you in danger? More so than what comes with being in Afghanistan?"

"No, not at the moment. At least I don't think I am. I'm being careful, and I'm staying mostly on base or at the orphanage where I have a lot of friends. And I have an escort wherever I go."

"What orphanage?" That was a new one. She hadn't mentioned that the last time they talked two weeks ago.

"Morning Star Orphanage. There are some hinky things going on here and I'm going to find out what."

"What kind of hinky things?"

"I suspect some black market adoptions, but I'm not sure. I've been watching the comings and goings of everyone at the orphanage, and when I haven't been able to be there, I've had someone on the inside watching. Her name is Kristin and she's an American as well."

He rubbed his blurry, rest-deprived eyes once more. It was getting hard to focus. "You need to come home, Sarah. This isn't worth your life."

"Says you," she said, her voice subdued. "Some things, some people, are worth dying for."

"But it doesn't have to be you!"

She fell silent. "I know you love me, Cade, but understand, this is something I can't just let go of. I've got months invested in this story. Finally, things are happening at warp speed and I'm making progress getting some answers."

Answers that others might not want her to find? Most likely. "So what are you doing at the orphanage exactly?"

"I'm sort of . . . um . . . undercover."

God help him, he was going to strangle her. As soon as he got her home safe and gave her a hug. "Undercover how?"

"As a part-time volunteer. As far as anyone there knows, I'm just another bleeding-heart American with too much time on my hands. My supervisor has cleared me—he knows what's going on."

"I thought you were a military journalist. What's this got to do with the military?"

"Tons. If what I've discovered is true . . ." She glanced over her shoulder and swallowed. "Look, I need you to talk to Brooke Adams and tell her to be careful. I tried calling her a couple of times, but naturally got the same results as when I tried to call you."

"What's with the new number? I didn't recognize it. Are you using your phone?"

"The government shut off my number and I had to get a new one under a fake name. I think that loud-mouth politician decided it would be fun to make my life miserable."

"You spoke against him. He was determined to get to you."

"I know."

"You should have come home then."

"He was just a side story. I had to give my editor something. And anyway, that guy didn't want to kill me, just drive me crazy."

Caden smothered a sigh for the umpteenth time since he'd taken Sarah's call. "I'll tell you who's being driven crazy," he muttered. "A poor long-suffering older brother."

"Cade—"

"Is it possible he's behind any of this?"

"No. There's nothing to indicate he's involved in anything I'm investigating right now. I just need Brooke to be careful and watch her back—and if she won't answer your call, then you're going to have to find her and tell her in person, because I overheard her name mentioned in regard to the soldier who died in the explosion. Isaiah Michaels. Her pictures in the burning café are all over the internet and someone was mighty interested in them."

He'd seen the pictures. They'd made national news and were probably going to win a Pulitzer. Brooke Adams was the woman in those pictures? Whoa. "Who mentioned Brooke's name?"

"An American soldier. I'm trying to find out his name. I was in the base cafeteria and two soldiers were talking. One of the guys wanted to know what Isaiah said to her just before he died."

Caden frowned. "Why would he care?"

"I've managed to uncover that Isaiah was going to be charged with treason the day he died."

The day *she* could have died. She'd been at that café only moments before the bombs went off. He shuddered every time he thought about it. "Why? What'd he do?" He refrained from asking how she'd managed to unearth that bit of information.

"Isaiah was at the hospital before the explosion. He took something or found out something related to what's going on at the orphanage."

"What'd he take?"

"Files or patient information, I think. I'm not exactly sure." She gave a slight shake of her head. "When I overheard Brooke's name, then Isaiah's, I started listening a little closer and they mentioned stolen files. They said something about the orphanage, but I couldn't make out exactly what. Then I followed these guys to the security office, where they watched some footage."

"What was on it?"

"I don't know. They shut the door before I could see."

He shut his eyes and prayed for patience. "Sarah, this sounds like a bunch of disjointed, disconnected stuff." Disjointed, unsafe stuff.

"I agree," she said, her frustration evident, "but I think it *is* connected somehow. I just don't know how to do the connecting. I don't have the resources, but . . ."

"But?"

"You do. You've got friends in high places—not to mention stationed here in Afghanistan. Could you have one of them find out what's on that security footage? I had a feeling one of them had seen it before and was just showing the other guy."

"I can try to get in touch with Felicia Wilson. She's a special agent based there. I'll give her your number and you can tell her what you need." He might also ask the woman to keep an eye on Sarah—if she could.

"Good. Thanks. I'm just concerned, because when they came out of the office, they were arguing."

"About?"

"Isaiah Michaels again. And then they saw me standing there. They both gave me a funny look, so now I'm really on edge."

"What?" The word exploded from him and he sat up, tension running a groove up the back of his neck and into his skull. "Sarah . . ." He closed his eyes for a brief second. "Did they say anything? Do anything?"

"No, I was wearing a white lab coat and a hijab and had a stethoscope around my neck. I was carrying my iPad too, so I looked like I belonged there. I don't think they realized that I was snapping pictures of them with the iPad, but again that look they gave me—"

"You were snapping . . ." Caden stopped and pressed his fingers against his aching head. Snapping. Yes. Something he was coming very close to doing. "And you didn't recognize them?"

"No, I'm telling you, I've never seen them before, but as you well know, that doesn't mean anything. There are several bases here. Anyway, I sent you their pictures. Can you see if you can ID them for me?" She paused. "I need to know who those guys are, and there's no one on this side of the world I can ask without worrying it's the wrong person."

The connection blipped for a moment before she came back on the line.

"Have you talked to Dustin?" he asked. Their other sibling was stationed not too far from Sarah.

"No. I've called and he hasn't called me back."

Caden frowned. He hadn't heard from Dustin in a while either. He made a mental note to call him. "Sarah, if Dad gets wind of this—"

"No!"

He grimaced at her shout.

"No," she said, softer this time. "He can't know about any of this. He'll wind up pulling some strings and I'll get sent home. I'm not ready for that to happen yet."

He gave a silent groan. Like he needed more stress. But she was right. Their father *would* pull strings, and as a lieutenant general, he had access to a lot of them. Caden raked a hand over his hair. "Wait for Felicia to call you before you do anything else. Please."

"Okay. Well, I mean, I'm still working at the orphanage, but I'll try not to rock any more boats until I hear from her."

She'd try. He could already see the boats rocking to the point of tipping over. "I'll find out who these guys are," he said, "and I'll talk to Brooke, but you need to stay in touch with me. I want you to check in every twelve hours. The same time every day. No texting. I want a phone call so I can hear your voice. If you're even an hour late, I'm going to assume something bad has happened to you. And if you find yourself in trouble and can't call, I want you to text me. Use the word 'snowball' in the text and I'll know you're in trouble. Understand?"

She went silent, and at first Caden thought she'd refuse—which had him wondering how to explain to his SAC that he was taking time off to go track down his sister. "All right," she finally said. "I think that might be a good idea—as long as I have service. What happens if I don't have service?"

"I'll have Felicia get you a sat phone." Should have done that the minute she'd enlisted and been sent to the Middle East.

"Yeah. That'd probably be a good idea."

Now he was really scared. The calls were simply for his peace of mind. If she wound up in trouble, there was no way he could act fast enough to help her in a timely manner.

His phone buzzed. A text from Zane.

The doctor that found the graves is in the clear.
We've still got work to do.

Caden reached for the roll of Tums in the front pocket of his khakis.

TEN

Brooke stared out the window, waiting on Heather to finish her shift at the hospital, while Asher made himself at home on the couch in Heather's den. He'd refused to leave even when she'd assured him she was fine. "I'll just hang around if that's all right," he'd said. "I don't think you should be alone until Ricci's partner is caught."

"I'm okay with that."

She'd texted Heather that she was there and made her way to the spare bedroom to gather her thoughts and take inventory of the clothes and other items she'd left there. Her friend had grown up in foster homes, bounced from one end of the state to the other, but with an iron will, a near-genius IQ, and an unstoppable drive to succeed, she'd graduated from high school and joined the Army so she could study medicine and squirrel away her pennies. As soon as Heather had saved up enough for a down payment, she purchased her first home and flipped it for a decent profit. Then did it again and again. And served her country while her bank account grew.

Brooke's phone rang. This time she recognized the number and tapped the screen to answer. "Hi, Kat."

"Brooke! Thank you for answering. I don't know how long I'll be able to talk. The power keeps going off and on—you know that, of course—but I didn't give my permission to print those pictures. I'd never, ever do that, I promise." Tears coated her friend's words and Brooke shut her eyes to hold back her own.

"Heather told me, but I . . . I should have known, Kat. I'm sorry I jumped straight to the conclusion that you'd betrayed me."

"I don't blame you a bit. The truth is, I wanted to show them to the world, but not this way. Not at your expense."

Brooke appreciated her friend's honesty. "How is everyone?"

"I know you won't believe this, but you're missed. I was snapping shots of the guys playing basketball—now, there's an assignment I'll never pass up—and they were talking about the shrink and how they missed her even though they'd never admit it to anyone but themselves."

"They said that in front of you?"

"I'm invisible when I'm behind the camera, I guess, and they had their guard down. But the shrink had to be you."

Gratitude flooded her. Maybe she'd made a difference after all. "And how's Sarah?"

"Sarah is Sarah . . . I haven't seen her in a while," Kat said, her tone changing, deepening. "Something's going on with her. Frankly, I'm worried. I need to call her."

"Why?"

"She's staying in touch, but it's like the power—intermittent. Whatever this story is she's working on, it must be huge. She's being super tight-lipped."

"She's been like that for months now. Keep an eye on her, Kat. If anyone's going to wind up in trouble over there, it's her. She's too impulsive."

"Boy, is that ever the truth. I'll see if I can find her and pin her down. Get her to talk to me."

"Just let me know that she's okay, will you?"

"Of cou—" The phone blipped and the call disconnected.

98

With a sigh, Brooke tossed the phone onto the dresser and said a quick prayer for her friends.

"You have your own room here?" Asher asked from the open door.

She jumped, his voice sending her heart pounding into triple time. She glanced up from the clothes she'd laid out on the bed, and for a moment she couldn't speak. She wasn't sure if it was because he'd startled her or simply because he was there. He looked so solid, so strong, so . . . safe.

"Brooke?"

"Uh, no. Not my own room, just a key to get in the house and access to the guest room. Which is what I am a lot of the time—the guest."

He eyed the clothes. "Who do those belong to?"

She flushed. "Well, me. But I just keep a couple of outfits here. Heather and I do a lot of spur-of-the-moment stuff since our schedules can be a bit crazy." She fingered one of the shirts. "Hers mostly. We've learned how to be flexible and make it work for us. The clothes in my guest closet"—she gestured to the ones she was wearing—"are Heather's. Fortunately, we're about the same size, although she's taller and I have to roll her jeans up."

"I noticed that."

Of course he had. It seemed like he noticed everything.

"She doesn't like roommates either, does she?" he asked.

"No."

When Brooke and Heather had discussed moving back to Greenville, neither had broached the idea of moving in together. They knew each other too well for that. Heather wanted her space, and Brooke needed her own too. But that didn't mean she wasn't perfectly comfortable using her key and letting herself into Heather's home while she got herself together and charted a plan of action. "When we were looking for houses to buy, we tried to find something we both liked in the same area, but she wanted to

99

be near the hospital and I wanted to be near downtown. So we're about ten minutes apart. Like I said, it works for us." She paused. "When do you think I can get back in my house?"

"Probably tomorrow. I think we gave them all the information they needed. The crime scene unit will process everything, and then someone will let you know when you can go back. Did you contact your insurance company?"

"No, I'm not filing a claim. Nothing was taken and all I need to fix is the window." The truth was, she wasn't sure she wanted to go back. Well, she did, but not until every possible entrance to her home had been appropriately wired. "I'll call the alarm company first thing in the morning and set up an appointment." She let out a deep sigh. "But for now, I'm hungry and I know Heather will be starving when she gets home. She probably hasn't eaten much today."

"You cook?"

"I love to when I have the chance—or someone to cook for."

"I'm willing to be a guinea pig."

His eagerness made her smile. "You don't have someone who cooks for you?"

"No, not really."

His eyes flickered with a look she couldn't interpret. She tilted her head and studied him, then walked past him into the hall and led the way to the kitchen. He followed as she'd figured he would.

"I dated someone for a while, but my . . . uh . . . issues seemed to be off-putting to her."

"Then she didn't deserve you."

He stilled at the instant response. She hadn't even had to think about what to say. It felt good. "Thanks."

She tossed a smile over her shoulder before rummaging in the cabinet for the large pot to boil water.

He leaned against the doorjamb to watch, and once she had the water going, he shifted. "Can I do anything to help?"

"Can you cook?"

"Depends on what it is."

"Chicken tetrazzini." She opened the refrigerator and pulled out the chicken.

"Ah, yeah, no. I believe that one's above my pay grade—or kitchen skills in this case. How do you know all the ingredients are here?"

Using the cutting board and a large knife, she began cutting the chicken into strips the way she liked it. "Because Heather has a shopper and she always fills the refrigerator with fresh meats and veggies on Tuesdays." She tossed him a smile. "And this is one of our favorites. Can you get the pasta out of the pantry?"

With a slightly bemused look on his face, he gave her a quick nod, then moved to do her bidding. Once she had the chicken prepared and in the oven, as well as the pasta boiling, she motioned to the table. He sat and she took the chair opposite him. "So, what's your story, Asher?"

"You know most of it."

Brooke let a short laugh escape. "I know next to nothing. Tell me about your siblings, your parents. What are they like?"

He cleared his throat and dropped his gaze to his hands clasped on the table. "My parents are Jonathan and Patricia James. They're good people for the most part. Well meaning, I think, and . . . nice. Very proper, thanks to my mother's British upbringing." Another nod, but this one more for himself than for her. "My father is a lawyer. I think he may have political ambitions, but he hasn't announced that yet. My older brother, Nicholas, is also a lawyer with Dad's firm, much to my parents' satisfaction—and probably relief. My younger sister, Lyric, graduates from college this year with her biology degree. She'll start med school in the fall."

"Very high-achieving family."

"Well, most of us. I'm the black sheep."

"Hmm. And your mother?"

"The perfect lawyer's wife. She's brilliant and was studying to be a physician when she met my father. At the time, she decided she'd rather get married and have kids than finish school. I think she regrets not finishing now, but all in all, she seems to be content."

She studied him. "They don't understand you at all, do they?"

He laughed—a short humorless bark. "And are completely confused as to where they went wrong with me."

"But they love you."

"Yeah, they do. Most of them anyway."

"Are they from Greenville?"

"No, Charlotte."

"So you wound up here because of the job with Gavin?"

"I did. What about you?"

She got up to check the pasta. "What do you want to know?"

"Same stuff. Siblings? Parents?"

"My mom left when I was sixteen. I haven't talked to her since."

"Oh, I'm sorry."

She shrugged. "I was, too, for a long time, but she didn't want to be a mother. Or maybe she just didn't know how. I've learned to let her go and can honestly say I hope she's happy. And . . . I've got two sisters and a brother." She drained the linguine. Once the chicken was finished, she'd add the pasta and it would be done. Her mouth watered at the thought. "My sister Veronica is twenty-four. She's the baby and is off exploring the world trying to find herself—and has been for the past two and a half years—so the joke is she's just really, really lost. My other sister, Misty, is on her third marriage. She has two kids from the first marriage and teaches fifth grade at an elementary school near her house."

"Three marriages?"

"It's not like we had a very good role model of what to look for in a husband." The words were out before she could implement the filters.

"So your dad—"

"Wasn't great. Very controlling, rigid, unforgiving. Sarah Denning and I often talked about the similarities between our fathers. Hers is much the same way."

"Ouch." They fell silent for a moment. "What about you?"

"What about me?"

"You're not married. Any significant other?"

"No." She couldn't help the clipped response in spite of doing her best to keep her mind from going to Kirkland Hatfield.

"But . . ." He drew the word out.

Brooke grimaced. "But nothing. Unlike Misty, I seem to have a harder time meeting someone."

"Meeting someone or committing to someone?"

"Meeting someone worth committing to. And anyway, the commitment issue wasn't mine." She hopped up and went to check the chicken in the oven.

"So whose was it?"

"It doesn't matter. He's in the past."

"Hmm. And the brother?"

"That would be Paul." She smiled. "He's the best and I love him. He's a pastor, believe it or not."

"A pastor? Where?"

"Here. In Greenville."

"What led him to that?"

"I think a lot of his search for God came from a . . . dissatisfaction with the father figure in our lives, so he went looking for a better one. He jokes that he found himself spending so much time with God that he figured he might as well get paid for it." She shook her head.

Asher laughed. Then blinked as though the sound surprised him.

"He was my spiritual influence," she said. "He'd found peace and life, and I wanted to know how he'd done that. It took a while for me to believe it could be real, but I discovered that it could.

Doesn't mean everything in my life is perfect, but at least I know I'm not alone in dealing with it."

"Have you called to tell him about what happened with Sharon?"

"No."

"Why not?"

Brooke planted her hands on her hips. "You're awfully nosy, aren't you?"

"How else am I going to find out what I want to know?"

"Right. I didn't want to worry him. He's a . . . well, he can be a helicopter brother, and I prefer to just stay quiet for now. So how well did you know Isaiah?" she asked. Two could play the change-the-subject game.

His eyes glittered with what she thought might be humor for a brief second. Because he knew exactly what she was doing. The humor faded. "Isaiah was one of us. Part of my unit."

"I'm sorry."

"I'm glad you were there for him in the end," he said, all trace of laughter gone. "Not glad you were hurt, but glad he wasn't alone."

"He was so concerned about being labeled a traitor. His last words were to make sure Miranda knew he wasn't a traitor." She bit her lip. "What if—" No. It was a crazy thought.

"Don't stop. What if what?"

"What if he wasn't the traitor, but someone in your unit was? And they set him up to take the fall?"

Asher reared back. "What? No. No way."

"I know. It's a harsh thing to say, but I keep going round and round about it and it's the only thing I can come up with. If Isaiah wasn't a traitor and there's evidence that says he was, then he was set up. It's pretty simple, if you ask me."

○ ○ ○

Simple? Hardly. "I know those guys and there's not one that could do that." He wouldn't believe it. Not for a second. And yet he wouldn't have thought Mario Ricci could have done what he'd done either. Still . . . "We ran missions together—good ones and a couple that went sideways. Every man in that unit has saved my hide more than once, including Isaiah. I can't see it."

"Can't or won't?"

The words were calm. Curious and nonjudgmental, but she might as well have shouted them. "Can't. Won't. What difference does it make? They like to blow off steam and they can be loud, obnoxious, and rowdy, but none of them would do anything that could be considered traitorous. Except Ricci, of course. His actions have gone against everything I'd ever believe him capable of, but the others? No way."

"But . . . what if?"

"There is no what-if."

"Asher—" The rumble of the garage door opening stopped her. "That's Heather."

He sniffed. "And I think the food's done." Grateful for the timely interruption, he rose to take the dish out of the oven, and while the friends greeted each other, he added the pasta to the chicken and set it on the table.

Heather tilted her head toward Asher. "It's good to see you."

"You too."

"I can't tell you how much I appreciate this," Heather said, dropping her purse and mail onto the counter. "It's been a very long, tedious shift, and to come home to this is an answer to prayer."

"Then let's eat," Brooke said. She went to the refrigerator and pulled out the fixings for a salad while Heather set the table. They worked together, not having to ask each other anything, they just knew what to do. Kind of like the guys in his unit.

"You two do this a lot?" Asher asked.

"A couple times a week," Heather answered with a smile.

It didn't take them long to demolish the meal, and Asher soon leaned back, his stomach full and his eyes heavy. If he'd been at home, he would have moved to the couch and slept—for as long as he could have anyway. He didn't dare fall asleep here.

"So tell me, what's going on?" Heather asked. "When you texted, you made it sound like it could wait, but apparently you downplayed everything and then you wouldn't answer your phone." She shot a reproving glance at Brooke. "The simple text you sent saying you'd explain when you saw me was decidedly not acceptable."

"I didn't want to distract you from doing your job," Brooke said. "And Asher's been with me every minute." She sent him a grateful smile and his heart thudded an extra beat.

What was it about her that drew him like a magnet? She was pretty, but not drop-dead gorgeous like Heather. While he noticed Heather's beauty, and even liked her personality and quick wit, it was Brooke he was drawn to. It was confusing—and bemusing.

He cleared his throat, then finished off his iced tea and leaned forward. "I think we need to talk about the elephant in the room."

Brooke sighed. Nodded. "All right."

Heather's gaze bounced between them as they related what had happened, but she didn't say anything. Only her expressions betrayed her shock.

Asher turned to Brooke. "Mario Ricci broke into your home."

Heather gasped and Brooke frowned. "What?"

"Uh . . . nothing."

"You know Mario?" Asher asked.

"Not really. Let's just say I know the name."

Brooke narrowed her eyes. "Okay." She glanced back to Asher. "And yes, he broke into my home."

"It appears that he was looking for something other than cash or stuff to fence."

"Again, yes. But what else could he have been looking for? I don't have anything."

"There's another possibility," he hedged.

"What?"

He really didn't like this one, nor did he want to share it with her.

"Come on, Asher, tell me," Brooke said. "I need to know."

"It could be he had no intention of leaving without you and was just seeing what he could find while he waited for you to get home." She paled.

"So if he was after something besides goods that he could easily unload on a fence," he continued, "I'd say we need to know what that something is in order to ensure your safety."

"Well, if he's still alive," Brooke said, "we need to go to Memorial. You have a connection with him just from serving in Afghanistan, if nothing else. If you play that up, you might be able to get him to talk."

He doubted it but could see it would mean a lot to her if he'd try. He hesitated, then caved. "All right, we can head to the hospital whenever they say he's awake." A pause. "If he wakes up."

"Yeah. If."

"Wait a minute," Heather said. "You mentioned Memorial. I had a GSW victim come through surgery. The only one tonight. Are you saying that's the guy who attacked and tried to kill you?"

"If his name is Mario Ricci, then yes," Brooke said.

"Um . . . I see."

"But you can't say," Asher said. "HIPAA and all that?"

"Yes, HIPAA and all that."

"Did he have any friends or family with him?"

"Not that I spoke to."

Brooke's phone rang. She glanced at the number and frowned.

"Who is it?" Asher asked.

"I don't know. I've gotten a couple voice mails from numbers I don't recognize. I guess I need to take care of those soon." She let this call roll to voice mail as well. "But I can do that later. I want to know how Mario is doing and if he can answer a few questions."

Asher nodded and slipped into the den to make the call.

ELEVEN

Heather turned to Brooke. "Are you okay?" she asked, her concern evident.

Tears gathered at her friend's question, and Brooke swiped at them to clear her bleary eyes, wishing she could sleep for a week. Without dreams or nightmares. "No, I'm not okay. Sharon is dead, and I think it was supposed to be me who was killed, not her."

"Why do you say that?"

"Because if you think about it, we look fairly similar. Like, if the killer had a rough description or a bad picture—"

"Like the one in the paper?"

Brooke frowned. "Yes, like the one in the paper. I can see how he might mistake her for me. Especially since she was in my office." She ran a hand over her face. "Probably fixing coffee for me like she's done every morning since I started working there." She pressed her fingers to her eyes. "She died because she was fixing coffee. For me."

"That's a big leap there."

"Maybe." She dropped her hands to her lap. "And I wouldn't

have even thought about it if someone hadn't been in my house when I got home. Now, I just don't know. I wonder . . ."

Heather narrowed her eyes. "Wonder what?"

"I had a client in Afghanistan. He was from this area and I had to send him home."

Her friend straightened and her eyes sharpened. "You think he's the one who did this? That he was coming after you because he wants revenge?"

"I don't know. What do you think?"

"I think it's not out of the realm of possibility and it needs to be checked out."

Brooke nodded.

"You need some sleep," Heather said.

"Yeah." Brooke lifted her gaze to meet Heather's. "Are you sure you're okay with me staying here tonight? You need your rest too, and I might . . . well, you know."

Heather scowled. "The fact that you even asked is insulting."

"I know."

"Good." Heather yawned. "I think I'm going to take a hot shower and grab some sleep while I can. You don't have to worry about waking me up tonight anyway. I'm on call."

"Bless your heart."

Her friend stood. "And I wouldn't mind if you did."

"What?"

"Wake me up. You know that, right?"

"I know."

Heather hugged her and Brooke cherished the sweet connection for the brief moment. God may not have blessed her with the kind of family she'd always yearned for growing up, but he'd made up for that in the kind of friends he'd placed in her life.

Heather stepped back, smothering another yawn. "Oh my. I'm tired. Thank you for the fabulous meal. Now I'm going to leave you with this positive thought."

"What's that?"

"If you can't make it as a shrink, you can always start a catering business."

Brooke tossed her wadded napkin at Heather as the woman left. Heather's lighthearted teasing never failed to lift her spirits. Today was no exception, in spite of the tragedy she'd just suffered.

But now her friend was gone and Asher was in the den still talking on the phone. As it didn't sound like a conversation with someone at the hospital, he was probably talking to one of his coworkers.

Brooke crossed her arms in front of her on the table and rested her head on them. The action pulled at the scars on her back, but she ignored the sensation and closed her eyes.

"Wake up! Wake up!" She shook him, but his eyes were locked on the ceiling above. Pop! Pop! The fire crackled. The smoke moved in, covering her like a weighted blanket. She coughed, unable to breathe. The pain finally registered and she looked down to see her arms engulfed. The right one fell off, then the left. Isaiah picked one up and held it out to her. She didn't understand. He was dead. He shouldn't be able to help her. He was dead!

She screamed.

A hand shook her. "Brooke, hey, Brooke, it's okay. Wake up."

Her eyes popped open. The flames and smoke faded. Her fingers—of both attached arms—curled into fists. Asher sat in the chair next to her, eyes full of compassion and understanding. "How long was I screaming?" she asked, her voice husky, thick with sleep. The fact that she'd basically passed out the moment she'd closed her eyes told her what she already knew. She needed to find a way to deal with the nightmares.

"Just once."

Her gaze flicked toward the stairs.

"Heather didn't hear it, I don't think. The shower's still running." He frowned. "And I think I hear music."

"She has a shower radio." Brooke pushed to her feet, cheeks heated, shame gripping her. "Sorry about that." She shouldn't have relaxed or let her guard down, but she was so tired.

She walked into the large den and eyed the refrigerator next to the bar in the corner.

"Don't start," Asher said. "It's too hard to stop."

"I'm not." She looked away. "I think about it, but I've seen what self-medicating with alcohol does and it's not pretty. As much as I might be tempted or want the oblivion I know it can bring, I just . . . won't."

"Your father?"

She gave one quick nod. "So I know better. But I can't say I don't remember the nights he simply passed out and didn't wake up until the next morning."

"He paid for those hours, though."

"You sound like you know that from experience."

His gaze met hers. "I do. My problem started in college. In Kabul, I knew I'd need my wits about me if I was going to survive." He shrugged. "My sister begged me not to die over there, and I knew alcohol would lessen my chances of coming home. So I haven't touched a drop since I joined the military. Not that I haven't been tempted sometimes."

She swallowed hard and let her eyes linger on his. "I'm sorry."

"Yeah, well, it's just one day at a time, right?"

Brooke huffed a short laugh. "Right. Are you sure you're not the one with the psychiatric degree?"

"Ha. Funny."

He gestured to the couch and she sat. "What did you find out about Mr. Ricci?"

"He pulled through surgery and is holding his own. He should be awake sometime tomorrow, and the nurse said we could come by and talk to him."

"How did you get her to reveal all that?"

"She's kind of a friend."

"Kind of?"

"I've been going to church with Gavin, and she's a member there. I simply told her the truth. That I was one of the people he tried to kill, wanted to ask him why, and could she tell me when I could do so."

"Okay, then we go first thing in the morning before we head to Columbia to see Miranda?"

"We?"

"Of course, we. I've canceled my appointments indefinitely. Marcus is working on getting everything—" The ringing phone cut her off. She snatched it and glanced at the screen. "It's the same number as before."

"Did they leave a message before?"

"Yes."

"Why don't you see what's so urgent?"

She sent the call to voice mail. "If it's so important, they'll leave another message."

Once the voice mail indicator popped up, she tapped the screen and listened. "Brooke, this is Special Agent Caden Denning again. I'm going to assume that you haven't listened to my earlier voice mails, so I'll start from the beginning. This is going to seem like a really strange request, but I talked to my sister, Sarah, and she said she thought you were in danger and you needed to watch your back. It had to do with something she overheard regarding your last inter-action with Isaiah Michaels before the explosion at the restaurant. Anyway, give me a call at your earliest convenience. If I haven't heard from you by tomorrow morning, I'll try again." He left his number, and it matched three of the previous attempts to reach her.

"Oh boy."

"What is it?"

She summarized the call from Caden Denning. "I need to call him back."

"Go ahead," Asher said. He stood and paced. "I'm just going to do a perimeter check around this place."

"Just so you know," Brooke said, "Heather's windows are wired."

He shot her a tight smile. "Good to know."

Her first attempt to reach Special Agent Denning went to voice mail. She left him a message, and almost before she could even hang up, her phone was ringing, displaying his number. "Hello?"

"Is this Brooke Adams? Sarah's friend?"

"Yes."

"This is Caden Denning, but I guess you figured that out."

"I did. I've heard a lot about you." She and Sarah had exchanged family histories over the course of serving together, but she'd never met the woman's family.

"Uh-oh."

"All good, I assure you. Sarah adores you."

"The feeling is mutual." He cleared his throat. "I'm assuming you listened to my messages?"

"I just listened to the last one. I'm so sorry I didn't pick up when you called, but it's been a very crazy day."

"What kind of crazy, if you don't mind me asking?"

She told him and he sucked in an audible breath when she finished. "Sarah said you might be in danger."

"I think we've figured that part out."

"Well, there's more." She listened to him talk about Isaiah Michaels and the fact that he'd taken something from the hospital just hours before the explosion had taken his life—and that two men were talking about her. But why?

"What about Sarah?" she asked. "Is she okay? Is she safe?"

"That's a really good question, but apparently something that happened between you and Isaiah has caught the attention of some people. Can you think of what that might be?"

"No. Seriously, the day's not even a blur until the very end. I remember the details vividly. All Isaiah wanted me to do was refute any accusations that he was a traitor. His dying words were 'Not a traitor. Don't let them say I am.'"

Caden fell silent for a moment. She could almost hear him thinking. "Someone was framing him?" he finally said. "Setting him up to take the fall for something?"

"I sure think so, but I don't have the first clue as to what—or who. He did say, 'I didn't know. I didn't know.'"

"You were his psychiatrist. He didn't tell you anything at all?"

She let out a harsh laugh. "No. He never said more than hello and goodbye to me most days."

"Nothing about his unit, his friends, his brothers, his family?"

She hesitated. Technically, according to HIPAA, she shouldn't say anything, but deep in her gut, she knew Isaiah would give her permission to use anything available to clear his name. "He . . . uh . . . yes, actually, one time. He mentioned his wife, Miranda, in the last session. I was asking him how he was going to deal with everything when he got home and had to adjust to civilian life. I asked him his plans and he blurted out something about asking for Miranda's forgiveness. Seemed mad that he'd said that, then said he had to leave—and did."

"What did he need forgiveness for? That seems to indicate he felt guilty about something."

"I don't know. He didn't give me any details. But I didn't get the feeling the guilt was related to being a traitor. I think it was something else because he kept saying 'I didn't know. I didn't know.' Like he'd done something and later found out it wasn't a good thing, and he regretted it but was justifying his actions because he didn't know . . . something."

"Like maybe he acted on information without having all the facts?"

"Yes, something like that." She sighed. "But I'm speculating. Again, it's just a gut feeling. I'd planned to ask him about the comment at the next appointment, but he never showed up—and truly, he probably wouldn't have told me anyway. I didn't see him again until the day of the explosion."

"Okay, I'm going to send an officer over for now to keep watch on the house and follow you around for the next twenty-four hours."

The door opened and Asher stepped back inside. "All clear," he said.

"Who's that?"

"Asher James. He was in Afghanistan with Sarah and me. He was actually there the day of the bombing and pulled me out." The images flickered in her mind, and she drew in a deep breath, focusing on the phone call. "I'm not at my house right now, Caden. I'm staying with Heather Fontaine. I'm sure Sarah's mentioned her."

"She has. All right. I'll send someone out there. Give me the address."

"I'm not sure that's necessary, but all right." She rattled it off for him.

"I think it might be necessary. Stay in touch with whatever you find out about Isaiah Michaels." He paused and she could hear keyboard keys clicking in the background. "I'm going to call CID and ask them to get involved in this." The Criminal Investigation Division was in charge of investigating any illegal activity within the Army.

"They were involved. Who do you think presented the evidence that nailed Isaiah as a traitor?"

Silence. "I see. All right, I have a friend who's CID. I'll ask her to unofficially look into it."

"You trust her?"

"I do. Actually, we have to. Because if someone set up Isaiah, then that someone is involved in something illegal and needs to be caught and stopped."

"And if he did that to Isaiah, he'll do it again to someone else."

"Exactly."

o o o

Asher paced from one end of Heather's living area to the other as he debated the events of this endless day. First Sharon's death, then Mario Ricci had tried to kill him and Brooke.

His friend from the hospital had called him ten minutes ago to let him know that Ricci's prognosis had taken a nosedive. He was now in a medically induced coma, so getting answers wasn't going to happen anytime soon. Which meant he and Brooke needed to find someone who knew what he was up to and why he'd been searching Brooke's home. They needed to link him to . . . something recent. Someone current. They needed to know where he was living and who he was living with and if he was working with anyone.

His phone buzzed and he pulled it from his pocket. Newell was finally calling him back. "Captain, thanks for returning my call."

"James, it's been a good while. How are you doing?"

"I'm hanging in there."

"Tough to transition back, isn't it?"

"Yes, sir."

"You're always welcome to come back. It's not the same without you and Black."

Asher shut his eyes. "Thank you, sir, I'll keep that in mind." Talking to the man brought everything back in force. The launch of the rocket that had taken out half their unit. The explosion at the café, killing Isaiah Michaels and two of his other unit members. A sniper making his head shot and obliterating Jasper Owens and the child on his back. *Nausea rolled, gunfire erupted.*

"James? You there?"

"Uh, yes sir, I am. Sorry, I was just . . . uh . . . remembering." And thinking that going back might not be a bad thing. He missed it.

"Right. So, what can I do for you?"

"Mario Ricci," Asher said. "You're good friends with Captain Gomez."

"I am."

"Well, Ricci just tried to kill Brooke Adams and me."

"What?" The hard bark hadn't changed, and once more Asher longed to be back there where everything was familiar and he knew exactly what was expected of him. "Who's Brooke Adams?"

"The psychiatrist who worked on base. You may have known her as Captain Adams."

"The one you pulled out of that café and wound up with her picture plastered all over the place?"

"That's the one." Asher explained the events that led to Mario's shooting. "He's still in ICU, but they expect him to pull through. When he wakes up, I plan on questioning him, but do you think you could talk to Captain Gomez and get some insight into why Ricci would break into Brooke's home?"

"Was he one of her clients?"

"No, she didn't recognize him. I did."

"I see." The man let out a low breath. "I have to say, I didn't think much could shock me anymore, but I'm pretty stunned at this news—about as shocked as when I got word that Isaiah Michaels was a traitor."

"I understand, I feel the same way. And for what it's worth, I don't believe Michaels was a traitor. If someone had evidence that he was, then he was set up."

Silence. Then . . . "What makes you say that?"

"I knew Michaels, sir, as well as you—or better. You know he'd never do anything to betray his country—or his unit."

"Yeah. But why go to all that trouble?"

"I don't know. Obviously, Michaels stumbled across something and trusted the wrong person with the information."

"You know who he talked to?"

"No."

More silence. "Okay, look, Ricci was let go with a dishonorable discharge. He and another soldier got into a fight, words were said, and that's why he's back in the States. However, I have no idea why he'd go after Brooke Adams. I'll look into Ricci," Captain Newell said, "and all of this."

"Thank you. I appreciate it."

"Tell Black we need him back here too." *Click*.

Unperturbed at the abrupt end to the call, Asher set his phone down and pinched the bridge of his nose. When his phone buzzed once more, he grabbed it. "Gavin, what's up?"

"I'm walking up to Heather's front door. Can you tell the cop out here that I'm a friend?"

"Yeah. Be right there."

Asher waved to the officer and led Gavin to the great room, where his friend settled himself on the couch.

"What's going on?" Asher claimed the recliner next to the fireplace and leaned forward, elbows on his knees, hands clasped between them.

"I was sitting outside Brooke's place just watching it," Gavin said, "thinking about Ricci and wondering if he was working alone or if he was taking orders from someone or what. About the time I was ready to leave, someone came by and started snooping around."

"Who?"

"Don't know. When I went to confront him, he took off and disappeared."

"On foot?"

"He had a motorcycle hidden away a couple houses down and he'd left the key in it. He simply vaulted over the back, into the seat, and off he went."

"Any plates on the bike?"

"No."

"Of course not. Did you report this?"

"I did. I don't think he messed with anything at the house, but an officer rode over to check it out."

"What did you find? Before the officer got there, I mean?"

"The place was boarded up," Gavin said, "but he could have gotten in if he wanted to." He paused. "Make that, if he'd had time to try."

Asher shook his head. "You know anything about Mario Ricci? Where he's from and what his story is? I know him, but not well."

"Same here. I hung out with him one night at that party Gomez threw for his unit after that particularly hair-raising adventure rescuing those two girls from the Taliban crew. I think Ricci's originally from Texas, though."

"Any family around here?"

"No."

"Then I don't get it. Could all this be connected to Afghanistan?"

"In what way?"

"Beats me."

"Yeah." Gavin eyed him. "So where are you sleeping tonight?"

"The couch. There's no way I'm leaving her here alone and unprotected." He ran a hand over his hair. "This is all messed up like a hot soup sandwich."

Gavin rubbed his chin. "Maybe Miranda Michaels can shed some light on that tomorrow when you go visit her."

"Let's hope so, because I'm at a loss as to what to do next—other than to somehow prepare for the next attack."

CHAPTER

TWELVE

The next morning Asher drove with confidence, his hands on the wheel, eyes on the road, although Brooke could feel him glancing at her every so often. "So," she said, "tell me about your unit in Kabul."

"Why?"

"Why not? Tell me about the men you served with."

He glanced in the rearview mirror and frowned. "They're good guys. Sergeant Mark Dobbs was our medic. The man's a genius when it comes to medicine and could improvise like no one's business if he had to."

"Where's he now?"

"Still serving. We text some, but mostly he's mad at me for getting out."

"Mad?"

"I broke up the unit."

"Oh. What about Gavin?"

"Oh yeah, we both get a snarky text every so often."

"I'm sure that's fun."

"I understand where he's coming from. He'll get over it in time. And then there's Jasper Owens. He was the youngest and most impulsive of all of us, but don't let that fool you, he was also probably the most deadly. Nerves of steel, that kid."

"You liked him."

"Yeah. A lot." He cleared his throat. "Unfortunately, he was killed by a sniper about two weeks before I flew home."

"Asher, I'm so sorry."

"It was supposed to be a routine mission. We were helping some children on the side of the road just outside the city and a sniper opened fire."

"Was anyone else hit?"

"One kid about nine years old. Owens was giving him a piggy-back ride. The bullet took them both out." He rubbed his eyes as though he could rub the memory away.

"How awful." Her heart ached. For the loss of life, for the people in Jasper's life who'd miss him. For it all. "I didn't know him. I saw him on base, of course, but I don't think I ever actually exchanged words with him."

"He was a bit of a hothead, but he was a good guy." He fell silent a moment, then blew out a short whisper of a breath. "Yeah. I miss him. His family misses him. It's sad and infuriating, but we know the risks when we sign up for the job. I think I related to Jasper because he reminded me a lot of myself, and his family reminded me a lot of mine."

"What about them?"

"We're just cut from a different mold," he said. "I have no idea how two people can create completely different kids."

"What do you mean?"

"Ah, well, my older brother, Nicholas, is a pain. He and I never got along at all. I used to think it was just that he didn't know how to have fun, but . . ." He clicked his tongue. "I don't know. I think he might actually be a sociopath."

"Wow."

"Yeah. He calls me the freak."

"Why on earth would he call you a freak?"

"Because I chose to serve my country rather than . . . do something else."

"Like what?"

"Anything that involved making a lot of money."

"That's sad."

"Indeed. But that's enough about my family. I like talking about the unit more. So, where was I? Oh, yeah. Mitch Sampson. He looks likes Paul Bunyan with a crew cut and no beard. He was our demo expert. Knows everything there is to know about explosives. It's weird, but he collects pieces of every bomb he survives."

"It's a coping technique," she said. "It probably makes him feel like God is on his side each time he walks away from something like that."

"Could be. I felt that way too but didn't want a souvenir as a reminder of how close I came to death."

"Different things work for different people."

"I'm not knocking him for it," he said. "I just found it weird."

"Is he still serving?"

"Oh yeah. The only way he'll leave the Army is by death or retirement."

"I'm voting for retirement," she muttered.

His gaze went to the rearview mirror once more.

"Something wrong?" He flipped the blinker to change lanes, and his white-knuckled grip worried her. "Asher?"

"Nothing's wrong. At least I hope not."

"Then why are you so tense your teeth are about to shatter?"

He shot her a scowl before his eyes darted to the mirrors again. "I think someone's following us."

"Really?" Her stomach dipped and she resisted the urge to turn and look. "Which vehicle?"

"A black van a couple of cars back. I'm going to take the next exit and see if they follow."

"Okay." Her right hand came up to grip the seat belt that crossed her chest, and her eyes went to the side mirror. Nothing. She watched the rearview mirror. "The black minivan?"

"Yes." Sweat beaded on his forehead.

"This isn't Kabul," she said. "May I hold your hand? Sometimes it helps to have that touch."

He shot her a swift look, hesitated, then reached over to grip her left hand. "Just until I need it again."

"Of course."

He continued to drive, but she thought he seemed calmer. She slid her right hand over to cover his wrist and felt his pulse beating beneath her fingers. A little fast, but nothing out of control.

"So the hand holding was for me, huh?" he asked without taking his eyes from the road.

"I was hoping it would benefit both of us."

He sat straighter. "All right, we're taking this exit." He adjusted the rearview mirror. "Can you see him?"

"Yes."

"Let's see if he follows."

Asher waited until the last minute to cut the wheel to the right and speed up the exit ramp. He passed two cars using the emergency lane, rolled to a halt at the stop sign, then made a quick left.

Brooke kept her eyes on the vehicle Asher suspected of following. "They didn't get off behind us."

"But the white SUV did."

"You think they're together?"

"We're going to act like they are."

The farther he drove, the more remote it became, with woods on either side of the two-lane road. "There's no one behind us."

"I'm sorry. I guess I'm just paranoid," he muttered as he slowed the truck to make a U-turn. "I'll circle back to the interstate."

Brooke wanted to chalk up his suspicious nature as a result of living on adrenaline for several years, but she couldn't help wondering . . . "You noticed that vehicle for a reason. What was it that stood out about it to you?" she asked.

He didn't answer right away but watched the road behind them. "I don't know," he finally said. "When I drive, I'm hyper aware of every vehicle around me and I spotted the van when we got on the interstate. It continued to stay behind us at exactly the same distance for the past twenty miles."

"And that white SUV is—"

"Coming straight toward us. Hang on, Brooke." He wheeled the truck to the right, but the driver of the SUV must have calculated that Asher would do that and managed to turn just in time to slam into them as they tried to pass him.

Brooke let out a low scream as the side air bags deployed, and her body rebelled at the impact. "Asher!" She looked over at him.

He had pushed up the side curtain air bag to see out his window. "Hold on! He's coming back!"

○ ○ ○

Asher gripped the wheel, grappling for control of the truck as the SUV backed up, then gunned the engine to make another pass at them.

"Call 911!"

"Trying," Brooke said. "I can't find it!"

He could hear the stark terror in her voice and silently vowed to get her out of this alive. Adrenaline pumped. Scenes from the past blipped through his mind and he did his best to shove them aside. *Focus. Just survive the moment. Think later.*

Anticipating a hard hit to the front of his truck, Asher spun the wheel and stepped on the gas, his only goal to get far enough ahead of the oncoming vehicle in order to take the collision on the truck bed instead of the cab.

He shot forward and the SUV hit behind the back door on his side. Asher lost his grip on the wheel—and control of his truck.

It spun once, twice, three times before it hurled off the road and into a large tree.

For a split second all was still and silent, then Brooke gasped, sucking in a breath.

Pain and shock held him motionless even while his mind ordered his body to move, to check on Brooke—and the location of the SUV. Finally, he pulled in a lungful of air and gave a quick glance back to see where their attacker was. The SUV was across the road, front end down and smashed up against a tree. No sign of the driver or a passenger. Yet.

Move! We have to move! "Brooke." Her name came out on a whisper and he cleared his throat. "Brooke!" Stronger this time.

She lay against the window, blinking. He straightened and unhooked his seat belt. A good distance away, a car approached from the opposite direction that the SUV had come from. An innocent motorist or someone looking for them?

With a groan, Asher leaned over and unlatched Brooke's seat belt. "Come on, Brooke, we've got to get out of here. I don't know if that's friend or foe coming this way, but I don't want to find out the hard way." His weapon still rested snug in his shoulder holster, but he didn't know where his phone was. It had flown out of the dash mount and he didn't have time to look for it. "Brooke." He rubbed her arm. The vehicle rolled closer on the flat stretch of road. "Come on, darlin', I need you to help me out here."

"Asher." She blinked up at him, the shock of the impact finally wearing off. She lifted a hand to her head and groaned. "That wasn't an accident."

"No, ma'am, that was definitely on purpose. The guy who hit us spun out too and went off the road into the trees on the other side of the road. We really need to get out of here before he recovers or his friends decide to come check on him." He glanced at the still-approaching vehicle, getting closer by the second.

"Right." She groaned again.

"Anything broken?"

"No. I don't think so. The seat belt did a number on me, but other than that, I think I'm all right. He hit on your side. How about you?"

"Nothing broken. Lots of bumps and bruises." He gripped her hand. "You're going to have to crawl over and come out my door." Her side was crunched up next to the huge oak tree.

With effort, she nodded.

"Yeah." He pushed open the driver's door, climbed out, and turned back to her. "Ready?"

"Sure."

He wasn't convinced she was being honest, but they were out of time. With a grunt, he helped her across the console and into the driver's seat. The car continued to close in on them and was finally near enough for Asher to make out that it was a black van.

"Hurry," he said, adrenaline spiking. "They're coming back to finish the job." With another pull, he had her out of the vehicle. Asher stopped long enough to make sure she had her feet under her before leading her around the front of his truck. A thought stopped him. He turned back to the truck, telling himself he didn't have time for this, but . . . "Hold on."

She stood still, swaying slightly when he let go of her.

Working quickly, he grabbed his registration and other identifying papers and stuffed them into the front pocket of his jacket. Not that they couldn't run his plates, but at least that would take more effort and time than getting his information from his glove box. He spotted his phone under the gas pedal.

An engine roared and a shot rang out.

Asher ducked and turned to find Brooke beside him. "Into the woods," he ordered, and pulled her after him as two more shots split the air.

CHAPTER

THIRTEEN

Brooke ducked, her war zone reflexes kicking in like she'd never left Kabul. Asher yanked her into the tree line. "Run!" The yell sent her stumbling after him, expecting to feel a bullet between her shoulders at any moment. Hand clasped in his, she held on, ignoring the throbbing in her head and back. Another bullet pinged off the tree beside her, and Asher made a sharp turn to the left.

Brooke stayed with him, but while she often used the punching bag in her basement to fight the memories and build her strength back up, she didn't go running. Simply because she hated it. It didn't take her long to grow winded. She pushed on anyway.

Finally, when she couldn't take another step, she yanked her hand from his and dropped to the wooded ground, dragging in oxygen with each gasping pull of her lungs.

Asher skidded to a halt and spun to hurry back and kneel in front of her. "You okay?"

"No, I'm not okay," she snapped and pressed a hand to her head.

He didn't seem to take offense at her shortness, he simply watched behind them. She sucked in another shuddering breath and stood. The ache in her side matched the one in her head. "I'm sorry."

"Don't apologize." He took three steps back toward the direction they'd just come from.

Brooke's harsh whisper brought him back. He shook his head. "Yeah. What?"

"I don't think the canoe fooled them. They're heading this way." She gripped his forearm and pulled him out the door of the office. "They're going to come in here and see the broken lock and know. What do we do?"

His mind clicked away from the past, and horror washed over him. His forays into the past . . . his hesitation . . . could get her killed. Chilled, he swallowed a surge of nausea and gripped her hand, centering his thoughts on just keeping her safe. "Come on."

"What are we going to do?"

"I locked the door when we came in. We'll have to keep an eye on them while we figure out what to do." He hurried to the door and flipped the dead bolt off.

"I think you're crazy, but now what?"

"I'm working on a plan. Up into the loft."

She frowned and glanced at the door but moved quickly and clambered up the ladder. He followed and pulled the ladder up after him. "Watch the door," he said. "When it opens, I'll need to know if one or both come in."

He didn't give her a chance to answer, simply hurried to the end of the loft, bringing the ladder with him. He pushed aside hay bales and stacked them, glancing at the door as he worked. Once he was finished, he made his way to the window at the top of the stack. Putting muscle behind it, he hefted it open—and turned to find Brooke at his side.

"When they walked across the yard," she whispered, "they were together. I don't know if they'll both come in, but at least one's going to be inside any second."

"All right, these hay bales are hiding the window and us from whoever walks through that door. If they both come in, we'll bust a move. If only one comes in, that's going to be a bit trickier." If one stayed on the outside, he'd be much more likely to notice the ladder—or hear them going down it.

Brooke peered around the bales. "Nothing yet."

Heart thudding, Asher carefully maneuvered the ladder out the window and onto the shingles of the roof over the main double doors of the barn. He turned to Brooke and motioned for her to follow him just as the door below squeaked open.

Asher stepped out onto the roof and held a hand back for Brooke. She hesitated, peering around the bales. Two seconds ticked past, feeling like five minutes for him, but she finally held up two fingers. He offered his hand once more. She took it and ducked out to stand beside him. He slowly closed the window, releasing a low breath when it slid shut without much noise. "It won't take them long to realize we were there and now we're not," he said. "I'm going to lower this ladder and we're going to climb down, okay?"

She nodded, dark fear in her eyes, as she stayed next to the window, back against the wall. Asher gripped the heavy wooden ladder and lowered it over the side to lean it up against the wall of the barn next to the roof's overhang. He hoped it would be harder to spot than if he'd placed it against the roof itself. "The first step is a doozy, so I'm going to have to lower you," he told her. "You ready?"

"I'm ready to get away from these guys."

"I hear you."

Brooke gripped his hands and swung her feet over the edge. He held her tight and lowered her to the top rung. When she tugged, he released her hands and down she went. Asher quickly followed, breathing a sigh of relief the moment his feet touched the ground.

"Can we steal their van?" she asked as they ducked under the pasture fence. Several horses grazed nearby.

He hesitated a fraction. It wasn't a bad idea, but . . . "If he has the keys, we'd be out of luck and I don't want to take the time to find out."

"Okay."

"How do you feel about horses?"

"Love them, why?"

"We're going to use them as cover. Grab part of the mane and walk on the far side of the horse, away from the barn." It was the best he could do in order to keep them from being completely exposed as they crossed the pasture.

Brooke moved to the first horse, hand outstretched as though she planned to feed one of them an invisible apple. The horse, a paint, lifted its head and let her approach. He gave her empty hand a snuffle, then shook his head in reproach. "Sorry, buddy," she said softly. "I guess that was kind of sneaky and mean, wasn't it? If I had an apple, I'd give it to you, I promise." Her soothing voice calmed the animal, and he let her scratch under his mane.

Another horse decided he needed his share of attention and approached. Asher curled his fingers around the halter of the second one and turned to Brooke. "Let's do this."

"Asher, look. They're outside the barn."

He glanced back and saw the two men in the yard once again, looking toward the main house and pointing. "Keep walking," he said. "Keep the horse between you and them. Slow and steady." She was already doing that, but it made him feel better to say it. Like he actually had control over something.

A shout caught his attention and he looked back once more. The two men raced toward the pasture, weapons raised.

CHAPTER

FOURTEEN

Brooke wondered how they were going to get out of this mess. Asher grabbed the horse's mane and swung himself onto the animal's back just as sirens sounded in the distance. "Get on," he yelled at her.

Still protected by the other horse, she peered up at him. "What? I can't do that! I don't ride!"

He held out a hand and looked back. "Come on, Brooke. They're right there at the edge of the fence."

She followed his glance to see the two men, one of them pointing in the direction of the sirens, then at her and Asher. Whatever they were arguing about was fine with her if it kept them from following—or shooting. "Put your foot on mine," Asher urged, "and I'll pull you up. Hurry, before they decide to start shooting and the horse spooks."

Brooke shut off the part of her mind that wanted to argue, grabbed his hand, stepped on his foot, and before she could blink, found herself seated in front of him. His arms snaked around her, and his fingers wrapped themselves in the strands of the horse's mane. Asher gave the animal a firm kick in the ribs and set them off in a fast trot. She squeezed her eyes shut and held on to Asher's wrists.

A single shot split the air and the horse leapt forward into a full-on run. Brooke squealed and ducked her chin against her chest as hooves pounded the hard ground. *Please, God, don't let them hit us or the horse. Please, please, please, please . . .*

"Hang on!"

He really didn't have to tell her that. She went with the motion of the horse. Down a hill, up a hill, down, then up.

The horse slowed and she opened her eyes, almost not quite believing she was still on top and not trampled underneath. The guys who'd been after them were out of sight.

"I think the cops are there," Asher said. "You can pull your nails out of my wrists now."

With a gasp she released him, appalled to see thin moon-shaped gouges seeping tiny spots of blood. "I'm so sorry!"

He smiled. "Didn't even feel it." He clicked to the horse and then trotted to the top of the next hill. Officers swarmed the area, weapons drawn. "Do you see them?" he asked. "Or the van?"

"It's gone. I'm sure they ran for it as soon as they realized officers were on the way."

"Most likely."

"What now?" she asked.

"Let's join the good guys back at the farm."

"I was hoping you'd say that."

He nudged the horse with his heels, and she gripped Asher's forearms for balance, making sure she kept her fingernails away from his skin.

"And what do you mean you don't ride?" he asked. "I thought you said you loved horses."

"I do. From a distance. They're beautiful animals, but I've never been on the back of one before today." At least this one was going slow now. She shivered, and he brought one hand up to rub her left arm, then slid his hand over hers. His palm was warm in spite of the chilly weather, and now that the danger was past, she could appreciate his nearness. The solid feel of him at her back gave her comfort in ways words couldn't express.

"Let's go see if they caught them," he said, "or at least have someone in pursuit."

"We came a long way," she said, letting herself relax against him. Yep, she liked being in his arms. And, oh boy, she needed not to like that. Right?

"Had to get out of range of the bullets," he said, "or at least out of sight. Once we were on the other side of the hill, they couldn't see us. You can't hit what you can't see."

"That was really smart using the horses. You bought us time, then you got us away from them. Thank you," she said, her voice low.

"Sure. You're welcome."

A police Range Rover with flashing blue lights drove through the gate and headed toward them.

"Keep your hands in sight," Asher said. "They might not realize we're the good guys yet."

She did as he said. "Whoa," Asher said, leaning back, pulling Brooke with him. The horse slowed, finally prancing to a halt. The vehicle stopped in front of them and the officer stepped out. "Brooke Adams?"

"That's me," she said.

He spoke into the radio, then dropped it into the vehicle. "That was dispatch wanting to know you're okay. She was worried when she lost contact with you."

"I'm fine." If you didn't count crashing adrenaline, shaky hands and knees, and the churning nausea at the back of her throat.

"I'm Asher James and we're really glad to see you guys. Did you catch the two in the black van?"

"No. And by the time a patrol officer got out to the scene with the white SUV, all that was left was evidence of the collision with the tree. Come on and I'll give you a ride to wherever you need to go."

"Back to see if my truck's drivable, I guess."

"We've got officers on the scene there. Once they're finished, you're welcome to drive away, call a tow truck, or whatever."

"Thanks."

"What was that all about anyway?" the officer asked.

Asher frowned. "I'm not sure." The officer nodded and stepped over to speak to a fellow cop. Asher glanced at Brooke. "Although, I can't help but wonder if yesterday and this incident are connected."

"They have to be," Brooke said. "And I have a feeling whoever's after us is just getting started."

○ ○ ○

Brooke's statement still rang in his mind as Asher cranked his truck. After detaching it from the tree with the help of the tow truck, he had found the truck drivable. Most of the damage had been done to the passenger side, but the engine and steering worked fine. He sliced the side air bags off with a knife from his glove box. And he'd found both phones.

Brooke was buckled in to her seat, looking weary but determined.

"Are you sure you want to visit Miranda today?" he asked. "We're about forty-five minutes away and the sun's going down in an hour and a half."

"I'm sure," she said and set her jaw. "I don't know what's going on—and I'll admit the lack of control over the situation is driving me batty—but this I can do. I can honor a dead man's last words and try not to feel guilty I haven't done it sooner."

"You had your reasons. Don't beat yourself up about that."

"But I do, Asher. I beat myself up every day because he's dead. If I had just—"

She fell silent, and he slowly pulled onto the road and waved a goodbye to the officer who'd driven them in from the pasture.

"Just what?"

"Nothing."

He glanced at her, but the closed expression on her face didn't invite him to press. For the next thirty minutes, he drove, watching the mirrors and even the sky. At this point, he was paranoid enough to believe he could be attacked from above.

The whomp-whomp-whomp *of the helicopters closing in for rescue sent a wave of relief over him. He stepped out to wave them in, only to realize . . . "Run! Run!"*

The rapid rat-a-tat-tat *of the mounted weapon blistered the air as the bullets chased him down the hill and around the protruding rock. Ducking behind it, Asher swiped a hand across his sweaty forehead and the bird banked off . . .*

He gasped and realized Brooke had laid a hand on his forearm. "Asher?"

"I'm fine."

He took the most circuitous route he could without diverting them too far off their path. He really wanted to get to Miranda's before dark.

"Tell me."

He stayed silent.

"Please," she whispered.

After a brief search for the right words, he finally clenched his fingers around the wheel, then made a conscious effort to loosen them. "I have . . . blips."

"Okay. Blips of what?"

"Blips of moments that I lived through." Barely. "I can function even as I'm having them. I can drive, walk, whatever, but I just sort of zone out for a few seconds." He drew in a deep breath. "Which is why I decided to see someone—well, between those and the nightmares. Someone who might experience some of the same stuff but know how to . . . deal with it." He shot her a sideways glance and caught her in a moment of intense vulnerability. Her expression was almost exactly like the one in the picture when she held the dying Isaiah in her arms. Only Asher wasn't dying—he just felt like he was sometimes. "Stop," he said.

Her eyes widened. "What?"

"Looking at me that way."

"Why?"

His jaw tightened. "Because I don't need or want your pity."

"Pity?" She jerked out a laugh. "Right. It's not pity."

"Then what?"

"Compassion . . . empathy. I've done exactly what you're talking about a few times—only mine's the same thing over and over. Mostly at night. Every once in a while during the day. So, no pity, just the intense understanding of what it feels like."

"What's yours?"

She hesitated. "It's . . . I'm . . . I've never put it into words before."

"Maybe it's time."

"I'm burning alive. And I watch . . ." Her heart pounded as the images swirled full force.

"Watch what?" His voice was barely a whisper.

"My arms fall off. My face melts and I'm finally just a skeleton."

A shudder rippled through him. He had a feeling that was the short, sanitized version. Before he could ask for more details, he noted the exit just ahead and knew there wouldn't be time to press her for more. He'd take a left at the top of the exit, then two rights, and Miranda's house would be in the neighborhood on the left. "I'm sorry."

"Me too. I wish I could stop seeing it, dreaming about it, thinking about it. But it's only been four months, so maybe one day I will. I hope one day you will too." She shot him a tight smile and Asher's respect for her rose a little higher. She blew out a low breath. "This is it, huh?"

"This is it."

○ ○ ○

Brooke steeled herself to meet Isaiah's wife. She had no idea if the woman hadn't called her back because she was still in the midst of grieving and adapting to life as a widow—or if she just didn't want to hear from Brooke.

If it was the second reason, Brooke was at a loss as to why.

Whatever the case, she was about to find out. The ranch house sat back from the road on about an acre of land. A thin line of trees surrounded the property. "Even though it's in a neighborhood, it's peaceful, quiet," she said.

"It's nice," Asher said. He pointed. "There's a car in the drive."

"And there's one of her kids peeking out the window."

The little face disappeared and the front door opened before Brooke or Asher got to the bottom step. A young woman in her midthirties dressed in jeans and a heavy sweater stepped out onto the porch. She wrapped a fleece blanket around her shoulders as the wind whipped her dark hair back from her face. "Hi. Can I help you?"

"Hi," Brooke said. "Are you Miranda Michaels?"

"I am."

"I'm Brooke Adams and this is Asher James. I've been trying to get in touch with you."

Miranda's eyes chilled. "I got your messages."

"Okay, then—"

"And I didn't call you back for a reason. I don't have anything to say to you."

"But why?" Brooke asked. "I don't understand."

"You're Army!" The snapped words hung in the cold air. "I don't want anything to do with the Army or anyone in it ever again."

"Ma'am?" Asher stepped forward and placed a hand on the

porch railing. "Isaiah loved the Army and everything it represented. What's turned your attitude about it?"

She clutched the blanket tighter against her throat. "They're saying he was a traitor, that he betrayed his country and his unit by selling information to the enemy about American troop locations and ops that would happen, allowing ambushes and lives lost." She tightened her lips even as a tear escaped to trail down a pale cheek. "Well, that's a lie. I may not know the details of what all went on over there, but I do know my husband. And he would never do something like that. And they're taking away his benefits. So, not only have I lost him, I've lost everything he's worked so hard for . . . died for. That's not the Army he loved and served, and it's not one I want anything to do with. My husband was not a traitor." Her chest heaved with her emotion, and Brooke's heart broke at the grief and betrayal—the sheer anguish in her words.

"I don't think he was either," Brooke said.

"Me either," Asher said.

Miranda stilled, her expression softening. She dashed away the tears. "Well, someone believes it."

"I know," Asher said. "Unfortunately, Isaiah never got a chance to refute the accusation."

"He did by text." She pulled her phone from her back pocket, tapped the screen, then turned it so Asher and Brooke could see the words.

"'Don't believe them,'" Brooke read aloud. "'I'm not a traitor. I know it looks bad, but—'" She looked up at Miranda. "I think he meant to say more, but he sent it only partially finished."

A wail came from inside the house. "Mama!"

Miranda glanced over her shoulder and took a step back. "You really believe he's innocent?"

"Absolutely," Brooke said.

Another cry sent the woman hurrying toward the door. "Look, why don't you two come in? I need to check on my kids."

Thankful for the thaw in the woman's demeanor, Brooke followed her inside to chaos. Miranda expertly dodged the scattered toys as though walking through a field of land mines. She glanced over her shoulder as she scooped an infant from the playpen. "The only thing I can think of is that he got interrupted and sent what he had," she said.

"Because he was worried he wouldn't have a chance later," Asher said, brows drawn over the bridge of his nose.

"Possibly." Miranda settled the child on her hip. "Actually, probably."

"What day and time did that text come through?" Asher asked.

One-handed, Miranda checked her phone and told him.

Brooke sucked in a breath. "That's the day of the bombing. The day he died."

"How did he know that he was under suspicion?" Asher asked.

The woman switched the child to her other hip, exhaustion and grief etched on her features like they'd been chiseled there. "I don't know."

Asher held out his hands and the baby practically threw himself into them. Brooke startled and Miranda breathed a sigh of relief.

"Mommy, I'm thirsty." The small voice came from the entrance to the hallway. An older toddler stood shyly in the doorway, one foot balanced on top of the other. Her dark eyes took in everything.

Brooke smiled at her and the child moved to her mother's side. "This is Erin," Miranda said, smoothing the child's hair behind her ears. "She's three, almost four."

Erin tugged on her mother's shirt in a silent reminder that she was thirsty. Miranda rubbed her eyes. "Your cup is in the refrigerator. I'll get it."

"I'll just keep this little guy for you while you take care of Erin," Asher said, expertly holding the boy against his chest.

"Okay, thank you. His name is Zac."

She and Erin disappeared in the small kitchen off the living area, and Brooke turned to scan the room. It looked like any other middle-class home. Pictures of family on the walls, in need of a good dusting, but basically clean and definitely lived in. Brooke pulled the charm bracelet from her pocket and settled it in the palm of her hand. She'd cleaned Isaiah's blood from it and now it gleamed innocently up at her.

A thud cut through her thoughts. Asher's keys had hit the hardwood floor. Zac lunged for them and only Asher's protective hold kept the child from going the same route as the keys. "This little guy is a wiggle worm," he said. He knelt and snagged the keys. Zac grabbed them with a giggle and shook them, narrowly missing Asher's right ear.

Brooke marveled at his complete calm in handling the little boy. "Where'd you get your kid experience?"

"I have a cousin with four munchkins I adore." He leaned over to take a closer look at the bracelet. "It's pretty."

"It really is. And unique. Each little charm is so different. Isaiah put a lot of thought into this." She closed her hand around it.

Miranda returned with Erin on her hip. The little girl chugged her drink.

"Did you survive Dr. Destructo?" Miranda asked.

Asher laughed. "He's fine. A very energetic little guy."

Miranda's eye roll pulled a smile from Brooke and she turned her head slightly to hide it. She couldn't figure out why Asher's "kid competence" impressed her so much. Maybe because she simply had no skills in that department whatsoever.

"So," Brooke said, "Isaiah never mentioned anything he was working on? Any special projects?"

"No, nothing. He didn't talk about what he did and I knew better than to ask."

Brooke held out the bracelet. "Isaiah gave me this the day he died. I think he wanted me to give it to you."

Miranda set the little girl on the floor. "You can go watch television for a few minutes, okay?"

"I can? Yippee!"

She skipped down the hall and Miranda gave a fond, if tired, smile. "I don't let her watch it very often." She took the bracelet from Brooke and frowned. "This wouldn't be for me."

"Why do you say that?"

She shrugged. "Because he already gave me one." She shoved her sleeve up and a matching charm bracelet wrapped her wrist. "I don't wear a lot of jewelry." She shook her wrist. "And especially not something that makes that much noise, but Isaiah brought it home for Christmas last year and I can't bring myself to take it off for long. I wear long sleeves and cover it up when I wear it—it helps me when I'm really missing him." She shook her wrist again and a small, sad smile curved her lips. "The noise makes me crazy. And yet . . ." She met Brooke's gaze. "Isaiah loved this kind of stuff and was always telling me I didn't know what I was missing. Maybe he got it for you. After all, you were the one helping him get past his PTSD—or at least you were offering coping strategies that he said were working for him."

Asher's flinch wouldn't have been noticed by the average person, but for some reason, Brooke was so in tune with him she couldn't help but see it. "He never said . . ."

"He wouldn't. Not to you. But he said you talked even when he wouldn't and he finally started listening and figured he'd try some of the things you recommended. He admitted it helped."

Brooke's throat tightened. The things she'd recommended had been shots in the dark. "I'm glad."

"So, what do I do with this?" Miranda asked, holding up the bracelet.

"What do you mean?"

"He didn't mean for you to give this to me." Her eyes clouded, then widened. "You don't think—"

"He wasn't cheating," Brooke said quickly. "His last words, his last thoughts, were of you and the kids—and the fact that he wasn't a traitor. He wanted me to pass that on to you and said to keep it safe."

Tears flooded the widow's eyes and she dashed them away as though the action was just habit now. "Thank you," she whispered and held out the bracelet for Brooke. "He bought it for a reason. Or maybe someone gave it to him to give to me."

"Why don't you keep it until we know for sure?" Brooke said. "If nothing turns up, at least you'll have it."

Miranda dashed away another tear. "Sure. I'll put it in my jewelry box with the rest of my stuff. You'll know where it is if you figure out what to do with it."

"Thank you. Well, I guess that's it," Brooke said, taking a step back toward the door. "I really just wanted to give you that and see how you were doing."

"My parents don't live too far away, so they're a big help. But I'm surviving. Just taking it one day at a time."

"Yeah," Brooke said. She understood that in her own way. "Will you call me if you think of anything else Isaiah might have mentioned that would lead us to figuring out why he was targeted and labeled a traitor?"

"Absolutely."

Brooke handed the woman her card and followed Asher out of the house.

Once they were back in his vehicle, he let out a low breath. "I need to talk to my former captain."

"Why?"

"He knows something about Isaiah. He was the one who had the evidence and sent us to the café to pick him up. I'll call in a bit and see if he'll tell me anything."

"He won't."

"Probably not, but it won't hurt to try. Where to now?"

"Home, I guess." She leaned her head against the window and peered out. Or she could go to Heather's again. While Asher was making a call, she picked up her phone and sent her friend a text.

> Are you at home?

Work. On the way to surgery. Can I call when I'm done?

> Sure.

A pause, and then Heather texted.

Everything okay?

Brooke hesitated. She wouldn't tell her friend about everything over text, but she didn't want to worry her either.

> Everything's okay. Just give me a call when you can. No rush.

Will do.

Brooke let her phone rest on the seat between her knees. "Heather's at work and I can't keep crashing at her place. Besides, if someone's after me, I don't want to put her in danger."

Asher shot her a glance that she saw from the corner of her eye. "You're sure you want to go home then?"

"Not really, but what choice do I have?"

"There's always a choice."

"Okay, then you make it because I think I'm done in." She leaned back and closed her eyes.

FIFTEEN

Asher's head pounded a steady beat behind his eyes, and when his phone rang, he jumped like he'd been poked. He grabbed the phone from the dash holder and switched it off the car Bluetooth to his earpiece. "Captain Newell, thanks for calling me back."

Static broke the connection for a brief moment, then finally cleared enough for him to hear the man. ". . . in a meeting. Can you hear me?"

"I can."

"Your message sounded important. What do you need?"

"First, anything on Ricci?"

"I would have called you if I'd found anything out. All I know is he was discharged for disorderly conduct. Nothing to tell me why he'd break into Brooke Adams's home. If I hear of anything else, I'll let you know."

"Yes, sir. Then I need to know what you know about Isaiah Michaels. I've just been to see his widow and they've cut off his pension, everything. What evidence is there against him?"

"That's classified, son. You know I can't tell you that."

"Sir, normally I wouldn't even consider asking, but this is a matter of life and death. I need to know."

Silence. Static. ". . . can't tell you! Now quit asking."

"Someone's trying to kill Brooke Adams over this. And me as well, if you want to get technical. Now I need to know what Isaiah knew that was worth killing over!"

Brooke stirred.

More silence from his captain, then, "Kill you?"

"Yes. I need to know what—or who—I'm fighting against and I need your help."

"James—" Asher heard the heavy sigh in spite of the bad connection. "Let me see what I can do. I'll call you back." *Click.*

Asher wanted to throw the phone.

"You okay?"

He glanced at Brooke. She'd been asleep the moment she shut her eyes and he didn't blame her. It had definitely been a rough couple of days. "Sorry, didn't mean to wake you."

Her eyelids flickered. "S'okay. He wouldn't tell you anything, huh?"

"No, but he said he'd see what he could do and call me back."

"I suppose that's something." Her eyes shut again. "I'm so sleepy. Why can't I stay awake?"

"Because your body is ready for some rest and you keep denying it."

"True." She shifted, gently slapped her face a few times, and yawned.

He glanced in the rearview mirror and caught her watching him. "How do you feel about getting a hotel room?"

She raised an eyebrow. "Okay, now I'm awake."

Heat flooded into his cheeks and he was glad it was dark. "Or two? You know, one for each of us. With a connecting door. So I can keep an eye on you." He gave a little groan. "I mean so I can help keep you safe and yet both of us can have the privacy we need to . . . Ugh." He was making a mess of a simple suggestion. A testament to his fatigue.

"It's okay, Asher," she said. "I know you're not suggesting anything inappropriate."

"I'm not. I'm simply wiped out and I don't feel like driving back. I thought you might feel the same."

"I'm so sorry. I should have offered to drive."

"You have to be awake to do that." He shot her an amused smile. "No way was that happening."

"There is that. A hotel sounds like a good idea," she said.

He could feel her studying him and kept his eyes on the road. "Why do I feel like a bug under a microscope right now?"

"While I'm sure you're exhausted, why do I have the feeling that your suggestion to stop at a hotel is coming from something other than fatigue?"

Was that amusement in her voice? "I can't be tired?"

"You were special ops. I'm sure you've been beyond tired before and I doubt you needed to find a hotel room."

"It's really scary how well you read me." What was actually scary was that while it made him a bit uncomfortable, he found he didn't mind her keen insight into him. Very weird. "Yeah, okay. I'll admit I'm a little concerned about driving back in the dark. Those guys had a reason for chasing us off the road earlier. And they did their best to track us down. I don't trust them not to try again."

"So what's your plan?" she asked.

"I think I want to call in some reinforcements."

"Who did you have in mind?" she asked. "Gavin?"

"Yes."

"What can he do to help?"

"He's got tools and resources that can help make sure we're doing everything possible to shut down these guys as fast as possible."

"Shut them down?"

"Meaning we catch them or set them up for the cops to do so. Either way, we need to get them in custody so we can find out why they've targeted you."

"How do you plan to do that?"

"I'm thinking on it. As soon as I have a plan, we go on the offensive."

"Works for me." She shut her eyes again and Asher stared. Just like that she trusted him to do what was best for her. For them. It kind of blew him away.

And scared him to death, as memories from his past rushed in to pound him.

Half of his unit had trusted him to lead them and do what was best for them on their last mission and they'd wound up dead. He swallowed. *God, don't let me lead her wrong. Don't let me lead her to her death. I can't handle another person dying on my watch.*

○ ○ ○

Victor looked at the map on his phone and glanced at the man in the seat beside him. Chester "Buzz" Howard. They'd been in Afghanistan together, but Victor hadn't realized he was involved in their secret. "How'd you get pulled into all this?"

"It's a well-known fact that I gamble. Unfortunately, I'm not very good at it. I guess word reached the powers that be and I was made an offer I couldn't turn down." The fact that the man had no trouble killing probably had been the only reference needed to ensure him a spot in the closed group—and a cut of the money coming in.

"Check this out." Victor passed him the phone.

Buzz studied it before lifting his gaze. "Were they headed to where I think they were?"

"Had to be. Nothing else around here makes sense, and I don't think it's a coincidence that Michaels's house isn't too far from here. He had a cookout there once and a bunch of us who lived around here went. They had to be going to see the widow."

"It's been hours. You think they've already been there or do you think they holed up to lick their wounds?"

"Only one way to find out."

151

Victor took another swig of his iced tea, then pulled out of the fast-food restaurant. They'd been regrouping since Buzz crashed the stolen white SUV. Victor had been trailing in the black van, keeping a good amount of distance since James had spotted him and would be looking for him. He'd picked up Buzz and they'd given chase, only to be outsmarted at the barn. "We underestimated her," he said.

"Not her. Asher James."

"Speaking of James," Victor said, "what was he doing in that office yesterday?"

"No idea." He shook his head. "I can't believe Ricci killed the wrong person."

"Whatever. We just have to get the right one or we're all done for."

Victor pulled onto Miranda's street and parked two doors down. He shut off the engine to wait while Buzz caught a nap. Victor didn't begrudge the man his rest. He was earning it.

When the light in the kitchen went out, he knew it wouldn't be long before they could make their move. She had two kids she'd want to keep safe, which meant she'd give them whatever he decided to ask for. As the dashboard's clock ticked toward midnight, he ate his protein bar and went over the plan in his mind.

He waited another forty-five minutes just to be sure she was good and asleep, then nudged Buzz, who opened his eyes, instantly awake. "It's time?"

The light in the kitchen went back on and Victor smothered a curse. "I guess not."

Buzz settled back against the door. "We'll give it another hour. There's no hurry. She's not going anywhere."

○ ○ ○

Asher lay on the double bed, hands tucked under the back of his head, gun at his side. He'd called Gavin, and after he'd filled his friend in on everything, Gavin promised to meet them at Brooke's home first thing in the morning.

Now he stared at the ceiling while the television on the dresser silently played the local news. Every so often, he'd glance at the screen and had caught the blip about the wreck with the white SUV. One thing he'd learned was that the vehicle had been stolen early that morning.

He ran the timeline of events through his mind, trying to make some sense of everything.

First, there'd been the dead woman in Brooke's office. That could have been a simple robbery gone wrong, but when one added in the facts that Ricci was in Brooke's home and someone had tried to run them off the road and shot at them . . .

In his book, that meant someone wanted Brooke dead.

But why?

He didn't have a fat clue and that bothered him, so he turned his thoughts to Brooke.

Brooke Adams.

He liked her name. Actually, he liked her. A lot. He'd noticed her once on base and had made a point to talk to her. She'd been friendly enough, but . . . distant at the same time. So he'd taken the sneaky route and learned her schedule, making sure to run into her occasionally.

And yes, he knew it sounded stalkerish, but he held no ill will toward her. He'd just wanted to get to know her.

And yet . . . he didn't. Getting to know her meant letting her get to know *him*. And that made him terribly uncomfortable.

And yet . . .

The more he learned about her, the more he decided she was way too good for him and he should just leave her alone.

If someone hadn't tried to kill her today—and if he didn't think she could help him with the nightmares—he might be able to walk away.

Darkness had fallen hours ago. Brooke was safely ensconced in her room next to his with the door between them cracked. The lights were off and he needed to follow her example and sleep while he could. His gun snug in its holster beside him, he laid his hand it and firmly shut his eyes, picturing the moment he'd first seen Brooke. She'd made him want to smile—and that had made him want to meet her.

His buzzing phone jarred him from the light doze he'd unintentionally slipped into, and he snagged the device from the end table. "Hello?"

"I decided not to wait until tomorrow," Gavin said, his bass voice a familiar friend.

"What do you mean?"

"Let me in. It's cold out here."

Asher rolled to his feet and walked to the door. He opened it and Gavin stood there, eyes hard, mouth tight. "You're making a habit out of this, aren't you?"

"What? Showing up to help? I should think so."

With a short laugh, Asher let the man inside. "What's up?" he asked and motioned for Gavin to have a seat on the couch under the window.

"I got to thinking about everything you told me and decided I didn't like you being on your own."

"I don't think we were followed to the hotel." He motioned to his weapon. "And I've got backup."

Gavin patted his hip. "Now you've got more backup."

"Fine, I'll take it. You can have the other bed."

"Don't think I can sleep just yet."

"Yeah, same here." Asher pinched the bridge of his nose. "So, let's look at this logically. One of us is the target. I'm thinking it's Brooke and not me for several reasons. One, it was Brooke's office that was the setting for all of this and no one knew I was going to be there that morning. No one."

"The dead secretary did."

Asher stopped. "True. But who would she tell?"

"Probably no one. I'm just saying there was at least one more person that knew."

"Now you're making me rethink things."

"I'm not trying to throw you off track. You're probably right. So let's say it's her. She's been home for four months and a couple of days and no one came after her until now. Why?"

"Exactly," Asher muttered.

"What's she been doing during that time? What's her timeline and what's happened during it? What triggered these attacks—or attempted attacks?"

"We'll have to ask Brooke for specifics. I know she was in the hospital in Germany healing from the burns she sustained in the bombing. From there, she was transferred home to the burn center near Atlanta."

"How long was she there?"

"Not too long, I don't think. She said most of her burns were second degree. All in all, I think she was in the hospital or the burn unit for two months."

"Then she came home."

"And moved into her new house and started working for Marcus Lehman."

Gavin leaned forward. "So, no issues for the two months she was in the hospital and rehab, recovery, et cetera."

"Right—and if someone wanted to get to her in there, I don't think it would have been too difficult."

"And no issues when she first moved into the house."

"No. Apparently, everything was fine until yesterday." Had it only been a day ago that he'd gone to find Brooke and found himself embroiled in a mess? "I just wish I knew why they're after her."

"I think I know why," Brooke said from the doorway.

Asher straightened. "Why?"

"It has to be the bracelet. We have to get that bracelet back from Miranda."

SIXTEEN

Brooke tried to call Miranda once more, but the woman still wasn't answering. "She must turn her phone off at night or something. Let's go. We're not that far from her house."

Gavin and Asher looked at her like she was crazy.

"Guys, assuming I'm right about the bracelet, these people have tried three times now to get it. First in my office where they accidentally"—she wiggled air quotes—"killed Sharon and then when they broke into my house, and finally, when they ran us off the road and chased us to the barn. Seems to me someone wants that bracelet pretty bad."

"If that's what they're after," Asher said.

"Yes. If. If I'm wrong, fine. But if I'm right, I don't want it in Miranda's possession a moment longer. If someone figures out we went to see her, she's in major danger."

"I don't see how anyone could know," Asher said.

"But what if they do?"

"Brooke—"

"What if, Asher? You want to risk her life on that? Her kids?"

He and Gavin exchanged a glance. Then Asher stood and Gavin

followed him to the door. Asher looked back at her. "What are you waiting on? Let's go."

With a huff, she grabbed her purse and hurried after the men.

Once she'd buckled up in the back seat of Gavin's Hummer, she laid her head against the rest, relaxed, and closed her eyes. *Please, God, I know I keep coming to you with panicked emergency prayers, but please keep Miranda—and us—safe.*

Asher's phone rang and he snagged it. "It's Caden."

"Put it on speaker," Gavin said.

"Caden, this is Asher. Gavin and Brooke are here too. What's up?"

"When Sarah called about Brooke, she also said she needed my help with something. I know an agent, Felicia Wilson, who's in Afghanistan training Afghan police in investigations. She got back to me about that security footage Sarah was talking about."

"What about it?" Brooke asked.

"Very clear footage of Michaels going into a Dr. Madad's office and sitting in front of his computer."

"So they immediately knew that Isaiah was on to something."

"On to Dr. Madad anyway. It looks like Michaels was downloading something, and just as he left, he dropped an item at the door before he picked it up and shoved it into his pocket. Looked like a bracelet of some kind."

Gavin shot a look at Brooke. "Guess you were right. It's the bracelet they're after."

o o o

Victor followed Buzz around to the back of the house. Most homeowners were conscientious about locking their front doors. Sometimes they left the back door open. He waited while Buzz tried it.

"Locked," Buzz whispered.

"Yeah, guess she's more careful because of the kids."

"Or she watched the news before she went to bed," the man muttered. "Nothing but home invasions and shootings. Even I check my locks before I go to sleep."

"Shut up and find a way in."

One by one they tried the windows. All locked. "Going to have to break one," Buzz said.

"Do the one in the kitchen then. It's farthest away from her bedroom."

"All the tools in the world and you don't have a glass cutter?"

"Just do this, okay?"

"So, does she need to die?" Buzz asked. "I'm okay killing her, but I'm not killing kids."

Victor had no desire to kill kids either. Hopefully, they'd sleep through the whole thing, but if not . . . "I guess it depends on how cooperative she is."

"Yeah."

Buzz pulled his fist back into his sleeve and gave the glass pane over the doorknob a firm tap. It fell to the tile floor and shattered. He reached through the hole and unlocked the dead bolt, then the knob. Victor stepped around the man and slipped inside. If Miranda heard the glass shatter and came to investigate, he wanted to be able to grab her before she could do something stupid like start screaming and alert her neighbors.

But no sound came from the back of the house. He swept the flashlight around the kitchen and noted the sink full of dishes and the laundry piled high in the corner next to a closed door he assumed hid the washer and dryer. Toys lay scattered over every surface. All signs of a grieving woman too overwhelmed to do anything except survive and make it to the next day. Too bad Michaels's family had to suffer for his actions. But . . . not his problem.

Buzz nodded toward the bedrooms, and Victor fell in behind the man. He didn't bother pulling his weapon. Two men in ski

158

masks would be terrifying for the young mother. He paused. Then again, she had two children she'd probably fight to the death for. He pulled the gun.

Buzz peered in the first room on the left. "Kid," he whispered. Second room was the baby's. The room across the hall had to be the master. The door was cracked. Buzz nudged it with his elbow and it opened on silent hinges.

Victor could see Miranda in the bed. He turned to Buzz and motioned for the man to stand outside the room. "Cover the kids, we may need to use them." He kept his voice low, almost non-existent, but the woman gasped and sat up.

Victor strode to her side and placed the gun against her chin. She froze, eyes wide, fully awake and so scared he wondered if she'd be able to tell him anything. She trembled but didn't make a sound. Probably afraid she'd wake her kids. Good. He needed her afraid.

A car door slammed, and without taking his gaze from Miranda, he jerked a hand at Buzz, who strode down the hallway.

"Now," Victor whispered, "we can do this the easy way or the hard way. It's up to you."

Her eyes flashed to the door, then back to him. "What do you want?" she croaked.

"The bracelet."

"Bracelet?" Confusion chased the fear from her eyes for a brief moment, and Victor wondered if they'd guessed wrong after all. Then her gaze hardened and slowly moved to her dresser. Elation swept over him. "Get it," he said. "Now."

She swallowed. "Who are you? Why are you doing this?"

Buzz returned to his side. "Three people in a Hummer just pulled up and they're standing on the porch," he murmured. "Looks like Asher James and Gavin Black. Couldn't see the woman, but it's probably Brooke Adams."

Someone knocked on the front door. Miranda hesitated.

Asher still held Zac, who'd fallen asleep without the bottle. Miranda thanked him, then sighed and raked a hand over her hair. "Will they come after me once they realize the bracelet isn't what they wanted?"

"I doubt it," Gavin told her. "I don't see how they could know there are two bracelets, so once they find nothing on the one they took, they'll probably figure they need to come back after Brooke since she's the last one who saw Isaiah alive." He grimaced at Brooke. "Sorry."

"Better me than Miranda and her children." She shuddered.

Asher was nodding. "I think you're right. They're going to figure even though they struck out with the bracelet, Isaiah passed information on to her about whatever it is they're after." His eyes locked on Gavin's. "Did you notice the same thing I did?"

"I noticed a lot of things."

"The way they left the house?"

"Yeah. They're military or law enforcement."

"I think I recognized one of their voices," Asher said, thinking back, trying to place it.

"Same here, but I can't put a face to it."

"So it's definitely someone we know," Asher said. "Makes me sick to think it."

The door opened once more and a couple in their late forties entered. The woman was strikingly beautiful, but anxiety pinched the lines around her mouth as she rushed in to wrap her arms around Miranda. "What in the world, honey?"

"I'm okay, Mom."

The woman pulled back and her gaze flicked to Asher, who still held Zac. "Where's Erin?"

"In my bed," Miranda said. "You can get her."

She darted down the hall.

Miranda's father stepped over to hug her, then took the sleeping baby from Asher while Miranda made the introductions and explained that it was only due to the good timing of Brooke and the others that she and the kids were okay.

The man swallowed hard, obviously trying to control his emotions. "Thank you," he finally said.

"Of course," Asher said.

Miranda's mother came back into the den carrying Erin, who'd snuggled down against her shoulder. "I told you we should have moved in here or you should have moved in with us."

"Mom—"

"But I'm so thankful you're all okay. Now let's get home so we can get these kids in bed and you can get some rest."

Once everyone was gone and Brooke, Asher, and Gavin were back in Gavin's Hummer, they sat in silence for a good minute.

"Okay," Asher said. "I vote we head back to the hotel and get a couple hours of sleep before we work on why this bracelet is worth killing for."

"Sounds good to me," Brooke murmured. She could feel a headache coming on, and the thought of closing her eyes for even an hour sounded blissful.

Asher insisted on driving since Gavin was a little loopy from the injection he'd been given. Everyone kept an eye on the mirrors, watching for a tail, but it seemed their pursuers were satisfied with their bracelet for the moment.

Brooke just hoped they could all get some rest before the attackers struck again. Because it wasn't a matter of *if*, it was a matter of *when*.

EIGHTEEN

Caden rubbed bleary eyes. He'd found the break room sofa and spent the night in the morgue after Clarissa had kicked him out of the autopsy room. She'd done it somewhat gently, but nevertheless hadn't been forthcoming with any information other than she was working almost nonstop to find something useful for him. Which he greatly appreciated, he just wished she would find it sooner rather than later. Like now. Too bad Joan had left. She would have been nicer. A fact he'd refrained from throwing in Clarissa's face simply because it would have made her mad.

A glance at the clock on the wall pulled a groan from him. Four o'clock. He shifted, trying unsuccessfully to find a comfortable position, and shut his eyes once more as he decided his partner was the smart one. Zane had opted for a hotel room.

Caden wasn't sure what made him stay. Almost a protective instinct. Like he didn't want to leave the victims, because if he did, he might miss something—or not learn something in time.

In time for what, he had no idea.

At five thirty, he gave up, read two "I'm fine" texts from Sarah, listened to a voice mail from her, and rolled to his feet. Sarah. Another reason he wasn't sleeping well these days. She was going to make him gray before his time. But it looked like she had electricity right now, so that was a plus.

Thirty minutes later, Caden stepped out of the men's room, dressed in clean clothes and carrying the backpack that held all of his essential toiletries.

His next stop was the autopsy room.

Empty.

Which meant Clarissa was finished. So why hadn't she called or texted? Tension threading his shoulders and the base of his neck, he walked to her office.

And found her seated in her chair, head on her desk, phone in her right hand. Worry spiked. He strode to her and placed a hand on her shoulder. "Clarissa?"

Her head popped up and she gasped. Then dropped her phone to rub her face. She blinked up at him. "Oh. Caden, I was getting ready to text you."

He wanted to know what she knew, but more importantly . . . "Are you all right?"

"Um . . . yes. I think so. Everything took longer than I thought it would because I had to check and double-check, then wake up one of the other pathologists to ask him some questions and I guess . . ." She picked up her phone and looked at the screen. "I guess I fell asleep. I'm sorry."

"Don't be. What is it you had to check and double-check?"

She hesitated. "They're still working at the site, but one of the bodies that was brought in while I was still working on John Doe A was a recent death. An adult probably in his early thirties. He was killed with a gunshot to the forehead and it wasn't self-inflicted."

Caden frowned. "Okay. So what does that tell you?"

"Nothing much other than he was murdered. Finding his identity will go a long way toward discovering who the rest of the victims are, though."

"Agreed."

"I sent his prints to AFIS but haven't heard anything yet." She covered her mouth and yawned. "I need coffee."

He went to the Keurig set up on a table in the corner and turned it on. "So, what else?"

"He was buried with a child who was probably in the ten-year-old range. I did the autopsies on both. The ten-year-old was missing both kidneys and a heart."

Caden stilled, a sinking feeling in his gut. "Okay."

"The girl, Jane Doe A, was much more decomposed, but I think she was missing a heart as well. It was really hard to tell, but definitely possible."

"Organ trafficking," he spat.

She held up a hand. "Maybe. It's a little too soon to call it, but . . ."

"But?"

"The adult had all of his organs intact."

"Were the two related? The man and the boy?"

"I wondered the same thing—and figured you would ask—and had the lab run an expedited DNA paternity test. Not even close. There's no way they're related. Not by blood anyway. The kid could have been adopted, I suppose."

"Okay." He scrubbed a hand down his cheek.

"I'm sorry I don't have more, Caden. After I grab a shower and a couple more hours of sleep, I'll get back to it and hopefully have a few more answers for you. Joan will be here too. I know you like her more than me."

"Hey, now, that's not true." It really wasn't.

"Uh-huh. She's a pushover for a pretty face." She winked. If she truly believed it, she didn't seem to care.

He gave her bicep a quick squeeze. "Thanks."

"Of course."

He called his partner and caught him entering the building. "I'm on the way down. You don't have to come up."

"Was it worth it?" Zane asked when he and Caden stepped outside.

"What?"

"That crick in your neck." He smirked.

Caden didn't feel like being ribbed this morning. "Yeah. It was."

Zane recognized Caden's mood, heard his report, and turned serious. "So, we pass this info on to Deveraux and the sheriff and then find out who the guy with the bullet in his skull is."

"That's the plan for now."

Caden's phone rang and Annie's smiling face appeared on the screen. He'd sent their tech guru the pictures Sarah had snuck of the two men. He tapped the green button. "Hey."

"Hey, so I finally got a chance to run these two down. They're military. Or ex-military as the case may be. They were discharged a little over two weeks ago for violence against fellow soldiers."

"But no prison time?"

"No. It's kind of weird. There's not a whole lot of information saying why they were discharged and there's no arrest record, no prison time, nothing. They were just kicked out of the military and sent home. Current location for both men is unknown. There've been no credit card transactions, no loans, no credit hits. They are definitely staying off the radar."

"Sounds like they cut a deal and disappeared together."

"Maybe—on the cutting-a-deal thing. That's not in here either. It's very vague and very secretive."

"Names?"

"Mario Ricci and Victor Hamilton."

o o o

Asher studied his vehicle while Brooke stood just inside the hotel door. He'd duct-taped a small compact mirror Brooke had given him to the end of an unraveled wire coat hanger. It wasn't a professional-grade tool, but it would do. In Afghanistan, he or someone else checked their vehicles several times each day for explosives. When he'd first returned home, he did the same every time he had to go somewhere.

Over the past month, he'd gradually forced himself to get out of the habit and now wished he hadn't been so determined to do so. He held the mirror under the truck and made his way around the perimeter. Then the wheels, the trunk, the bumper, the roof. He returned to the back and noticed the license plate looked . . . off. He wiggled it. One screw was tight, the other moved. Asher unscrewed the loose one and the plate swung down.

And there it was.

A flat GPS tracker about one inch in diameter. He pulled the device off and crushed it beneath his heel before replacing the plate. "Let's go see Ricci." Asher's friend from the hospital had called and said the doctors were bringing Mario Ricci out of his medically induced coma and he was showing signs of waking.

"Okay." She climbed into his damaged truck and fastened her seat belt.

An hour and forty-five minutes later, with security leading and trailing behind, Asher and Brooke stepped out of the elevator and followed the signs to the intensive care unit.

Caden waited at the electronic doors, talking on his phone. When he turned and saw them approaching, he hung up. "Good to finally meet you two in person."

Asher shook the outstretched hand and introduced him to Brooke.

The agent was tall. Easily six feet five and built like a linebacker. Dark hair and with emerald green eyes and a five-o'clock shadow, he no doubt drew stares from men and women alike simply because he looked like he should be in a magazine—or on a movie screen. Right alongside Heather Fontaine.

Frankly, Asher didn't care what the man looked like as long as he could get them back to see Ricci. The fact that Brooke's eyes lingered shouldn't have sent a dart of jealousy shooting through him. But it did. The fact that he didn't see a hint of interest there calmed the green-eyed monster. He cleared his throat. "Appreciate you meeting us."

"Of course. Somehow this guy is connected to Sarah and whatever she's investigating. And now his name shows up in conjunction with the two of you? I don't think that's a coincidence. I've got other cases on hold at the moment to see if we can figure out the connection."

"Works for me," Brooke said.

Caden slapped the button on the wall, and the doors swung open. Asher took in the setup of the unit. A row of offices to his left, patient rooms to the right as well as the far side of the nurses' station planted securely in the middle. A monitor station at the rear with an exit to the stairs just beyond. His brain registered all this in seconds.

The nurse looked up from her station and smiled. "May I help you?"

Caden flashed his credentials. "We're here to see Mr. Mario Ricci."

The woman's smile slid into a frown. "The officers have already changed shifts."

"We're not here for shift change, just to—"

Asher let the two hash it out while he draped an arm across Brooke's shoulders and took a few steps back. Brooke frowned up at him.

"What are you doing?" she whispered.

"No one's watching, so I figured we'd wander down here and see what we can see."

"Asher, I don't think—"

He placed a finger on her lips and she fell silent. "Room 6," he whispered. "I think it's on the other side near the monitor station."

When they reached room 6, Asher stopped. Frowned. She looked up at him. "What is it?"

"Thought the nurse said they'd switched out guards."

"She did."

"And yet there's no one on the room." He dropped his arm from her shoulders and strode to the door to look in the large window. Ricci lay in the bed, attached to numerous machines. A police officer stood at the side of the bed, looking down at the patient.

Asher narrowed his eyes. That was no cop. He backed away before the man could see him.

"What is it?" Brooke asked.

"Get Caden. Victor Hamilton is in the room with Ricci. He's dressed as a cop. Now I know why I recognized the voice. He was the one at Miranda's house and was probably one of the guys chasing us in the black van. I'm going to need backup. And hospital security."

She spun on her heel and darted off. Asher stepped up to the door once more and looked in. Hamilton hadn't moved and Asher couldn't read his expression. The man looked up to catch him watching. Alarm flared, then settled into resignation. Asher nudged the door open, keeping his hand on his weapon.

"What's going on?" Caden asked, stepping up beside him.

"Special Agent Caden Denning, meet Victor Hamilton," Asher said. "He and Ricci and I served together overseas. I've got lots of questions for you."

Hamilton nodded. "I'm sure you do."

"Like why you're impersonating a police officer, but most importantly, what's so special about that bracelet you and Ricci and the other guy were so desperate to get your hands on."

The man fingered the badge. "Doesn't matter." He took another look at Ricci as the machines beeped and whirred. "He saved my life, you know."

"I was there. He saved mine at the same time, remember?"

"Let me see your hands," Caden said.

In a swift move, Hamilton raised his right hand. His weapon pointed at Asher. Asher's muscles tensed, and the agent next to him slid his hand into his jacket.

"No, no," Hamilton said, waving the muzzle of the gun at Caden. "Leave it alone."

Caden lowered his hand. "Put it down," he said. "You're not getting out of this one."

"Maybe not, but I've got to try. Now move away from the door. Get up by the head of the bed. Go."

Asher and Caden moved.

Hamilton's eyes flicked to the man in the bed once more before returning to Asher.

"Ricci spotted the bomb strapped to the guy as I was walking up to him," Hamilton said. "And he yanked me behind that hill just as the bomber detonated it." He sighed and shook his head. "I can't do it. I told him I could, but I can't."

"What? Kill him before he wakes up to talk?" Asher asked.

Hamilton gave a low, humorless chuckle. "Yeah."

"Who gave the order?"

A cold hardness stole over his face. "That doesn't matter either."

"Did you kill the secretary?" Asher asked in an attempt to keep him talking while waiting for security—or to take the man down. "At Brooke's office?"

"Not me. Ricci. He thought she was the shrink."

So Brooke had been right. Sharon had died simply because she'd been in the wrong place at the wrong time. "What did Michaels find that warranted him being set up as a traitor?" he asked.

"I'm not talking, so you might as well quit asking." Hamilton grabbed two pairs of handcuffs from his belt and tossed one set to Asher. "Cuff yourself to the bed. Now." The other pair he threw to Caden. "You too. Glad I chose to steal a uniform from a cop who likes to be prepared." Most cops carried two sets of cuffs. He backed toward the door. "If you get loose and chase me, I'll start killing people I pass. You may get me in the end, but I'll take a lot of people with me before you do. If you let me walk out of here, no one else dies. No one will even know I was here. I'm going to back out of the room and I'll be watching the window. If I see either one of you before I reach the exit, someone will die. If you alert the cops that I'm here, someone will die. Am I clear?"

"You have to pass in front of the monitor station," Asher said. "Someone's going to guess something's wrong if they see you walking away and leaving the room unprotected."

"I'll be gone by the time they figure out what—as long as you two behave."

"Where's the cop?"

Hamilton stilled. "What?"

"The cop who was wearing the uniform you stole."

The man scowled. "Don't worry, he'll wake up with a headache, but he'll live." With that, he slipped out of the door, tucking his weapon into his armpit, effectively hiding it, yet leaving the barrel clear so he could fire off a round if he needed to.

Caden yanked on the cuffs. "I've got a key in my pocket. Can you reach it?"

Since Asher had cuffed his hands below Caden's, he simply slid his wrists down the pole next to the agent's pocket. It was awkward and it used up precious time, but he managed to twist his fingers and grasp the key. After two failed attempts, he got it out. "He'll do it, you know," he said. "He might not have been able to kill Ricci, but Ricci saved his life more than once. Hamilton has no connection to the people out there and won't hesitate to do what he said."

"We can't just let him walk out of here."

"Of course not," Asher said, even as Caden was attempting to pull his ringing phone from his pocket. "Be still, will you?"

Caden sent the call to voice mail. "We can't let him escape, but we can't let him know security is looking for him either."

"He'll head for an exit—probably not the nearest one." He paused and the lock clicked on Caden's cuff. He turned the key on his and was soon free, then handed the key back to Caden, who released his other wrist from the steel bracelet. "The only reason he didn't kill us right here," Asher said, "is that he didn't want to cause a hospital lockdown."

"He thinks he's going to walk out of here."

"Yeah—and he knows we're going to follow as soon as we're free. He also knows we'll try to be discreet because we don't want innocent people dead. Which makes him believe he can get out of the hospital and escape before a full-on search is called for."

The door to the room opened and a frantic nurse pulled to a stop. "A woman said the cop wasn't really a cop and he had a gun pulled."

"Great," Asher said. "Call security and tell them not to confront him and not to lock the hospital down." Caden hesitated and Asher gave him a hard look. "I know this guy. He's a trained soldier with the heart of a killer and he won't let a few dead people stand in his way to freedom."

Caden placed the call while Asher bolted to the door's window.

"You see him?" Caden asked.

"No, he's gone."

"Is this security?" Caden identified himself. "Good. Yeah, yeah, the guy with the reported gun. Don't let him know you're on to him." He gave a quick explanation of the situation. "Cover all exits and try to get everyone away from them. He's armed and dangerous. Don't let him know you have him spotted, but don't lose sight of him. I repeat, he will shoot. Keep your distance, help is on the way." Asher and Caden stepped out of the room. "I'm going after Hamilton, you stay with Brooke," Caden said and darted for the exit.

Asher didn't bother responding as the man disappeared before he could blink. He looked around and his pulse pounded. Staying with Brooke might be a problem since she wasn't anywhere to be seen.

He rushed to the monitor station and found two men and the young woman who'd entered Ricci's room to tell them about the gun. They talked in hushed tones, obviously trying to decide what to do. "Did you see a woman about five feet six inches with blonde hair? Really pretty?"

"I did," the woman said. "She's the one who reported the cop with a gun in room 6, then went out the door to the stairs just about a minute or two ago." She pointed. "The same way the cop left. He also looked like he was in a hurry. Why did he have his gun out?"

"Don't worry about it, it's being taken care of and you guys are safe." He backed toward the exit.

"Wait a minute," she called, "where's the officer who's supposed to be guarding the patient? Sir? Sir?"

"Call security and get someone on his room! Just tell them the other officer had an emergency and you need coverage." Not really concerned that the man so near death would be a threat, Asher pushed open the door to the stairs and followed after Caden and Brooke. Only Caden wouldn't realize Brooke was ahead of him.

He sure hoped Victor Hamilton didn't know she was behind him.

NINETEEN

Brooke dialed Asher's number while she waited for the door to the second floor to shut behind the man who'd been part of the attempt to kill her. Once she heard the click, she hurried down the next flight of stairs.

Back in the ICU, she'd been watching through the glass and had witnessed the confrontation between the men—as well as the weapon Hamilton had pulled on Asher and Caden. She ran back to the monitoring station to report what she'd seen and was waiting for security. Then Hamilton was backing out of the door, his hand under his arm, hiding his weapon. He headed toward the exit and Brooke stepped sideways toward him, watching from the corner of her eye, not wanting to attract his attention but not wanting to lose him either.

When he exited to the stairs of the monitoring station heading out of the ICU, she glanced back at the room. Where were they? If she ran to check, Hamilton might get away. "Check on room 6, will you? I'm going after him."

She'd followed Hamilton without thinking about the potential danger, only that she wasn't going to let him get away without at least seeing which way he went.

"Brooke!" Asher's voice reached her through the phone.

"Sorry," she muttered, realizing he'd been calling her name since he'd answered. "He's on the second floor." She pushed her way through the door and stepped into the hallway. Nothing to her left. To the right, she caught a glimpse of his uniformed back as he disappeared through another door labeled with an exit sign. "He just went out the door next to the cafeteria. There are stairs that lead down to the basement area. If he goes up, that's another problem."

In the background, she heard Asher passing the information on. "Brooke? You need to stay put. If he realizes you're following him, he won't hesitate to kill you."

Hamilton exited the stairwell and continued his hurried escape—and no one stopped him. The uniform parted people like Moses had the Red Sea.

"Brooke?"

"I'm following him, Asher. Now hush."

She thought he might have growled at that. "Where is he?" he asked.

"Heading straight for the main entrance—or exit in his case."

"Is security there?"

"Yes, but that doesn't seem to bother him."

"We told them to let him go. He's prepared to kill anyone who tries to stop him—or anyone who gets in his line of fire."

Hamilton strode confidently across the lobby floor, his weapon still tucked out of sight.

The security officer on the left saw him coming, nudged his coworker, and drew his weapon. "Stop right there!"

Hamilton's weapon barked and the officer's knee exploded. Screams from the people in the lobby echoed as everyone scrambled to get away from the shooter.

Brooke swallowed her own scream and ducked behind the large information desk. She crawled to the edge and peered around it in time to see the other officer hold his hands up, surrendering because he had no place to hide. Brooke pressed her palm against her mouth, wondering if Hamilton would shoot him anyway.

The man held his fire and backed out of the glass doors, pausing. He made eye contact with Brooke, then looked past her. She turned to see what had caught his attention. Asher and Caden were rushing into the lobby.

A shot, followed by a thud, sounded near the entrance and Asher's eyes went wide as he and Caden skidded to a stop. More screams.

Brooke spun back to see a red mist covering the double glass doors, Hamilton's face pressed against the one on the right. His empty eyes stared back as he fell over and was still.

○ ○ ○

Once again on a video call, the large man strode to the back of the room, looking for a modicum of privacy. If he walked outside, he'd lose internet. His gaze centered on Buzz sitting at a table in a hotel room. "Well?" He didn't think his nerves would settle down until this was all over.

For a moment, he let himself wonder how it had come to this. He hadn't wanted to use Buzz unless it was absolutely necessary. The fact that it had come to that said things were spiraling out of control.

The sound of his name pulled him into the here and now. "I'm here. Just thinking."

"Right. Well, it's done."

"What's done?"

"Hamilton's dead. Ricci soon will be."

"I . . . see." He closed his eyes for a moment and drew in a deep breath. Thought for a moment.

"What's our next move?" Buzz asked, impatience edging his voice.

It had to be done. "I've got four more coming your way tomorrow night. You get them where they're supposed to be, then I have one more project for you. It will pay well, don't worry."

"I wasn't worried. What do you have?"

Once again, the man breathed heavily. Thought about what he was planning and decided there was no other way. Brooke Adams, and now Asher James, had to be stopped. "Here's what needs to happen . . ."

○ ○ ○

Asher paced from one end of the hotel room to the other. Once they'd finally finished up at the hospital, making sure Ricci was under heavy guard, Gavin met him, Brooke, and Caden at a hotel. They'd gotten a two-bedroom, two-bath suite, with a living area and a small kitchen situated between the sleeping areas. Room service had been ordered and the smell of fresh coffee permeated the air.

The knock on the connecting door turned him in that direction. Caden stood on the other side, holding his iPad.

Asher stepped back. "Come on in."

Caden took a seat at the table. "First things first. We've got agents and CID out at Ricci's place. They're going over it with a fine-tooth comb."

"Where does he live?" Brooke asked.

"He and Hamilton were sharing a house in Lexington. Neighbors said they were quiet and kept to themselves. Didn't seem to be home much."

"Of course they weren't. They were too busy terrorizing, kidnapping, and killing," Brooke muttered.

Caden grimaced. "Right. Anyway, hopefully we'll hear something soon about anything found in their house. Also, I've gotten the information off that bracelet," he said, stepping into the room. "Everything had been downloaded to a small microchip hidden inside one of the charms. Our tech guru, Annie, had to locate an adapter for it before she could see what was on it."

"And?" Brooke asked, lacing her fingers together in front of her.

"And at first, it looked like gobbledygook."

"Gobbledygook," Asher said. "Is that the official term now?"

"Her word, not mine. But this is what she eventually managed to get." He tapped the screen of the iPad he'd brought and turned it around so Asher and Brooke could see it. "It's a spreadsheet. In the left-hand column, there are numbers. She thinks each number represents a person."

"Why would she think that?"

"Because the next column seems to indicate blood type, since all of the values are things like A+ or B- or O, et cetera. This next column here, all of the numbers are zero to seventeen."

"So you've got a number that represents a person, blood type, and . . . ages maybe?"

"Could be. The next column is a list of names. It's in Pashto, but she thinks it's couples."

"As in married people?" Gavin asked.

"Yes." Caden swiped the screen. "Look at this. The whole couple-names thing works because of this file that was also on the chip." He pulled up pictures on his iPad. "And here, I give you couples."

"They're all . . . what? Muslim?" Brooke said.

"Yes." He swiped. More couples, smiling and holding hands or praying together. Some with children, most without.

"Who are they?"

"Actors," Caden said. "Models."

Brooke blinked at him and Asher raised a brow. "Okay. What?"

"Annie said some of the pictures looked off to her. Photoshopped. She did an image search and found the pictures had been copied from various websites advertising for churches, mosques, private schools, whatever."

"But . . . why?" Brooke asked.

"Well, Annie's amazing, but some things are beyond even her capabilities."

"What about those last two columns?"

"Don't know. Numbers and letters that probably make sense if you know what it's referring to. And finally, the last column. Four numbers. Could mean anything."

"So how do we find out what all of this is referring to?"

"Annie's still working on it," Caden said. "Your friend Isaiah sacrificed his life to get this stuff. He had a reason and I need to know why more than ever now."

Brooke studied him. "Sarah?"

"I talked to her about an hour ago and finally got more information out of her." His jaw tightened and his eyes flashed. "If she'd told me this stuff earlier—" He stopped and waved a hand. "Nothing I can do about that now—and in her defense, she was making sure she had her facts straight before she said anything. But when she originally called to tell me about the men discussing Isaiah and asked me to get in touch with you, she said she was undercover in an orphanage and occasionally at the hospital because she was keeping an eye on a doctor who worked between the two places."

"Which was how she found out the men were after me?"

"Yes. And it was at that same hospital that Michaels downloaded that information."

"Which computer?" Brooke asked. "How did he know which office and computer to get it from?"

Caden rubbed his eyes. "Sarah gave him the name of a doctor. For some reason this guy tripped her investigative alarms and she began watching him, looking into him. Somehow, she got a copy of one of his bank statements—and I don't even want to know how she got that—and he's been making some pretty big cash deposits."

"Everything's always done in cash," Brooke muttered.

"Can't make it easy for us, right? Anyway, apparently Sarah's been working undercover at the orphanage where this doctor comes by on a regular basis. She established a pattern between his visits and . . ."

"And what?" Asher asked.

"And the adoption of the kids that he was there to see."

Brooke gave a subtle snort. "Let me guess. They weren't adopted."

"It's not looking like it. Each of those cash deposits was made exactly three days after one of the children from the orphanage was supposedly adopted. Sarah went looking for some of the children, just to check up on them. And she couldn't find them. All she found were bogus addresses and fake names. It was all untraceable—including the kids—so she went to Isaiah with her suspicions that the children were being sold into slavery. She couldn't figure out how they were being transported or where they were going or who was taking them, but she was pretty sure this doctor was involved with everything—and she'd seen American military vehicles on the property several times the day a child was adopted. Isaiah told her to lay low and that he would look into it. Sarah said he must have found out something—which we now know he did—because he went AWOL on her for a few days. She tracked him down and he told her to stay away from him, that being around him could be dangerous."

"So someone was watching him," Brooke said softly, "knew he was digging into something that he shouldn't, and decided to set him up as a traitor."

"And probably planned to have him killed while in custody," Asher said, his jaw tight.

"Only the bomb went off in the café," Brooke said, "and they didn't have to follow through with their dirty work."

"Until they saw those pictures of you and Isaiah in the paper and realized he might have passed on the evidence he'd stolen."

Brooke went still, and Asher could practically see her mind working. "What is it, Brooke?"

"Do you remember what you told me about those pictures?"

He frowned. "I said a lot of things about them. What specifically are you talking about?"

"You said you recognized me because you'd been there, but if you'd just seen me on the street or whatever, you never would have recognized me."

Asher immediately got what she was trying to say. "So the only reason they knew who you were in the picture was that they were there when the explosion went off."

"Or they saw my picture in the paper with Isaiah, determined to find out who the woman was, and asked around until they found someone who saw me that day and knew it was me."

"Or that."

"We just need to interview everyone who ever met me while I was in Kabul."

"No," Asher said, "we just need to find out who was there that day and saw you. Then find out who was asking about the woman in the picture."

"Well, that narrows it down," she said with a disgusted sigh.

Caden rubbed his chin. "I'm going to send this stuff to Felicia, one of my Bureau contacts in Kabul. I'll ask her to look into it. And maybe she can check with some of your buddies over there if anyone was asking about the woman in the pictures."

"I think that's a good place to start, just make sure she's careful who she talks to," Asher said. "At this point, I wouldn't be trusting anyone."

"She can handle it."

"Of course. In the meantime, we need to figure out who's after Brooke here in the States. Because if we find one, I have no doubt he'll lead us to the other."

CHAPTER

TWENTY

Caden paced the length of his hotel room as he waited for Clarissa to pick up the phone. She'd texted and said she needed to see him—that he needed to see something.

I'm in Columbia. Can we FaceTime?

Sure. You won't get the full effect, but it'll do. Let me get set up and I'll call you in five minutes.

His phone rang. Finally. He swiped the screen and Clarissa's angular face filled the space. "Hi."

"Hi. Hold on a second, I want to put you on the tripod. I need my hands." The picture bounced a few times before steadying, and he had a good view of her workspace. Two reconstructed skulls stared back at him. "These are two of the victims." She appeared beside one and brushed the dark hair away from the brown eyes she'd pressed into the sockets. "This is the one who interests me most. And I think will interest you as well."

He looked at the face. "How old is she?"

"Thirteen, or fourteen at the most, according to her teeth and bone growth. She's been dead for a while. Just a skeleton with clothes on."

"Anything on the DNA?"

"Not yet. I've requested it be rushed, but so far nothing. I've put her through all of the databases and come up with the same. Nothing." She shot him a ferocious look. "Who doesn't report a missing kid?"

She appeared on screen once more, a frown creasing her forehead.

"Someone who doesn't want her coming home? An abused kid?"

Clarissa made a sound that he thought might have been a growl. Then her eyes softened and she ran her fingers over the skull's head as though smoothing her hair. "*Someone, somewhere* has to be missing her, don't they?"

"You would think," he said. "But come on, Clarissa, you've been in this business longer than I have. You've seen it all too."

"Doesn't mean I have to accept it. She's a child. A girl. If she's a runaway, surely there's a report. If she was kidnapped, same. If she was living on the streets, someone had contact with her."

"True, but she could be from anywhere. Just because she was found here doesn't mean she disappeared from here."

"I know that."

He knew she did. "What else?"

"Something really interesting. She's Caucasian. The bones I had were healthy and intact except for her ankle. It was broken at some point and she had a plate and screws put in it."

"Okay. Can you zoom in on her a bit?" She did and Caden took his time studying the girl's features. "You've given her a Middle Eastern look. Why?"

Clarissa reappeared. "Because the plate had some writing on it. In Pashto."

"Pashto?" He frowned as he processed that. "Are you saying she had the surgery in the Middle East?"

"Well, it sure wasn't in North America."

"Okay, that's good. Send me the information on the plate, and we can probably trace that to where it was made—and possibly who it was implanted in. That helps narrow things down a bit. What about some of the other victims? Any progress there?"

She sighed. "We've been working in shifts nonstop, day and night, for the past couple days. We finally have all of the bodies in the morgue. I've done two of the other autopsies. I think our initial conclusion is correct. You've stumbled across victims of organ harvesting."

Caden's stomach twisted again. He hadn't said anything to the others about this case simply because it wasn't any of their business, but now Isaiah's files immediately came to mind, and incredulous as it seemed, he wondered if the two cases could be connected. "I was hoping you were wrong."

"I was hoping so too."

"So someone is identifying people who need organs, probably charging them a fortune, then finding live 'donors' and taking their healthy organs, then burying the evidence."

"And pocketing a whole lot of money."

Caden dropped his chin to his chest. "I've seen a lot of evil in my law enforcement career, but this may take the spot as the worst."

She swallowed hard, eyes shadowed.

"Has anyone been able to match up the other victims with a missing persons report?"

"That's the weird thing. We've run six of the twelve victims through the databases. And nothing."

"Nothing. I can see one or two not being reported missing, but six?"

"The only one we've been able to identify is Carlos Garcia, the adult male you found buried with the young boy." She went to her desk and pulled a file from the top. "He was in the Army and

He, Asher, and Gavin took a seat at the table. "One of the victims that was dug up is a young girl probably thirteen or fourteen years old. I learned a few hours ago that she'd had surgery that required a plate and screws for a broken ankle. The plate had a serial number on it written in Pashto."

Asher froze. "How is that possible?"

"It's the next picture."

Asher flipped to it and stared at the plate. He easily read the inscription. "But that means . . ."

"Exactly. It took a while, but with Annie's help, we traced the plate to the manufacturer—and the hospital where it was used. She had that surgery in Kabul, Afghanistan, three years ago."

"Then how did she wind up here in the US, buried with a guy who was in the Army in Kabul?"

"Now, that, my friend," Caden said, "is the million-dollar question. Or at least one of them. Who is she? How did she get here?"

"And *why*?"

Caden clasped his hands in front of him on the table. "We think we know the answer to that one. She was too far decomposed for us to be sure, but a few of the other more recent victims were missing organs. Clarissa said they'd been surgically removed. Like by a doctor or someone who knew what they were doing."

Asher slumped back against the chair. "Organ trafficking?"

"That's what it's looking like."

"Man." He paused. "But how'd they get here? They'd have to have passports and money and adult supervision." He trailed off on the last word. "Garcia? Could he have brought them?"

"Well, not all of them. He died before some of them, but it's very possible he smuggled in a few."

"But that's not possible, is it?" Asher grimaced and continued without giving Caden a chance to answer. "Never mind. Of course it's possible, but how would he do it? And why would he do it at all? I remember him well and he was a good guy. Smuggling people into the US to steal their organs doesn't fit with the guy I knew."

"We ran a check on his financials. He had one big cash deposit of forty grand into a checking account that was opened three days prior to the deposit. But he never touched it. In fact, there were never any transactions made on that account after the money went in."

"Because he was killed before he could spend it?"

"I'm thinking so. The timing fits."

Asher rubbed his eyes. "I still don't see Garcia being involved in leading kids to their deaths."

Gavin sat silent, looking over the files. Asher knew the man was processing every scrap of information available.

Caden's phone buzzed. "It's Annie."

"She's working overtime, isn't she?"

"We all are." Caden stood by the window, off to the side. "Hi, Annie. Hold on, I have a couple of friends here who need to hear whatever you've got. I'm putting you on speakerphone." He tapped the screen. "Go ahead. You must have something important."

"Oh boy, do I. I know who your girl is." She paused. "Oh, sorry. Hi, friends."

"It's Asher James and Gavin Black," Asher said. "And hi."

"Nice to meet you two. Sort of."

"So, the girl," Caden said. "The one with the plate?"

"Yes. Her name's Tasneem Asmahd. She was an orphan living at the Morning Star Orphanage in Kabul."

Caden went still and his face paled by about three shades.

Asher raised a brow. "Caden? You okay?"

"Yes, but that just confirmed something I suspected. That's the orphanage where my sister is doing what she calls her undercover work." He raked a hand over his head. "Annie, I've got to go. If you find out anything more, call me. Thank you." He hung up and immediately punched his screen. "With Sarah's connection to Ricci and Hamilton—the two guys she got pictures of with her iPad and overhearing them talk about Brooke, and now a girl in a grave who was a resident of the orphanage where Sarah's working, it's all connected in some crazy way. I've got to reach her and tell her to get out of there."

"Brooke said she was working on a story and that she didn't want to leave even though she had the chance to do so."

"That's right." Caden held the phone to his ear and paced in front of the couch. "Pick up, pick up," he whispered. Then raised his voice. "Sarah, call me as soon as you get this. I need you to call me, understand? Please, call me." He hung up and rubbed his eyes, then turned to Asher. "Something major is going on and we need to figure it out fast."

"We need a place to stash Brooke," Gavin said.

Asher exchanged a glance with Caden. "Stash her? Why?"

"Think about it. Organ trafficking is a hugely lucrative business. According to this article"—he waved his phone at them—"kidneys are the most sought after. These people are making millions, so whoever has been coming after Brooke isn't going to stop until someone stops them. We need to focus, and only by knowing she's safe will that happen." He kept his eyes locked on Asher's for a brief moment.

Asher nodded. He wouldn't deny his growing feelings for Brooke, but he hadn't realized he was so transparent. "I know where she'll be safe."

"Where?" Gavin asked.

"With my parents. They have the room and a top-notch security system."

"Sounds good to me," Caden said, still pacing and muttering at his silent phone.

"She's not going to like it," Asher said.

"Then you'll have to talk her into it," Gavin said, "because things are about to go to the next level."

○ ○ ○

Brooke could hear the men talking in the other room. It was six in the morning and her stomach rumbled. She wanted pancakes topped with strawberries and whipped cream, a side of bacon, and a bowl of cheese grits. And coffee. Lots of strong black coffee. She thought she could smell the coffee.

She rose and brushed her teeth with the toiletries she'd gathered from the front desk when they checked in. She dressed in the clothes she'd placed at the bottom of the bed before crashing in it and made her way into the living area, where she found Caden, Gavin, and Asher gathered at the table.

"Morning," she said.

"Morning." They each mumbled it to her and she frowned at their bleary-eyed appearance. "Oh, come on, you didn't." She barely resisted placing her hands on her hips.

"What?" Asher asked.

"You found out something last night and let me sleep right through it, didn't you?"

"More like three o'clock this morning," Gavin said. "Caden's the one who's been up all night."

"Grab some breakfast," Asher said, "and we'll fill you in."

Bacon, eggs, grits, and an assortment of pastries sat on a cart in the kitchen, and she decided that the pancakes could wait. She fixed her plate and joined the three men at the table.

She took a bite of the still-warm eggs and Caden jumped right into it. "From the evidence presented to us, it looks like Sarah's investigation led her to the orphanage and the hospital located not too far from it. She and Isaiah were friends and she trusted him. When she found out she was in over her head—for the first time—she went to him for help."

"With what?" A swig of coffee chased a bite of bacon.

"At first she thought the orphanage was involved in black market adoptions. Then she discovered some things weren't adding up and decided children were being sold into slavery by the director and a certain doctor who has a lot of involvement with the children there—and it looked like some soldiers were also involved in the transport of those orphans."

Her appetite left and she set her fork on the edge of her plate. "Which would explain why her boss allowed her to continue to investigate. She told him about the soldiers' involvement."

"But she didn't even tell him everything." Caden drew in a breath. "And now it looks like Sarah's investigation-slash-story is related to mine."

"What?"

The three men exchanged looks.

Brooke wadded her napkin into a ball and placed it on the table. "Tell me. Please."

She listened as he told her about the mass grave site containing bodies of mostly children, about the plate in the teen's ankle and the fact that she'd once been a resident of the Morning Star Orphanage.

"Wait a second," she said. "How did Sarah know something was going on at the orphanage in the first place? What made her start investigating?"

"One of the orphanage's workers, Kristin Welsh, was concerned with the high number of adoptions that were taking place at such a fast rate," Caden said. "She said adoptions were so rare that it was hard not to notice when one actually happened, but for this number to occur in such a short amount of time—"

"How many?" Brooke asked.

"Twenty-seven within a year."

Her brow rose. "Oh." Okay, she hadn't expected that one.

"Kristin wanted to make sure the children were being sent to good, reputable homes or, in some instances, back to family."

"That's not so odd, is it?" Brooke asked. "For a child to be returned to a parent after a stint in the orphanage?"

"No, not odd, but again, it was the increase in numbers she

was seeing that caught her attention. She and Sarah had met at a park and become friends. Eventually, Kristin asked Sarah if she would like to volunteer at the orphanage. Sarah said she would and that was that."

"So, Sarah and Kristin were investigating where the children were going, and . . . ?"

"They're not being adopted. They're being trafficked for their organs."

Brooke's stomach did a complete flip and nausea kicked in. "No," she whispered. "Please, that's not even . . ."

"I know," Asher said. "I know. Makes me sick too, but we're calling in all the agencies on both sides of this. I've notified agents in Kabul and they're already investigating. They're looking for the doctor involved and plan to pull in the director of the orphanage for questioning, of course."

"I see. And what about those who are working on this side of the world?"

"Again, the alphabet soup agencies are involved."

"We're gathering all the security footage from every camera in the vicinity of the places you were attacked," Caden said. "We're asking homeowners for any footage they may have on their private systems, everything."

"But how long will it take to watch it all?" she asked.

"It'll take time," Caden said, "which is why we think it's best you not go home right now."

"All right, then where do I go?"

Asher cleared his throat and she looked at him. "Uh . . . it might be a tad awkward, but how do you feel about staying with my parents?"

She let out a shaky laugh. "I think that might be more than a tad awkward."

"They have the best security system money can buy and round-the-clock staff on the premises. It might be awkward, but it would be safe."

199

A wave of dizziness hit Kristin and she stumbled to the bed to sink onto it, mind swirling. No, it was a mistake. It couldn't be true. "What are you talking about? Please explain," she whispered.

"That was Caden, my brother. He called to ask if I'd find out about the girl."

"Tasneem?"

"Yes." Sarah hesitated, seeming to be searching for words.

"Just say it, Sarah."

"She's . . . dead."

"No!" Grief crashed over Kristin.

Sarah sat next to her and gripped her hands. "I'm so sorry."

"Go on," she said, her voice rough with unshed tears.

"She was found buried in a grave, one of many, in South Carolina. The autopsy on her revealed that her heart was missing. And her lungs. And"—Sarah drew in a breath—"her kidneys."

A numbness began to invade Kristin and she welcomed it. "But how did she get there?"

"Caden said he believes that the children are being told they're headed to the United States for adoption. There's someone who escorts them with forged or faked documents, including passports." She paused. "The passports might actually be real. Anyway, once they reach the States, they're taken somewhere and . . . killed. For their organs."

"But . . ." Kristin pressed her hands to her temples. "I can't process it." She looked up. "It can't be true. There must be a mistake."

"Look, Kristin, you were right when you asked me who I was not long ago. You know me, the real me, but not my real profession."

Kristin stilled and looked at the woman she'd considered a friend. "I don't understand."

"I'm with the Army. I'm an investigative reporter."

"What?" It was too much. Her brain couldn't take in any more crazy.

"I live on the base and the guy who escorts me here every day is an American soldier. He sits outside the orphanage waiting and watching. And he takes me back and forth to the hospital so I can keep an eye on Dr. Madad."

"Wait a minute. How did you know all this was going on here? I asked you to come work here as a volunteer."

"And in the beginning, that's all I was. Until you brought up the fact that the children were being adopted really fast and you were suspicious about it—and you were trying to find the families these children were adopted into but couldn't. It got my nosy reporter brain spinning and I started looking into it."

Kristin felt like she'd been blindsided. "But the hospital? Dr. Madad would recognize you as being from the orphanage. Wouldn't he be suspicious?"

"Only if he saw me. I made sure he didn't. I've followed him from here a couple of times and he goes straight to the hospital each time. And you know what he does there? He goes to his lab, where he stays for hours."

"So? He's a doctor. Of course he would go to his lab."

Sarah's eyes never wavered. Her look was a cross between compassion and determination. "On the files that Isaiah Michaels downloaded from Madad's computer, there's evidence that he's testing blood and tissue samples, along with DNA and everything else necessary to match up these kids with a paying recipient. A very well-paying recipient, because he's got money rolling in."

"How do you know all this?" Kristin whispered.

"My brother Caden is an FBI agent and he's in touch with agents here in Kabul. They're working with the Afghan police force, looking for Madad right now to bring him in for questioning. I told Caden to let them know he was here at the orphanage."

"They took Paksima," Kristin said. "Mr. Yusufi just told me she was being adopted." She rose and grabbed her purse and the keys to the orphanage van. "I have to get to the airport."

Sarah's eyes widened. "You can't go without an escort."

"I have no choice. I have to stop them from taking Paksima! If what you say is true, they're going to kill her!"

Sarah let out a groan. "All right, then, let's go."

"No, not you. It's not safe."

"Exactly. That's why you're not going alone." Sarah shut the door behind her. And Kristin heard her friend mutter, "Caden's going to kill me if someone doesn't beat him to it."

Two steps into the hallway, Kristin pulled up short. Dr. Madad stood there, weapon held in front of him. Mr. Yusufi stood behind him.

"Back in the room," Dr. Madad said.

Adrenaline humming so fast she thought she might faint, Kristin stepped back and felt Sarah behind her. "What are you doing?"

"Getting rid of a problem." His gaze flicked to Sarah. "Two problems."

"You're going to kill two Americans?" Kristin asked. "Do you know how much attention that will bring down on this orphanage?"

"She's right," the director said. "We can't do this here."

Frustration, rage, indecision whipped across the doctor's face. "Then clear this hallway and make sure no one comes this way. I'll hold them here while you do it. Then we'll get them away from the property and arrange for an accident." He scowled. "Lots of accidents have been known to happen around here."

Kristin sucked in a breath, terror sweeping over her, but mostly Paksima's sweet smile kept flashing in her mind. If she didn't do something, the child would die. And Sarah. "Her brother is an FBI agent," Kristin said. "Do you really think killing her will make this disappear?"

The director shifted, sweat beading his brow. "Doctor, I don't know—"

"We'll worry about the ramifications later. One thing is painfully obvious. These two can't live to talk."

"I've already talked," Sarah said. "To a lot of people."

"Go!" the doctor snapped. "Clear the hall as best you can. You two, follow him. Walk. Stay beside me and don't do anything stupid, because if you do, then obviously other people will have to die."

Kristin gripped Sarah's hand. Sarah shook her off and stuck her hand in her pocket as she obeyed the man's order to walk. At first Kristin was hurt, then noticed Sarah stayed slightly behind her. She just prayed whatever the woman was doing, it was related to bringing help before it was too late.

o o o

Asher rang the bell to his parents' home. He might use the code to the gate without thought, but he never just opened the door—front or back—and walked in. For one thing, it was usually kept locked, but regardless, it didn't feel right.

"You grew up here?" Brooke asked, eyes wide.

"No, this was a celebratory purchase after Dad won that big case and put Oliver Loft behind bars."

"The famous basketball player?"

"And serial killer. Yeah. That's the one. He became the firm's golden boy and was turning away work after that. Then he opened his own practice, became a judge, sold the practice, and the rest is history, as they say. Right now he's on the short list for the Supreme Court."

"Whoa."

"Don't let this change your view of me," he said, his voice low. "This isn't who I am."

She lifted a brow. "You don't have to worry about that with me."

His heart walls crumbled just a little more, and he had to look away from the eyes that would be easy to get lost in.

Focus, man. Asher rang the bell again, although it wasn't necessary. It was a long walk to the door from any part of the house.

He'd called ahead and made his request, and his father agreed after Asher had answered a dozen questions. He was vague on most of the answers but didn't fudge on the possible danger hosting Brooke could bring to their doorstep.

After a significant pause—during which Asher fully expected the man to say no—his father had said, "Bring her. The property is gated, the dogs are out, and I'll add two more guards to the outside. She can have the bedroom next to Lyric's."

"Bedroom" wasn't quite what he'd call the space that also held a bathroom and sitting area with a large fireplace and three walls of books. If it had a kitchen, one would call it an apartment. "I appreciate it, Dad."

"Are you going to be staying here as well?"

"For the night." Just to make sure Brooke got settled. Her green eyes flashed to mind and the thought of anything happening to her shot fear straight to his very soul. How could he feel so deeply about someone he'd never even been on a date with? Then again, facing death together would probably intensify feelings.

"Asher?"

He shuddered and realized she'd been calling his name and squeezing his hand for several seconds.

Amanda Grissom, dressed in her work uniform of black pants and long-sleeved blue sweater that signaled she was an employee of the household, frowned at him. "Are you all right, Mr. James?"

"Yes, of course. Sorry. Got caught up in . . . thoughts." At least they weren't bad ones. "And I've told you, it's Asher. Mr. James is my father. And brother."

He waited for Brooke to cross the threshold and followed her inside.

Amanda shut the door. "This way, please."

Brooke leaned close to him. "You don't know the way?" she whispered.

Asher choked on a laugh and he thought he might have heard

Amanda do the same, but her ramrod-straight back never twitched. She led them into the sitting area. Two wingback chairs bookended the mammoth fireplace in the corner that blazed with a lively flame, giving the room a warmth he didn't think was possible in this home.

He placed a hand on Brooke's lower back when he realized she wasn't moving to sit. Even with his light pressure she didn't move. Her eyes were locked on the fireplace.

"I'll turn it off," he said. Ten steps later, he flipped the switch and the flame flickered, then disappeared. He turned in time to see her panicked look fade.

She took a deep breath. "Sorry, I have issues with fire. And fireplaces. And heat. And smoke."

"Understandable."

"Asher?"

He spun to find his father watching them from the doorway. "Hi, Dad."

The man's gaze flicked over the two of them before a forced smile curved his lips. "Welcome."

"Thank you, Mr. James," Brooke said. "I can't tell you how much I appreciate this."

The smile thawed a fraction. "Well, any friend of Asher's is a friend of ours."

Asher frowned. *Since when?*

"I hear you're looking at a Supreme Court nomination in the near future," Brooke said. "Congratulations."

"Ah, yes, I am," his father said, surprise tingeing his voice. "I didn't realize Asher was up-to-date on my career."

"Of course. He's very proud of you."

Another flash of surprise. Then his father cleared his throat and turned to Asher. "Nicholas and Lyric will be here for dinner. I hope you brought appropriate clothes."

"Sure did."

"Amanda will show you to your rooms."

With a nod of dismissal, the man left.

Brooke leaned in next to him. "Are you sure he wasn't in the military?"

"I've always kind of wondered."

"This way, Ms. Adams," Amanda said. "Asher, I'll leave you to find your own way."

"I can show her, Amanda."

The woman stopped, then swept out a hand for them to proceed. "Of course."

She hurried away, and Asher directed her toward the curved staircase off the kitchen. "Up those and to the right."

"I'll follow you."

He led the way, shaking his head as he went. He didn't mind a big house if one could afford it but found his parents' place over the top. However, for now, he'd be grateful for it—for the security it would offer Brooke. He found the room Brooke would use and opened the door. She looked inside and smiled. "It's lovely."

"Most important, it's comfortable."

She stepped inside and set her small bag on the rose-colored comforter. "It's very generous of your parents to let me stay. I'm grateful."

The fact that she voiced his earlier thoughts stilled him. He reached for her hands and clasped them. They felt small and soft in his callused ones. They felt like they belonged there. He liked that. "You don't have a boyfriend, right?"

She blinked and laughed. "No."

"Potential?"

"Uh . . . again, no."

"Why not?"

TWENTY-TWO

Brooke bit her tongue on the stammered response that threatened to spill out and took a calming breath before releasing her words. "I was dating someone before I left for Afghanistan. He didn't want me to go." There. That sounded reasonable enough. She tugged her hands from his.

"And yet you did. Why?"

She gave a tiny shrug. "Because I'm a bit of a brat."

"Huh?"

"The guy I was dating was someone my father approved of. I wasn't sure how I felt about that. I mean, I liked Kirk. He was a perfectly nice man."

"But?"

"My father liked him. That one fact really threw me. And so I kept looking for things to dislike. I finally found one."

"Which was?"

"He was nice to me, but he was nice to several other women as well. Turns out he wanted to 'keep his options open, but I was in the lead' when it came to his favorites."

"You're kidding me."

"If only."

"What a jerk." Anger flashed in his eyes.

"He was definitely that."

"I hope you punched him."

"No, I didn't resort to violence." His look said he would have. For her. It made her stomach do strange things to know he would do something like that on her behalf. Not that she wanted him to punch anyone, but the fact that he would stand up for her touched her in ways she'd forgotten existed.

"What?" he asked. "What's that look?"

"The only man who's ever really offered to defend me is Paul."

"I like Paul."

"And Paul didn't like Kirk."

"In fact, I love Paul."

A giggle slipped out and she covered her mouth. "How can you make me laugh when I'm telling you about one of the lowest times of my life?"

"It's a gift."

It really was. "Anyway, when I found out, I wasn't too happy about it, as you can imagine. We were supposed to be having a dinner party with some of my father's friends and associates. My father came into the room when he heard us arguing. He might be a strict, hard-nosed man, but he's not stupid. He figured out pretty quickly what the topic of our argument was. He told us to suspend the discussion—his word, not mine—until after his guests had left. We did. The guests left, and before Kirk and I could get into it again, my father pulled me aside and said that men sometimes strayed but most came home to the wife and I should let it go. Kirk would be a good provider and had a promising career ahead of him." She clicked her tongue. "Which would, of course, make my father look good."

"He sounds a lot like my father." He shot her a small smile. "Maybe that's why I like you so much. You understand what it's like to grow up with a man like that."

"Well, I wasn't having any of it. Told them both I was going to Afghanistan with the Army and Kirk was welcome to take a long walk off a short pier." She grimaced. "It wasn't original, but I was mad and it was the first thing that came to mind."

"Sounds appropriate."

"Hmm." She studied him, suddenly realizing what he'd said a moment ago. "You like me so much? You do?"

He stilled and let his eyes linger on hers. She could sense the turmoil boiling beneath the surface. "So very much," he said, moving closer, lowering his head. "I've never met anyone quite like you before. You fascinate me."

"And that's good?"

"I sure think so." He hesitated while Brooke's heart hammered in her chest. "Then again," he said, "I don't know if this is a good idea."

"What?"

"Kissing you while we're in the middle of such craziness."

"Right."

His hand lifted and his fingers trailed down her cheek. "So soft. How do you keep your skin so soft?"

"Um . . . moisturizer. I have a really good one, although I haven't had much of a chance to use it lately." Brooke wanted to smack herself. Had she really just said that? She cleared her throat gently. "Asher?"

"Yeah?"

"If you kiss me, you can't be a client. Just . . . putting that out there."

"I'm okay with that. Are you?"

"I'm okay if you're o—"

His lips settled on hers. Soft, gentle, exploring, curious. Her pulse thundered in her ears while her knees went weak and her stomach flipped a three-sixty. His hand slid under the back of her head and tilted it, granting him better access. She leaned into him, sliding her arms around his waist, reveling in his closeness and the care he took while kissing her senseless.

"Well, well, little brother. I thought you were bringing a damsel in distress to hide out for a few days. Guess I know where to find you if you go missing in the middle of the night."

Brooke had frozen at the first words and opened her eyes to meet Asher's dark ones. Without taking his gaze from hers, he stepped backward and with one hand, slammed the door in his brother's face. Then he pulled in a deep breath and dropped the other hand still resting at the base of her head. "That was Nicholas."

"He's charming." Brooke was proud she was able to speak with a steady voice.

"He can be. Until he chooses not to be." Thunderclouds rolled behind his eyes, defusing the sweet, if heated, moment.

"You didn't punch him," she said.

"Just say the word and I'll be happy to." He looked like he would enjoy it. "But truly, all he's looking for is to get a reaction. One he can tell our father about. He's not worth it."

"I'm just teasing. I don't want you to punch anyone, especially not your brother. Don't worry about him. I can hold my own with him." She wouldn't mind asking him to have better timing. Being in Asher's arms, kissing him, had been even better than she'd imagined—and she had a good imagination.

"He can be vicious, Brooke. Don't underestimate him."

"I've worked with people like him before. It's okay. I'll just treat him like a client."

"Except he won't want your help."

"He doesn't have to know I'm offering." She sighed. "Seriously, most of the people I've tried to counsel in the past nine months haven't wanted my help. I'm used to it."

He winced and she squeezed his hand. "Soldiers are a tough group," he said.

"No kidding."

With a sigh, Asher pulled her into a hug, and she laid her head against his chest. She never wanted to move.

"That felt good," he murmured.

"What? The kiss?"

"Well, that, yes. I've been wanting to do that for a while, but I have to say, slamming that door in Nicholas's face ranks a close second."

Brooke snickered.

Asher did too.

Brooke's snicker turned to a giggle, then a full-on laugh. Asher stepped back and looked down at her for a moment, obviously fighting his own grin. Then laughter rumbled from him, and they held each other until tears of mirth tracked Brooke's cheeks. She swiped them away. "Asher?"

"Yeah?"

"It wasn't that funny."

"We needed the laugh." Asher pulled her back against his chest. "Was kind of funny, though. Wish I could have seen the look on his face."

She took comfort from his embrace and the feeling of being safe. Cherished. "What now?" she asked.

"First, dinner, then we sleep, and tomorrow we figure this out and take down a group of killers."

o o o

Kristin slid down the wall and pressed her palms to her eyes. "We have to get out of here."

Halfway down the hall, they'd been interrupted by the administrative assistant looking for Dr. Madad. One of the children was seizing and they needed him immediately.

At his hesitation, her eyes had widened. "Doctor? He needs help. Please!"

He'd pointed and told her to get back to the child. "I have to

215

get my bag. I'll hurry. Now get back to him. Stay with him until I get there."

She'd spun on her heel and bolted.

The good doctor, with the director's help, had shoved them into a large, mostly empty, supply closet with a warning hiss. "Director Yusufi will be outside. Make any noise and I'll start killing the children—one by one."

"Don't do this," Kristin said. "You're a doctor!"

The door slammed in her face and she heard the click of the lock.

The minutes ticked past while Sarah paced, her phone in her hand, dialing. Kristin watched her, saw the fear on her face, the shaking in her hands, and the sheer determination to figure a way out of their current—and dire—situation.

"We're too late, aren't we?" Kristin asked. "She's going to die, isn't she?"

Sarah stopped. "I don't know, Kristin, but if we don't get out of here, other kids will for sure." She stilled and listened. "Felicia, this is Sarah. Dr. Madad and the director, Abdullah Yusufi, have gone off the deep end." She explained the current situation. "They're using American soldiers who probably think they're doing something good—or maybe they're a part of the whole thing, I don't know—to transport these kids somewhere—"

"Tajikistan," Kristin said.

Sarah frowned at her. "What?"

"I overheard them say something about Tajikistan. It makes sense."

"Okay, we suspect they're crossing the border into Tajikistan with these children and turning them over to someone who's probably acting like they're adoptive parents from the United States. They'll have passports and all the right paperwork. You need to stop them from getting on that plane. Okay. Thank you." She hung up and looked at Kristin. "Help is on the way, heading here and the nearest airport, but we're going to have to do our best to save ourselves until it can get here."

Kristin nodded.

Sarah grabbed a bottle from the shelf with one hand and pulled the mop from the bucket with her other. "Here." She gave the mop to Kristin. "Whoever opens the door, shove the mop into his stomach. It'll distract him long enough for me to throw this ammonia in his face. Then we'll deal with anyone with him."

"You think that's going to work?"

"I think we have to try."

"Okay, then."

The lock clicked and Kristin sucked in a breath. "Get ready," she said.

When the door swung open, Kristin jabbed with the mop.

Dr. Madad yelled and doubled over, curses ringing. Sarah threw the ammonia. It missed Madad but hit Director Yusufi. He hollered and went to his knees, holding his eyes.

Dr. Madad shoved his way past her and ran at Sarah, who backed into the corner, keeping the shelving between her and the doctor's gun. Kristin grabbed a glass bottle from the shelf behind her and swung it at the man's head. It cracked against his left ear. He howled, whirled, and fired the weapon.

Pain shattered through her chest. She heard Sarah's cry. Saw Paksima's beautiful smile even as she saw Sarah throw herself at the doctor. The gun clattered to the floor. Fire radiated through her and she rolled toward the weapon with a groan. Her hand closed over the grip. She turned to see Madad with his fingers clamped around Sarah's throat.

Kristin lifted the gun, aimed, and pulled the trigger.

Dr. Madad dropped. Mr. Yusufi was still trying to breathe through the ammonia fumes and clawing at his eyes.

Kristin slid to the floor, gasping, her gaze on Sarah. "Find her," Kristin whispered. "Take care of her."

"No," Sarah croaked. She crawled over the dead doctor's body and reached for Kristin's hand. "Hold on."

The pressure on her chest intensified, and she realized Sarah was leaning against her wound. "Promise me. Find a way to save her."

"I promise, now be quiet. I think I hear sirens."

And all Kristin saw was darkness closing in. One last electric flare of agony whipped through her and she sank into the blackness.

○ ○ ○

Dressed in black, he blended into the dark background of the night, but the streetlamps would be his downfall if he wasn't careful. He noted the security system, but that wouldn't be a problem. He'd just have to be fast once he was inside.

He'd received his orders and had watched the house for two days, run the plan through his mind, written it out, studied it, practiced it in his head until he figured he could do it with his eyes closed.

The sounds of television laughter drifted from behind the windows of the living area, and he approached quietly from the side so he could see in. The woman sat on the couch, watching a sitcom. A blue bowl had been discarded to the floor. Had it held popcorn? Probably. A Coke bottle had been drained, along with several water bottles that would most likely make it into the recycle bin before she turned in for the night.

He let his gaze run over the home. A large brick house set in the middle of two acres, it was private, quiet, peaceful. Everything he'd ever envisioned for his own life. Maybe one day. He almost felt sorry for the occupants, but orders were orders and it was his job to follow them.

As soon as the last light went out, he pulled on the black ski mask, then removed the weapon from his pocket and screwed on the suppressor. It was go time.

o o o

Sleep. His few hours of dreamless oblivion had been nice. Wonderful. Then the dream had hit him.

Asher halted mid-pace, the nightmare fading as he thought about Brooke and that amazing, earth-shattering kiss.

Wiping the sweat from his face and chest, he dropped into the chair next to the window and pressed his palms to his eyes. He really had to get a handle on the nightmares.

Although, strangely enough, it did seem they'd gotten better since he'd been working with Brooke and doing his best to keep them both alive. Maybe he was an adrenaline junkie and needed the rush that being in constant danger brought.

He frowned and hoped not. Most likely it was just because he wasn't sleeping as much.

A buzzing sound pulled at him, and he blinked away the fog of interrupted thoughts as he picked up his ringing phone. "Yeah, Asher James here."

"Mitch Sampson here, you loser."

"Samps, good to hear your voice. Wish I could see your ugly mug."

"Now, that's the pot calling the kettle black."

Asher frowned. The words were right, but the tone was different. "What's going on, Sampson?" He and Sampson had talked occasionally since Asher had left the Army but not usually during the middle of the night. "You forget how to calculate the time difference?"

"Sorry, man, but this couldn't wait and we're getting ready to head out on a mission. I don't know when I'll get another chance to call."

"Of course. What is it?"

"Captain Newell's wife was murdered late last night. He's on his way home now."

Asher could only stand there staring at his old bedroom wall. "Asher?"

"Yeah," he grunted, the momentary paralysis leaving. "I heard you, but, man, I'm . . . stunned."

"I know. You're not the only one."

"What happened?"

"Home invasion. She fought, and he shot her."

"And the kids?"

"They're fine. Well, devastated, of course, but physically unhurt. They weren't supposed to be there that night. They had some kind of church function. A lock-in or whatever. But Monica wasn't feeling well and PJ brought her home. Apparently, he decided to just go on to bed. Yvonne's mother is with them for now." The background noise intensified. "I also gotta tell you one more thing."

The man's voice was so low, Asher could barely make out his words. "Speak up, man, can't hear you."

"I'll text you. It's getting crazy around here."

"I remember. I miss you guys."

"Then come back. We need you and Black. It's not the same without you. Look for my text." He hung up and Asher rubbed a hand down his face and resumed his pacing. He wouldn't be going back to sleep anytime soon.

Captain Newell's wife? Yvonne? How could this be? He stopped. And was her death somehow related to everything going on? He had no idea why his mind immediately went there, but Yvonne's death couldn't be a coincidence, could it? So, did that mean Newell knew something and they'd retaliated? But why go after his family?

Or . . . it was a simple home invasion and Yvonne had gotten caught in the middle of it.

His phone buzzed. Mitch's promised text.

Bomb parts from the ambush match the bomb
parts from the café in Kabul. Out of all the

parts I've collected, these are the only two
that match—because they weren't Afghani.
Parts are American military grade. I've let the
captain know, but he's headed to your part of
the world. Maybe you can talk with him and see
what he has to say about that?

Asher processed the information, then typed back.

Will deal with on this end. See what you can
find out on that one. And be careful who you
trust. Don't get your ugly self killed. People are
dropping like flies.

He got a thumbs-up emoji in response.

Asher dropped his chin to his chest. *God, protect them, please.*
He pulled up his captain's number and sent a text.

I know you're still in the air heading home. I'm
so sorry. Yvonne was the best. I can't believe
this. I know you'll probably stay in close touch
with CID while they investigate her murder.
If there's a lead you want me to run down or
whatever I can do, just ask. If you need me to
hang out with your kids for the day or whatever,
I'm here.

He sent the text and rubbed his eyes. A glance at the clock made
him groan, but he knew he was up for the day. He showered and
dressed and couldn't shake Sampson's words. American materials
had made both bombs? His main questions were where had the
stuff come from and who had gotten their hands on them?

Coffee. He needed something to push the fog out of his brain.
He made his way downstairs to the kitchen using his phone to
light the way.

As he pulled a mug from the cabinet, a footstep behind him

spun him around. He hefted the mug, ready to let it fly like a missile until his eyes landed on Brooke. She stood there, hair tousled, eyes wide. She had on sweats and a T-shirt and looked adorable.

He lowered his arm. "Sorry."

"I didn't mean to scare you. I was just thirsty."

He opened the fridge and pulled out a bottle of water. He handed it to her and took another look at her. "You're not sleeping."

"No."

"Have you even tried?"

"Um. No."

Because she was afraid she'd wake up screaming. "Drink your water and come on."

She uncapped the bottle and took a long swig. "Where are we going?"

"The sitting area in your wing. The couch is comfortable and there's a great selection of movies."

"Oh. Okay."

He returned his mug and took her hand. She followed him to the sitting area, and he sat on one end of the couch and patted the cushion next to him. With only a slight hesitation, she sank onto it. He wrapped an arm around her shoulder and picked up the remote. "Favorite movie?"

"Well, it's not my all-time favorite, but I feel it's appropriate."

"What's that?"

"*One Flew Over the Cuckoo's Nest.*"

He barked a short laugh. "I'd say it's very appropriate. And I know we have it because my sister is a huge classics fan."

Soon, he had the movie playing. "Now, I want you to let your eyes close when they feel heavy." He took her hand. "If you start to get restless or make noises, I'll wake you up."

Brooke shifted to look up at him. "What about you? You have to sleep."

"I actually did and I'm wide awake right now—which is why I was in the kitchen getting ready to make a pot of coffee."

"Nightmare?"

"Yes."

"And?"

"I got a phone call. Nothing to do with you, so don't worry about it. Just rest, okay? You need to or you're not going to be alert." And that could be deadly for her.

"You're sure?"

"Positive."

With a sigh, she settled against him and focused her gaze on the screen. Within minutes, she was completely relaxed, her breathing even. Asher leaned his head back and closed his eyes even while he made a list in his head of everyone who had access to military-grade bomb materials.

He didn't like the list at all.

TWENTY-THREE

Brooke woke slowly, not wanting to give up the feeling of comfort. Peace. Safety. All of those thanks to Asher, whose strong arm was around her, keeping her snuggled up against him, her head still resting on his shoulder where she'd leaned against it last night. Or early this morning.

"Asher?" she whispered.

"Yeah?"

"You awake?"

"Yeah." Amusement tinged his answer. "Are you?"

"Uh-huh."

"Okay, can you shift a little? I can't feel my arm."

She gasped and lurched into a sitting position.

"Well, you didn't have to move quite that fast, but thanks." He held his phone in the other hand. From what little she could see, he'd been scrolling through his texts.

"I fell asleep," she said.

"About three seconds after the movie started."

A laugh escaped her. "I didn't dream."

"That's because you were too busy snoring."

"What? I don't snore!"

"You do, but it's a cute sound."

She gaped, then gave his arm a light punch. He leaned over and kissed her nose, moved lower, and she went still. "Don't you dare kiss me."

He pulled back, frowning, looking a little hurt. "Um . . . okay. Ouch."

"At least not until after I've brushed my teeth."

The hurt faded, replaced by amusement. That also faded. She stood and Asher caught her hand. The sad look in his eyes stopped her. "What is it?"

He pulled her back down next to him. "I got a call last night from one of my buddies. Mitch Sampson."

"The Paul Bunyan guy?"

A smile flickered for a nanosecond. "He'd be so proud of that reference. But yes." He groaned and rubbed his eyes. "There's no easy way to say this."

"What? Just say it."

"He called to tell me that Captain Newell's wife was murdered the night before last."

"What?" she whispered. "No. Oh no."

"Yeah." He waved his phone at her. "I was just reading updates from him. I'm not sure where he's getting his details, but he's passing them on to me." Another groan. "This is awful. Newell's got two kids. Monica and Phil Junior."

"But . . . why kill her?"

"Looks like a random break-in. The kids were in their rooms asleep. Yvonne was up late, cleaning the kitchen, it looks like. She had a light on over the sink, but the rest of the place was dark. The guy probably thought she was asleep too. He broke the glass on their back door and was inside in a flash. Apparently, Yvonne saw him. He took her outside, placed the gun to her head, and pulled the trigger."

"Because she could identify him?"

"Probably."

"But wouldn't the shot have alerted the neighbors? Woken the kids?"

"The kids said they never heard anything. Neighbors either. If that's the case, then he had to have been using a suppressor."

Brooke shook her head. "I didn't know her, but I remember Captain Newell from our brief encounters. I'm so sorry."

"I am too." He closed his eyes for a brief moment. "I'm going to head over to his house. He should be landing any minute now."

"Those poor kids." She hesitated. "Would it be weird if I came with you? To be there for them and you?"

He reached for her hand and gripped her fingers. "There's no one I'd rather have by my side than you."

And she couldn't think of any place she'd rather be. "But isn't that sort of defeating the purpose of me being here at your parents'?"

"Maybe," he said softly, "but I can't help thinking this isn't random—that it has something to do with the case. No matter where we turn, everything keeps pointing back to Kabul. Having your insight may be helpful. And . . . it won't hurt for you to be there in the event that he might need you and your expertise."

She thought about that. "You think he'd even acknowledge that I might be able to help him? This soon anyway?"

"Well, if not him, then his kids. It's possible they may need someone to talk to. His family means everything to him, and he's not going to know how to help them."

Brooke drew in a breath. "All right. Can you tell me a little about him? His personality? His mind-set?"

Asher looked away and frowned.

"What is it?" she asked.

"I'm realizing I don't know how to answer that. Let me see . . . his personality and mind-set. Captain Newell is an extremely private person. He can come across as a hard man, crass and blunt and difficult to get to know, but underneath that exterior is a man who cares. At least I think so. He's always been professional, an excellent leader, brilliant in his assessment of a mission and what needed to be done to complete it successfully, but he's not one to mix professional and personal lives. His daughter was really sick about a year ago. Maybe ten months ago? I can't remember. He never said what was wrong with her. The only reason I knew she was ill was because I overheard him on the phone with his wife telling her everything would be okay and that he'd be on the next flight home. I asked him if I could do anything. He just said his daughter was in the hospital and his wife was overreacting. But he went home. Was back two weeks later saying nothing. But he was more quiet than usual, more withdrawn from the rest of us. I guess he got tired of us harassing him about what was bothering him, because he finally told us that his daughter was sick. Said he didn't feel like sharing the details, but the doctors were handling it and she'd be fine. He said his wife was amazing and keeping him updated, but for now, everything was being taken care of and we needed to focus on the reason we were there. And that's the last I heard him say anything about her other than to let us know she'd recovered and was doing well."

"Okay, that helps me get a handle on his personality," she said. "Very private, doesn't share easily, driven in his profession but loves his family."

"Nice summary. Accurate. Like I said, he's a hard person to get to know, but he's always put his unit first. If one of us had a problem, we could go to him and know he'd do his best to help us—and he usually took care of the issue."

"You have a lot of respect for him."

"I do. And I care about him and his family. That's why I think having you there would be emotionally helpful for them."

"Okay. I'll do whatever you think is best."

"I'll call Caden and let him know. Maybe he can arrange some protection with the local officers."

"Sure. I'm just going to jump in the shower and put myself together."

"You look put together to me. I don't see anything you need to improve on."

"Asher . . . um . . . never mind." She patted his cheek, feeling the rough morning whiskers under her palm. "You're sweet. Clueless, but sweet."

"Hey, what does that mean?"

"I'll see you in about twenty minutes."

Poor guy looked completely confused. Then he shrugged. "Okay. Meet me by the front door?"

"If I can find it." She headed for the bathroom, the momentary lightness fading with the heavy sorrow she felt for the grieving family.

Fifteen minutes later, she decided she'd set a new record for getting ready and stepped out of the bedroom, crossed the sitting area, and let herself into the hallway.

Only to come face-to-face with Nicholas James. He shot her a tight smile and looked her up and down in a way that made her skin crawl. But she lifted her chin and met his gaze.

"Good morning, Nicholas."

"What do you see in him?"

She didn't pretend to misunderstand. "A lot. Kindness, compassion, strength, determination, loyalty . . . do I need to go on?"

A funny look crossed his face. "I've never seen what you're talking about."

"Have you looked? Or have you just been so jealous of him that you've been blinded to the fact that he'd love to have a relationship with you?"

His jaw dropped before he could snap it closed. "Me? Don't make me laugh. I'm his brother, but he has to go to the ends of the earth to find complete strangers that he calls brothers. So, right. I'm not buying that. He's a loser. Always was and always will be."

Brooke debated the wisdom of arguing with the man, but everything in her rose up in defense of Asher. She stilled. Thought. "Okay. What makes him a loser in your eyes?"

Again, Nicholas looked like she'd taken him by surprise. "Well, um . . . he joined the Army. Who does that unless they have no other option?"

"A lot of good men and women who believe their country is worth fighting for?"

He rolled his eyes.

"Like my father," she said.

A sneer twisted his lips. "So that's it. The only real man is a guy who wears a uniform?"

"No. A real man is one who cares more about the people he loves than himself. Asher saved my life. More than once. He's saved countless lives. Those of women and children and other men who, through no fault of their own, have been born into a world of violence and misery. He gave up a lot to be a part of something bigger than himself in an effort to bring peace to an area of the world a lot of people don't care about. I find that honorable and admirable. I have a lot of respect for him."

A hint of something flashed in his eyes, and for a moment she saw into the depths of his heart before he covered it with a grunt of disgust. "You're just like every other female who's ever crossed his path. Doing whatever it takes to get his attention, not just because of his bad-boy attitude and appearance, but because of who our father is. Oh yeah, don't think I don't know that you and everyone else sees dollar signs when they look at him. Well, let me tell you this—I'm the one who'll inherit. I'm the one with the future. I'm the one with self-control, not a freak who can't even be in the same room when a loud noise goes off. You really should get away from him while you can."

Brooke struggled with the dual desire to lash out at the man and the need to feel sorry for him. "Wow. You've got a lot of deep-seated issues when it comes to Asher, don't you? Have you ever thought about talking to someone about those?"

He snorted and let out a guffaw. "Me? Talk to someone? You've got to be kidding. I'm not the one jumping at every little sound."

"Let me ask you this, Nicholas." She did her best to keep her voice even. He was a man who found his self-worth in tearing others down, pushing buttons, and getting a reaction. She wouldn't give him the satisfaction.

"What?"

"Has Asher ever hit you?"

He frowned. "What?"

"Just answer the question."

"No, he's never hit me. At least not since we were teens."

"Then I'd say he's exhibited an amazing amount of self-control. You might want to think about that."

She brushed past him and made her way to the front door with only one wrong turn.

○ ○ ○

From Asher's parents' house in Charlotte, North Carolina, to Captain Phillip Newell's home in Greenville, South Carolina, it was only about an hour-and-a-half drive. Brooke shot him a frown. "Wait a minute. Isn't their house a crime scene? Why are they still able to stay there?"

"The crime scene people got what they needed and let them come back."

"Oh." Her frown remained, and he could almost hear the wheels of her brain spinning.

"What is it?"

"Nothing."

"Something."

"Well, it doesn't make sense. Who goes to break into a house prepared with a suppressor for his weapon? That just sounds weird to me."

"I know. It sounded weird to me too." He shot her a quick glance. "Let's just reserve judgment until we have more details, okay?"

"Sure."

Asher pulled to a stop at the curb of the stately brick home with the manicured lawn.

"Wow, he does well," she said.

"Yvonne did well. Actually, they did well together. She was the manager of a fairly large bank in downtown Greenville. Add in the captain's salary and yeah, they can afford a house like this."

He glanced behind them, noting three police cars. Nothing subtle today. He wanted it plain to anyone watching that it was going to be hard to get to him or Brooke. Caden had called ahead and let the detective in charge of Yvonne Newell's murder case know they were coming.

Gavin stepped out of his truck and headed their way. "Just in time."

"Yeah," Asher said. "Let's do this."

Asher took Brooke's hand and led her past the neighbors congregated on the edge of the property. Some were genuinely concerned, others were rubberneckers. Family and close friends were inside.

He didn't bother to knock on the door but slipped inside, with Brooke following right behind him and Gavin bringing up the rear. Asher stood in the foyer and guessed there were about twenty people in the house. He had no idea who was family and who wasn't, but most looked military. He let his gaze land on each person, looking for a familiar face, and finally found one in George Slocum. "Hey," he said to Brooke, "I'm going to talk to George for a few minutes. Why don't you see if you can find Monica or PJ?"

"Sure."

"But please, whatever you do, don't leave the house. In here, I feel like you're pretty safe, but the minute you step outside, anything could happen."

"I won't go outside."

"Good. I'll be right in this area if you need me."

"Asher?"

231

"Yeah?"

"Go. I'll be fine."

Asher nodded, then caught Gavin's eye, and they walked toward one of the men they'd served with under Captain Newell. "George, how are you?"

"Doing okay. Stunned that this happened."

"We all are. Is he here yet?"

"Yeah. Been here for about an hour. He's in the den with his kids. He'll be glad to see you. You always were his favorite."

Asher raised a brow. "That's the first I've heard of it."

Gavin snickered. "He's right."

"Shut up."

"Trust me," George said, "I know what I'm talking about. You could say things to him that none of the rest of us could get away with."

"Right." After giving the man a mock salute, he turned and made his way through the throng of people and into the den. He spotted the captain on the sofa with his seventeen-year-old son, PJ, sitting next to him. Phil Junior was a carbon copy of his father. Military haircut, razor-sharp blue eyes, and the physique of an athlete. His sister, Monica, was nowhere to be seen.

Newell's red-rimmed eyes met his and widened a fraction before he stood with an outstretched hand. "James? Black?"

"Sir," Asher said. "I can't tell you how sorry I am." He shook the man's hand and nodded to PJ. "Hello."

PJ bobbed his head in return, his lips tight, shoulders rigid.

"I got your text," Captain Newell said. "Meant a lot. Thanks." He cleared his throat. "Black, good to see you. Civilian life seems to agree with you."

"Most days."

Newell turned to his son. "Where'd your sister go, PJ?"

"To her room. Said she couldn't handle one more person giving her a hug."

232

The man sighed. "Yeah."

"Brooke Adams is with me," Asher said. "Thought it might be a good idea to bring her in case anyone wanted to talk with her."

"Who's Brooke Adams?" PJ asked.

"A shrink," Newell said. "I appreciate the gesture, but I think we're all right."

"Of course." He thought he'd seen a flash of interest in PJ's eyes that was quickly squashed at his father's instant dismissal.

"Anything you need?" Gavin asked.

"I need my wife's killer caught." Captain Newell closed his eyes. "Sorry."

"Don't apologize, sir," Asher said. "We just wanted to come by and offer our support in any way possible."

"And I thank you for that." The words were appropriate, but an odd look crossed his face.

One that Asher couldn't quite interpret. "Sir?"

"Nothing, nothing. It's just . . . you're a good man. I've always admired you."

"Even though I quit the unit?"

"Even though. Now, Black, on the other hand . . ."

"Aw, come on, Captain, you know I was your favorite." Gavin kept his tone light, but a slight frown creased his brow, and his eyes conveyed his sorrow for the situation.

Asher let the two of them continue the conversation while he let his gaze run the large open-concept living room. When he didn't see Brooke, his nerves started to itch.

TWENTY-FOUR

Brooke couldn't help feeling a bit out of place. She'd wanted to come with Asher, and yet, deep down, she'd known the captain wouldn't be willing to talk with her. His kids? Maybe. She found the room she'd been looking for. And the person she'd hoped was in it. She rapped on the open door. "Hi."

Monica Newell lay on her bed, staring up at the ceiling. At Brooke's greeting, she turned her head. Curiosity flickered. "Hi."

"I'm Brooke Adams. I was in Afghanistan with your dad for a while."

"Oh."

"I didn't know him very well and I'd never met your mom, but I'm so very sorry about what happened."

A tear slipped down the girl's cheek. "Yeah. I can't believe I slept through it," she whispered. "That's what I can't believe. How could I not hear that she was in trouble? How could I not wake up?"

"There's no reason you would have heard it," Brooke said. "It happened outside."

"I know, but . . ." She shook her head. "I should have heard something. How can someone kill your mom and you sleep through it?" The tears came faster.

"He used a suppressor," Brooke said. "I don't know if I'm supposed to tell you that, but yeah." No one had said not to say anything about it.

Monica froze, gave one last hiccuping sob, then sat up slowly to meet Brooke's gaze. "He used a suppressor?"

"Yes."

"Then I wouldn't have heard the gunshot."

"No." Brooke went to the bed and sat on the edge, feeling very awkward in her attempt to comfort the young teen she'd never met before.

More tears dripped down her cheeks. "I thought . . . I thought . . ."

"What?"

"I'd been drinking," she whispered. She must have seen Brooke's eyes widen. "I know, I know. I'm only fourteen. It was the first time I'd ever tried it. It was at Melissa's. We snuck some of her father's scotch." She grimaced. "It was horrid, but I drank it anyway. Just one glass. I wasn't drunk, but I thought . . ." She threw herself into Brooke's arms.

Surprise held her motionless for a split second before Brooke wrapped an arm around the child and reached up to stroke her hair. "You didn't hear it because there was nothing to hear, not because you'd had too much to drink."

"I was blaming myself," she said on a hiccuped sob. "I thought for sure if I'd just not been drinking, I would have heard something and could have helped her."

"No, honey, there was nothing you could have done even if you'd heard something." Nothing that wouldn't have earned her a bullet as well most likely.

"I'm never touching alcohol again."

"That might be wise, but again, it wasn't to blame for you not hearing anything."

Monica pulled back and swiped a hand across her cheeks. "My dad can't know this."

"I don't plan to tell him."

"Thank you," she whispered.

"Of course."

"I'm sorry for dumping that on you."

"You dump away. Anytime."

A beeping sound caught Brooke's attention and she noticed the slim watch on Monica's wrist. The girl shut the alarm off. "I have to take some medication. Excuse me."

"Sure. I probably should go back to the den and see if my friend is ready to go."

Monica slipped into the en suite bathroom. Brooke released a slow breath, saw a pad and pen on the girl's nightstand, and grabbed them. She wrote her name and number down, then hurried to the open bathroom door and knocked. Monica looked back over her shoulder. She held a medicine bottle in one hand and a bottle of water in the other.

"Okay, so maybe it's weird because you barely know me, but I just wanted to say that if you find you need to talk or anything, this is my number."

Monica took the paper with a slow nod. "Thank you."

"Monica?"

The girl jumped, her gaze swinging to the door. "Dad."

"What's going on?" The captain's gaze flicked between Brooke and his daughter.

"I was just getting ready to take my meds." She gave him a tight smile. "See? Being responsible and all that." She looked at Brooke. "He preaches a lot. Very big on responsibility."

Unsure how to respond to the obvious teen angst, Brooke simply smiled. "I'll be praying for you."

"Yeah, you do that." Monica's expression thawed. "Thanks again, Brooke."

"Sure thing."

Monica crossed her arms and stared at her father with a frown.

"What are you doing in here?" the man asked.

Brooke jumped at the snappy tone. "Oh, sorry. I came with Asher James and you were all talking, so I . . . wandered. I found Monica here and we chatted."

"She helped me figure something out, Dad. Chill."

"Figure what out?"

"Doesn't matter. Can I have some space now?"

His eyes glittered, then his expression softened a fraction. "No, you can't. Your cousins from Oregon are here and are asking about you. Come on."

Monica slipped out of the room and Brooke followed. Seeing no one around, she turned back to the captain. "Asher asked me to come and see if you or the kids wanted to talk. He figured it was a long shot but wanted me to come anyway. He said if you weren't interested, one—or both—of the kids might be. So that's why I was wandering. I was looking for Monica."

"I see."

"So, anyway, if you find you need to talk or bounce things off someone, I'm here." She held up a hand. "Just offering. I understand that you're a very private person, but . . . if you find you need to. It's my job. I'm trained in counseling and grief management, so before you write me off, just think about it."

He shot her a tight smile. "The guys you worked with back in Kabul had good things to say about you."

Brooke drew in a breath. "Thank you."

"I know they weren't easy to work with or be around, but they liked you."

"I liked them."

"Even though they made you pull out your hair?"

"Touché. But, yes, even though."

He nodded and made his way back into the den. Brooke followed and found Asher and Gavin next to the kitchen door.

Asher looked from her to the captain, then back to her. "Everything all right?"

"I think so," Brooke said, turning back to the captain. "Again, I'm so sorry for your loss. Please reach out if you need to. Monica has my number."

"Thank you," he said.

"Ready to head back to my parents' place?" Asher asked.

"I'm ready."

He took her hand and led the way out of the house and back to his truck.

"He's not going to call, is he?" she asked.

"No."

But maybe Monica would.

o o o

Caden's phone rang and he grabbed it as soon as he noted the international number. "Caden Denning."

"Caden, this is Felicia. We've got trouble and it's heading your way."

He tensed. "Tell me."

"Everything's blown up over here."

"Literally or . . . ?"

"I got a call from your sister. She's okay. But she and the assistant director, Kristin Welsh, were kidnapped and locked in a storage closet this afternoon. They got out and Sarah didn't sustain any injuries, but Kristin's been shot."

Caden closed his eyes. "Thank you for leading with 'Sarah's okay.' And?"

"Our team arrived and contained the scene. Kristin's headed to the hospital, but your sister says there are four orphans with fake papers on their way to the US to be used as organ donors. We've got Madad and the director in custody and receiving medical care, but—"

"Medical care?"

"Sarah and Kristin put up a good fight. Anyway, Madad is not expected to live and Yusufi claims he has no idea what's going on or why anyone would think they're involved in something other than legal adoptions. I've got to tell you, so far the paperwork all looks legit and it's a she says/he says kind of thing. Although the weapon that was used to shoot Kristin belonged to Madad. But that's understandable. Everyone in this place carries. Sarah said Kristin had a bullet in her and grabbed the gun while Madad had his hands around your sister's throat. She's giving Kristin credit for saving her life."

Caden blew out a long sigh to give himself time to get his thoughts together. *Sarah, Sarah.* "All right, I think you need to check out Madad's computer at the hospital."

"Already on it."

"Of course you are. Where's the plane?"

"In the air."

"I'll have agents meet it when it lands."

o o o

"James! Wait up."

Asher turned to see Captain Newell rushing down the porch steps. "Sir?" Brooke was already in the passenger seat, buckling her belt. "Be right back."

"Sure."

Asher loped back over to the man and met him in the middle of the yard. "What do you need, Captain?"

Newell pressed a thumb and forefinger to his eyes, then blinked at Asher. "Uh, look, I hate to ask, but . . ."

"Anything, Captain, name it."

"Right. Um . . . PJ asked me what you did, how we knew each other. I told him, and he wants to talk to you."

"About?"

239

"Being in the Army. He says he wants to be a Ranger or Special Forces."

"I'm happy to talk to him, but I'm not sure what I can tell him that you can't. I was never a Ranger. You were."

Newell shook his head. "It's not the information, it's the source."

Asher smiled. "Gotcha. And yeah, man, sure. I'm happy to talk to him, answer his questions. Anytime."

"Thanks. All right if I give him your number?"

"Of course."

"Appreciate you coming by."

"Sorry it had to be because of this."

"Yeah, me too." The captain retraced his steps back into the house, and Asher climbed into the truck.

His phone rang the same time Brooke's buzzed. "It's Caden," he said, swiping the screen and putting the phone to his ear. "Asher here."

"Calling to give you an update and ask you a quick question."

"Go ahead."

"Did you ever notice any of the guys in your unit working extra shifts or doing odd jobs for extra money?"

"Uh . . . no." He laughed. "Not supposed to do that."

"Okay, then what about doing favors for people and coming back with money?"

Asher frowned. "No. What's this about?"

"That's where the update comes in. Looks like the Morning Star Orphanage in Kabul was using US soldiers to transport kids to Tajikistan where they were met by supposedly adoptive parents and flown to the US. Once here, they were taken to a medical facility—still trying to figure out which one—where they were sold for their organs and then killed and buried."

"What? No way!"

Brooke looked up from her phone, her face ashen. How had

she heard what Caden said? But she looked back at her phone, then back at him, holding her phone out, clearly wanting him to see it. "Caden, hold on a second." The man went quiet. "What is it?" he asked Brooke.

"Sarah texted. She said there's a girl on the flight—a six-year-old named Paksima. She's not sure who the other children are but wants to be sure someone's there to talk to them—and she thinks I'm the one to do that."

"They'll be taken into custody by child protective services. They'll have a counselor there for them."

"But how long will that take? And how scared will they be? And will that person be able to speak their language?"

Asher blinked. "You speak Pashto?"

"Enough to make myself understood and understand them."

"Did you hear that, Caden?" Asher asked.

"I heard. Bring her to the airport. It can't hurt. Stay outside and wait for us to let you know when we've got this wrapped up and are ready for her. We don't know which flight they're on. There are three different choices. We're covering them all at the moment. Just know that it could be a long wait."

"Got it."

Asher hung up and drove toward the airport, his mind spinning.

"Do you have the information, that spreadsheet thing with all the data?" Brooke asked.

"Yeah, I've got a printout of it in my backpack. Why?"

"I want to look at it again."

"Well, you'll have time when we get to the airport. Not sure how long we'll be waiting."

She glanced in the side mirror. "Gavin's following us?"

"Yep. So are a couple of other cops. I don't want any more attempts on your life."

"And yours?"

"I'm okay with no more on mine too."

241

She shot him a tight smile.

At the arrivals area, Asher pulled behind one of the officers who'd been part of their escort to the airport. Another officer closed in behind them.

"And now we wait," Brooke murmured.

"I'll get that printout for you." Asher reached into the back seat and pulled his backpack into his lap. Within seconds, he found the paper and handed it over to her. "What are you thinking?"

"That we're not seeing something that should be obvious."

"Well, you're a genius if you can figure it out."

"Why? The people who made this weren't geniuses, were they?"

"Not that I know of."

She squinted at the paper. "I need a magnifying glass." She fell silent as she worked on the chart, and Asher scoured the area, watching, waiting. Finally, he texted Caden.

You figure out which one?

Should be the one that lands in an hour.

Good. Thanks.

He glanced at Brooke. "See anything?"

"I see a lot. Nothing that I understand."

"Talk it out if you want."

"Okay, we've already decided the first column of numbers represents a child, right?"

"In lieu of a name."

"Yes. And then blood type, tissue type results, and then a couple names and more letters and numbers. The names are fake since couples aren't really adopting, but," she said, her words measured, "what if the passports aren't fake?"

"What do you mean?"

"Madad and the director would have to have someone meet them in Tajikistan and escort the children, right?"

"Yes. Of course."

"Then it has to be an actual couple."

He gave a slow nod. "That makes sense."

"They're going through security multiple times a month. Seems like they would start to be recognized. If they were using fake passports there, it would eventually raise a red flag. Someone would recognize that they were using a different name."

"True."

"What if you have Felicia ask the airport workers in Tajikistan if they know of a couple who comes through with children and papers for adoption on a regular basis?"

He stared at her. "Are you sure you're not a cop?"

She gave a light snort. "Quite, but hanging around you military guys as long as I did might have rubbed off a bit. And besides, it's common sense."

"Then why the different names on the list?"

She poked her bottom lip out and sighed. "I don't know. My theory could be completely wrong."

Asher's phone rang. Caden. "Yeah?"

"Nothing. They're not on the plane."

"What do you mean they're not on the plane?"

"I'm not speaking Greek here."

"Great. Now what?"

"We step back and regroup. And hope Mr. Yusufi starts talking before too much longer."

TWENTY-FIVE

Brooke waited while Asher and Caden talked. She knew Caden didn't have to keep Asher in the loop, but he did so with the expectation that they would do the same. And besides, Caden had arranged for her "protection detail" while she was away from the security of Asher's parents' home.

But that detail was a limited thing, a favor from Caden's friend, the sheriff, Mickey Daniels.

She half listened to the men talk, her mind tumbling the information over and over. When Asher touched her arm, she looked up at him.

"I'm going to take you back to my parents' house," he said. "Caden is going to join us and we're going to go over—" He stopped when he realized she wasn't listening. Brooke's focus was on the electronic flight schedule posted on the marquee over the parking garage. "Brooke?"

"They're flights," she said.

"What?"

"The numbers and letters after the couples' names. They're flights. I think. Look. These here are the same for these three people. The next four are the same. Then the next two. And look up at the flights. TA. That could be Turkish Airlines, couldn't it?"

"Yeah," he said, looking over her shoulder. "It sure could."

"They're spreading everything out," she said, looking from her phone to the list. "They're rotating airports. Charlotte, Asheville, Greenville, Atlanta . . . I don't know what that one is."

He looked. "Charleston, South Carolina."

"There's a pattern. They leave from different airports in Tajikistan and land in different ones in the US. They're only in the same airport a couple of times a month. That's why they weren't there today. They're . . ." She jabbed the paper. "In Charlotte, North Carolina, today. And I bet they're using multiple passports. Probably for each airport they go through, they'd use a different name with a matching passport. They'd go through security and everything so rarely, no one would remember them."

He dialed Caden and filled him in while Brooke continued to think. When he hung up, he squeezed her fingers. "Good job."

"So?"

"So Caden's checking it out. In the meantime, we'll go back to my parents' house and get you settled."

"Then?"

"We'll figure out where we go from there."

"Like where they're taking the children once they land?"

"Yeah. Like that."

"It can't be to the same hospital, can it?"

Asher drove, heading for his parents' house. "I don't know. It would almost have to be."

"Then . . . a private facility? The doctor would need a team of people to help with the surgeries. I mean, it's not just some back-woods facility. If the doctor is involved and knows the organs are black market, then . . ."

"A private facility would make more sense."

"But there have to be a thousand of them."

"Maybe not a thousand, but definitely a lot."

His phone rang and this time he answered on the car's Bluetooth. "James here."

"This is Caden. Just catching you up. Agents on the ground at Charlotte said the plane landed two hours ago. Everyone is gone."

Brooke groaned and grief hit her for the children who would die unless someone found them. "Thanks, Caden."

"We're not giving up. I'll keep you in the loop, but for now, I recommend you guys get someplace safe and stay there. I'm not going to be able to keep a security detail on you for much longer."

"We're headed back to my parents' estate. At least for now."

"Good plan. Talk later."

Caden disconnected the call. "Unbelievable," Brooke muttered.

"Well, at least this will be the last group that manages to get through that airport. There won't be any more after this."

"It's not good enough. There are other airports. We have to stop them from killing anyone else."

"I know. I agree."

Brooke leaned her head against the window and prayed as she caught sight of Gavin behind them and a police car behind him. She closed her eyes. *Spare the kids, please, God. Don't let them die.*

When she opened her eyes, Asher was pulling through the gate of his parents' home with Gavin right behind him. Two of the cruisers left, but one stayed parked across the street. "How long will he stay there?" she asked.

"Not sure, but someone will give us a heads-up when it's time for him to leave."

Brooke looked at the looming house and gave an inward grimace. She hoped Nicholas wouldn't put in any more appearances for the duration of her stay. Then again, if she could help bridge the gap between the two brothers, she'd be okay with that.

This time when the door opened, a beautiful young woman stood there smiling. Dark waves of thick hair cascaded over her left shoulder, and her blue eyes glinted with good humor and life. "I've been waiting on you," she said.

Asher hugged the girl, then pulled Brooke into the marble foyer. "This is my sister, Lyric. Lyric, this is Brooke."

"So nice to meet you." Brooke held out a hand but found herself engulfed in a hug equal to the one Lyric had just given her brother.

"What are you doing here?" he asked when she released Brooke. "I thought you moved out."

"I did. I'm just here to help Mum plan that charity event—raising money for care packages to soldiers overseas. If I drop in frequently enough, it keeps the parents off my case. Now, come on in the den and say hi. Mum wants to meet your . . . friend."

Bemused, and loving the faint British accent in Lyric's voice, Brooke followed the siblings into the large living area. Three leather sofas had been strategically placed in front of the floor-to-ceiling rock fireplace. Flames danced from the gas logs.

"This is one of the coziest rooms I've ever seen," Brooke said, eyeing the flames. It truly was. She swallowed, gritted her teeth, and refused to allow the memories to overshadow the comfort of the room.

Asher looked around. "Huh. Yeah, I guess it's nice."

Lyric rolled her eyes and Brooke forced a smile.

"You want me to turn the flames off?" Asher's barely there whisper in her left ear sent shivers through her.

She cleared her throat. "No, it's okay." Maybe. Possibly. As long as she didn't get too close.

Here she was in the comfort of a multimillion-dollar home that made her want to gape, but no matter the beautiful surroundings, she wouldn't take her mind off the poor orphans being driven to their deaths. *Please let the police be on time.*

"Brooke?"

She blinked. "Oh, sorry. I was thinking about something."

"This is my mother, Patricia James."

Surprisingly, Asher's mother didn't look anything like Brooke had envisioned. But she could see where Lyric's blue eyes and dark hair had come from. Mrs. James was about five feet six inches tall and about twenty pounds heavier than she probably wanted to be. She smiled and held out an elegant hand to Brooke. "I wasn't home when you arrived yesterday, but I'm so very glad to meet you."

Her British accent was very pronounced, and Brooke was surprised Asher didn't really have one—unless he talked about his family. "Thank you. I can't tell you how much I appreciate you opening your home to me."

"Oh, luv, we're glad to do it. Now, don't let us keep you from whatever it is you need to be doing. You're welcome to join Lyric and me in filling these boxes or you can simply go to your room and rest. Please, make yourself comfortable."

"The boxes look amazing," Brooke said. "I'm sure the soldiers who receive them will appreciate them very much. I know I would have."

"What's all this about, Mum?" Asher asked. "Since when did you do . . . this?"

"Since I decided that it was time to support both of my sons. I may not *understand* you, my dear, but I do *love* you."

Asher's throat worked and Brooke thought he might turn and leave the room. Instead, he crossed it and wrapped his mother in a bear hug that lifted her off her feet. She laughed like a teenager and swatted Asher's solid shoulder. "Well, if I'd thought I'd get that kind of reaction, I would have done this ages ago."

Asher set his mother on her feet and kissed her cheek. "Thanks, Mum."

"Of course. Now, either sit down and help or scram. We've got work to do."

Asher's phone rang. "Saved by the bell," Lyric said in a sing-song voice.

"And I have a call I'd like to make too," Brooke said. "I think I'll go to my room and do that. Thank you again for your hospitality."

She turned and headed out of the den, hoping she could find her way.

Asher fell into step behind her, the phone pressed to his ear. "I see. Thanks. Yeah, I'll tell her. Bye."

He hung up only to have it ring once more. He ignored it for the moment, his jaw tight, eyes hard.

"What is it?" Brooke asked, forgetting she'd planned to tease him about calling his mother Mum.

"Mario Ricci died about an hour ago."

She gasped. "What? Killed?"

"No. Succumbed to his wounds."

"Oh. I'm sorry. I think. Mostly because I wanted to know what he knew." His phone buzzed the last time before it would go to voice mail. "You need to get that?"

"Yeah." He swiped the screen and Brooke found her way to the kitchen. The stairs were familiar and she headed toward them, pulling her phone from her pocket. She had text messages from Heather and Kat just checking on her and one from her sister, Ronie, saying she was in France and thinking she might make it a permanent thing.

Inside her room, Brooke answered them, then collapsed onto the bed, staring at the ceiling. She called Sarah Denning's number and grimaced when it went to voice mail. "Sarah, call me. I need to ask you something." She hung up, then closed her eyes to pray.

□ □ □

The next morning, there was still no word about the missing orphans or the people who'd flown with them from Tajikistan. Asher looked at the security footage from the airport Caden had shared with him. Footage that had been released to all major news networks with still shots of each of the six faces. A manhunt was in progress, and they needed the public's help to locate the couple and four children.

An 800 number flashed at the bottom of the screen. This was the hot topic in the news, and Asher was glad to see it there. He could only pray it worked.

He finished the last bite of eggs he'd found under a warming light in the kitchen. Lyric sat opposite him at the table.

"If you're going to keep coming home, what's the point in having your own place?" he asked her.

"I like having it. It's my escape pad. My happy place." She tossed him a smile. "But I also like to see you, so I thought I'd pop over and fix you breakfast. I know you never skip it."

"Nope. I don't know how you turned into such a fabulous cook when Mum can't even find the pot, much less boil water."

Lyric grinned. "I took lessons."

"From who?"

"A girl at school. Her dad was a professional chef, and she picked up a few things and passed them on to me."

"I'm just glad I get to benefit."

"What are your plans for the day?"

"Well," he said, "I think I'm taking a young man fishing." Captain Newell had texted and said PJ was acting out, throwing things and threatening to run away.

"Who?" Lyric asked.

"My former captain's wife was killed a couple of days ago. His son, PJ, needs a break." Asher could only hope he was doing the right thing in saying yes. Sounded like he needed to talk to someone like Brooke more than him.

"What about Brooke?"

"She's going to stay here until I get back."

"Very good. I'll entertain her with your baby pictures."

Asher narrowed his eyes. "You wouldn't dare."

"Wouldn't I?"

"You know I'll get even."

"Hmm. I'll think on it and decide if it's worth it."

"Lyric—"

"Good morning, you two," Brooke said from behind him.

He looked over his shoulder, and when his eyes landed on her, longing hit him, taking him by surprise. "Good morning." Yep, the more he looked at her, the more the feeling grew. He'd like to see her every morning. Have breakfast with her. Watch over her. Wake up next to her. Take care of her. Do life with her. If only—

"Ash?" Lyric prompted.

He cleared his throat. "Sit down and have a bite. Food's under the covers, thanks to Lyric."

Brooke grabbed her food and slid into the chair next to him. While she dug into the restaurant-worthy fare, he inhaled the scent of her freshly washed hair. Something vanilla with a hint of peaches. He jabbed his food with his fork. What was wrong with him? He needed to get it together or she was going to have him carrying on like a besotted fool. More so than he already was doing, if the look on Lyric's face was any indication. He crossed his eyes at her like he used to do when they were children.

She gaped, then giggled.

Brooke's head lifted and her brows rose as her gaze bounced between them. Lyric dropped a kiss on the top of his head and breezed past him and out of the kitchen.

"Your sister is a doll," Brooke said. "I really like her."

"She likes you too. But that's not hard."

The gentle smile she tossed his way wasn't helping him ignore the fact that he was losing his heart to her. "How'd you sleep?" he asked.

"I didn't much. You?"

251

"No, not much. I kept waiting for Caden or someone to call and say they'd found the children, but no one did."

"Same here." She stopped eating and pushed her plate away. After a sip of coffee, she dropped her head into her hands. "I want to do something to help."

"You have. You figured out the airports pattern."

"But sitting around here is driving me nuts. I want to do more."

"You're a fixer, aren't you?"

She looked up at him through her fingers. "How'd you guess?"

"Your choice of profession might have something to do with it."

"I called Sarah last night."

"And?"

"She didn't answer and hasn't called me back yet. I'm worried."

He slid an arm around her shoulders and pulled her against him. "Caden is keeping close tabs on her. As for the orphans, they'll find them. Are you going to finish your breakfast?"

"I heard there was food in here," Nicholas said from the doorway.

Asher shut his eyes for a brief moment at his brother's voice but didn't release Brooke from his embrace. "Good morning, Nicholas." He couldn't think why Nicholas would be at the house so early but wasn't about to ask. He stood and carried his and Brooke's plates to the sink.

Nicholas fixed his plate and sat at the table. "Dad asked me to stop by. Said he had some client he wanted me to meet. Is he here yet?"

"I don't think so."

Nicholas turned his attention to Brooke. "Dad's hired extra security and had a metal detector installed at the back entrance to his office."

"Oh my," Brooke said with a sigh.

"You're really worth all of this trouble?"

She coughed to cover a small laugh—and maybe a wince. "Apparently, but I was hoping it wasn't going to be a lot of trouble."

"You're no trouble, Brooke," Asher said with a glare at his brother. "How about we head into the library?" She stood and Asher took her arm.

"And leave me to eat alone?" his brother asked. "Thanks so much."

Brooke hesitated.

"I think you'll be all right," Asher said. "Better chow down, you don't want to miss Dad's client."

He led her out of the kitchen, down the hall, and into a small room lined with bookshelves. Brooke gaped. "Good grief, how many books are in here?"

"At least a couple thousand. They're mostly Lyric's."

"What an amazing room. I could stay in here forever and never be bored."

"So, listen," Asher said. "I'm going to take PJ fishing. The captain said he's been having a hard time and thought I could help. Here's the text he sent me." He held out his phone so she could read it.

He's angry at me for not being here when his mother was killed. He's blaming me, said if I'd been here, it wouldn't have happened. I'm at my wits' end and can't get through to him. I know it's a lot to ask but was wondering if you would try while I go pick out a coffin.

"Oh, that's sad. I'm glad you're taking the time to be with him."

"Are you going to be all right staying in this house with my kinda crazy family?"

"I'll be fine. I'm going to focus on trying to get Sarah on the phone again. I really want to talk to her."

"Of course. And I'll text and check in with you while I'm gone—which will be early afternoon."

She studied him. "The waiting and helpless feeling are driving you as crazy as they are me, huh?"

He swiped a hand down his chin. "Beyond. I feel like I need to be out there with Caden or . . . something."

"You're doing what you need to do. Go make a young man feel important and distract him so he's not missing his mother so much."

"You're sure? I feel like you'll be perfectly safe here, but I don't want to leave you if you're at all uncomfortable with the idea."

"I'm a big girl, Asher. I can handle it."

He nodded. "Okay. But you'll stay here, right?"

"Of course."

"Call me if you need anything."

"Asher . . . go."

"Right."

He kissed her forehead and went to his room to gather his things. When he returned, he found her in the library, sitting in the corner, book in her lap, phone in her hand.

"What is it?"

"I think Sarah tried to call me. It went through, but then dropped. I'm just waiting on her to try again."

"Okay, I'll be back soon. I've got my phone on and the house is secured."

"I know. Bye." She set down the phone, then looked up at him again. "Hey, if you see Monica, tell her to give me a call if she wants to talk more. She seemed interested yesterday, but I think her father spooked her from saying anything."

"I will."

Asher left. In the car, he texted Caden.

Anything?

Caden's quick reply dinged.

No, we're still looking for them. No luck on
finding the person who might have recognized
Brooke from the pictures in the paper, but
we're still hoping the director will start talking.

Asher started his truck and put it in Drive. One last look at his
parents' home convinced him he was doing the right thing, that
Brooke was safe behind the walls and gates. He pressed the gas
and headed to Greenville.

TWENTY-SIX

Brooke's phone rang, and she'd been so engrossed, she nearly fell off the chair. The book she'd been reading hit the floor with a thud. She ignored it and grabbed her phone. "Sarah!"

"Brooke? Are you okay?"

"Yes, yes, but how are you?"

"Okay. It's a bit crazy around here. I know they haven't found the orphans yet and I'm scared to death they won't in time. I found out who the other three are and sent Caden their names."

"So you haven't learned any more on your end?"

"No, but Kristin is beside herself. She loves all the children, of course, but Paksima is special to her. She was trying so hard to figure out a way to adopt her."

Brooke closed her eyes and fought the despair that wanted to overtake her. Reading had distracted her for a few moments, but until she heard the kids were safe, she wouldn't be able to fully relax. "Sarah, these children are being transported to some kind of medical facility. Can you think of anything you might have heard about which one or where?"

"No, nothing. And believe me, I've been looking. They've assigned a new director to the orphanage who seems to be on the up-and-up. The FBI, Caden's friend Felicia, has searched the office and everywhere else we could think of, and so far there's nothing."

"What about his home, his computer, his phone?"

"Yes, of course. They've got all that. One thing Felicia said was interesting about his phone is that he was making calls to someone in South Carolina over the past few days."

"Who?"

"They can't figure that part out. It's one of those prepaid phones."

Brooke sighed. "Of course it is."

"They've recently discovered that the recipients were using a dark web site. They did get that out of the director."

"Great. That's completely untraceable, isn't it?"

"So everyone thinks, but Caden said they've got their professionals working on it. That's all I know. I'm sorry, Brooke. I'm not much help."

"I guess you've already done your part. It's up to the authorities at this point."

"I guess. I've got to go."

"When are you coming home?"

"I'm not sure, but Kristin is being transported back to the US to heal. Her parents will meet her at Eglin Air Force Base in Florida and take her home. She's from Orlando."

"Okay. Stay safe."

"Always. You too."

"Always."

She hung up and stood to pace, her shoes silent on the wood floor. How could she figure out where the children were being taken? She scoffed. If the FBI and everyone else working this couldn't figure it out, why should she be able to?

But there must be something—

Her phone buzzed and she didn't recognize the number. She stared at the screen, then decided to answer. "Hello?"

"Is this Brooke?" a soft voice asked.

"Yes."

"This is Monica."

"Oh, hi, Monica, I'm very glad to hear from you." Silence. Then a rustling sound came over the line. "Are you there?"

"Yes. Sorry, I had to move into another room. My dad and one of his weirdo friends are here."

"Weirdo friend?"

"Some guy he used to work with. I can't stand him, so I just disappear when he comes over."

Well, that didn't sound good. "Does he ever . . . hurt you?"

"No, no. I just think he's creepy. He probably doesn't even know I exist."

That was a relief. "So, what can I do for you?"

"Can you meet me?"

"Um . . ."

"I . . . I mean, if you're busy, it's okay. Never mind. I'm just—"

"No, I wasn't hesitating because I don't want to or I'm too busy, I just don't have a car here and I'm about an hour and a half from you."

"Oh." She sniffed. "It's okay. I don't want to put you to any trouble. I . . . I've been thinking and I'm trying to figure out why I'm even alive . . ." Her voice caught on the word and Brooke's heart thudded.

"Oh, Monica, I can assure you, there are so many reasons why you're alive."

"Name one."

"You're alive because God decided you would be an amazing addition to the world."

The teen huffed a watery laugh. "God, huh? Can we do this without bringing God into it?"

"Well, I suppose we can try." But Brooke knew the conversation would circle back to him. Assuming she could figure out a way to get to Monica. "What about your dad? I got the feeling he didn't want you talking to me."

"He thinks everyone can deal with stuff without talking about it. Like he does. But I'm not like him. And by the time you get here, he'll be gone. I overheard him talking to what's-his-face about needing to go meet someone in about thirty minutes. I just thought it would be nice to talk to you again since you . . . um . . . helped last time, but forget it. I'll just—"

"What about FaceTiming?"

"No. Never mind. I'm bothering you. I didn't mean to. I seem to bother everyone these days. I think it might be better if I wasn't here."

"Monica, I gave you my number. If I thought you were a bother, I wouldn't have done that. I meant it when I said you could call me." Brooke paused. "What do you mean if you weren't here? Do you mean at home?" Or something else?

"I mean on the planet!"

Suicide. "Okay, you're hurting, I get that. I've been there, and it *will* get better. So let's talk about some things you can do in the meantime."

"I just . . . never mind." Voices in the background reached her. "Hold on a minute . . ." The voices faded. "They're gone. I'm all alone now. Dad said he'd be gone for several hours."

Brooke closed her eyes. *Don't say it, don't say it, don't say it.* "I'll be there in two hours, okay? Give me a bit of time to sort out transportation and I'll be there."

A pause.

"Monica? Promise me, if I come all the way to Greenville, you'll be there."

"Okay," she whispered. "I'll be here. Just . . . can you hurry?"

She hung up, her mind in a whirl. No, she shouldn't do this. She needed to stay put.

But . . . no buts.

She pulled up Monica's number from the list of recent calls and let her thumb hover over it. *Just tell her you can't come, that it's too dangerous and you're staying put.*

But . . . what if the teen was suicidal? That was the impression she'd given her.

Brooke closed her eyes. *Please, God, I don't want to do anything stupid.*

What if she didn't go and Monica did something? Like try to kill herself? Could she live with that, knowing the girl had reached out for help and Brooke had refused? Or put it off?

"Ugh . . ." She had to. Of course she did. She couldn't help the poor missing orphans, but she could help Monica. Or at least attempt to.

She went looking for Lyric and found Nicholas in the kitchen, grabbing a fruit drink from the refrigerator. "Oh, sorry," she said. "I was looking for Lyric."

"She left to run some errand for Mum. Anything I can do for you?"

Brooke frowned and narrowed her eyes.

He laughed. "Oh, come on, I can be nice. I only say the things I say to get a rise out of Asher." He bowed. "I'm at your service."

"Hmm." Brooke had to admit she had no idea what to think of the man, but . . . "Could I borrow a car?"

He blinked. "What? That's a bit cheeky, isn't it?"

"I know I'm asking a lot, but I need to get to Greenville and Asher isn't here to take me."

"I don't think you're supposed to be going anywhere. Isn't that the whole reason you're here?"

"Yes, yes it is, but . . ." She sighed. "Look, this is important. I need to go. I made a promise to a young girl that I would help her. I plan to ask the police officer outside to follow me."

"You can't do this over the phone?"

"Apparently not." She really wanted to see the girl face-to-face. If she was truly suicidal . . .

"What do you think Asher would say about this?"

"He'd probably tell me to stay put. And he'd be right, I probably should, but—"

"But you're going anyway."

"Yes, because I have a feeling this girl doesn't have many people she can reach out to—if any, now that her mother's been murdered. So, do you have a car I can borrow or do I need to pay for an Uber?"

"Ouch. That would be a tidy sum, wouldn't it?" He capped his bottle and pulled keys from the front pocket of his khakis. "Well, come on. I'll take you."

"What?"

"Get your purse and coat. I'll take you."

"What about your client?"

"My father's client. They'll never miss me." A muscle jumped in his jaw until he forced a smile.

"But I really shouldn't leave the security. No. This is a bad idea." She raked a hand through her hair. "I'll stay here and figure something out. Never mind."

"What if we have security with us? Would that help?"

"Tremendously."

He headed for the garage. "I'll let them know. I'll be in the red Beemer when you're ready."

Three minutes later, Brooke climbed in beside him. "I'm not sure I should let you do this, but I'm desperate."

"You really know how to stroke a guy's self-esteem, don't you?"

She grimaced. "Sorry."

He backed out of the garage, and Brooke soon found herself on the interstate heading toward Greenville.

Nicholas fell silent and Brooke wondered if she was supposed to talk. "Why are you helping me?" she asked.

"Because it will stick in Asher's craw that you left the house."

"You do understand that I've had people trying to kill me."

He flicked her a glance. "Are you sure about that? Sounds like it's just Asher's overactive imagination."

Brooke frowned. "I'm pretty sure the bullets flying in my direction were real."

"Bullets? Seriously?"

"Seriously."

"But no one knows where you're staying, right?"

She shook her head. "As far as I know. We were really careful when we drove here. Took a very long and circuitous route."

"I don't know. Asher always liked to exaggerate things—even as a kid. It's his way of getting the attention he craves. Like joining the Army. So common."

"Is that still a thing?" she asked.

"What do you mean?"

"The whole snobby thing. Commoners versus the upper class."

"Well, it is in my family."

"So you're an aristocrat? You hold a title?"

He laughed. "Not really, but Mum is descended from the royal family. It's a very far descent, but . . ." He shrugged.

And he milked that for all it was worth. "Asher doesn't care about that sort of thing. Why does that bother you so much?"

"Because it's a reflection on the family," he snapped. "He's always doing things to drag our name through the muck."

"Hmm. So you're only doing this to make him mad?"

"Well, I could tell you really thought you needed to come, so . . ."

She glanced at him. "You're not such a bad guy, are you, Nicholas?"

He tsked. "Now, don't go ruining my reputation. That's Asher's job," he added with a sniff.

"You really should sit down with him and talk. He just wants to get along."

"I'll think about it. Are you going to call Asher and tell him where you're going?"

"I probably should, but I don't want to ruin his time with PJ. That's not fair to either of them. And if we have security around us, then I think I'll wait a little while before I call him."

"Right. Security." He studied her for a brief moment before turning his gaze back to the road. "So tell me about this whole thing with the orphans and the people who are trafficking them?"

Brooke talked until they pulled to a stop in front of Captain Newell's home. Monica stood on the front porch wrapped in a blanket.

She turned to Nicholas. "You don't have to wait. I'll let Asher know where I am and he can give me a ride back to your parents' house." She glanced around. "I don't see your security people, Nicholas."

"They wouldn't be very good at their job if you could see them, would they?"

She didn't like the uneasy tone in his voice but let herself be distracted by Monica, who was waiting on her.

He stopped her with a hand on her forearm. "Brooke—?"

"Yes?"

"Um . . . nothing. Just . . . uh . . . nothing."

She frowned. "What?"

"Be careful."

"Of course."

She slipped out of the vehicle and shut the door, then hurried up the front porch steps.

o o o

Asher packed the gear and fishing rods into the cargo box in the back of his truck, then climbed behind the wheel.

"So, I have a question that I've been wanting to ask," PJ said.

"Go for it."

"What happened to your truck?"

Asher glanced at the teen and twisted the key. "Someone ran me off the road."

"Dang, that stinks."

"Yep." Asher pulled away from the parking area and got on the road that would lead them back to the Newell home. They'd fished for a while in silence, then Asher had asked a few general questions to get the kid talking. He figured he could cover anything else on the ride home. "Now, my question for you. Why'd your dad think this would be a good idea? You and me getting together?"

PJ laughed, a rusty unused sound, but a laugh nevertheless. "Who knows, man? He's had something eating at him even before Mom was killed."

"Like what?"

PJ lifted a shoulder a fraction, then dropped it. "I don't know. Stuff like keeping things short on phone calls when they managed to connect, and about a week ago I heard him yelling at her about something and she started crying."

"Is that why you're so angry with him?"

Another shrug and silence.

"He said you wanted to join the Army, be a Ranger," Asher said.

"Thinking about it, but he won't even discuss it with me. Every time I bring it up, he says, 'I'm not a Ranger anymore.' Either that or he's got somewhere to be or someone to see."

Asher frowned. "It's a tough career. Maybe he wants you to really think hard."

"Might have more to think about if he'd discuss it with me. The more information I have, the better decision I can make, don't you think?"

"I can't disagree with that." It was actually a very mature observation.

"Look, Asher, I've got a good head on my shoulders, thanks to my mom. I know what I want, and in six months I'll be eighteen and he doesn't get to have a say in it." PJ paused. "Doesn't mean I don't want his blessing, though."

"Yeah, I know what you mean."

"So why does he dodge the topic every time I bring it up? Do you know?"

Asher considered the heartfelt question. "I have an idea why."

"I'm listening."

"He's already lost your mom. And he had a bad scare with Monica's illness. Being a Ranger's tough. Dangerous a lot of the time. Could be, deep down, he's afraid if you go after that particular career path, he'll lose you too."

PJ fell silent. "Maybe, but I get the feeling it's more than that. Like he doesn't want me to go into the Army. Period." He sighed. "Which I don't get because most career Army are more than happy when their offspring follow in their footsteps."

"Most. I can think of a few exceptions. Look, you've just lost your mother. Give him some time to get things arranged for you and your sister. It could be that he's just really stressed right now."

"Sure."

"I'm not making excuses for him, PJ. He can be a hard man to know and talk to. I figured that out about ten minutes after meeting him. I'm just saying give him some grace right now and let him deal with everything related to your mom before you try to talk to him about this again."

PJ fell silent. "Yeah, you're probably right," he finally said. "Thanks."

"Sure. So what do you think about doing this again? I mean, if you can stand to hang around an old guy like me."

PJ shot him a half smile. "I think I'd like to give it a try."

o o o

Dr. Geraldine Frasier washed her hands, dried them, then walked into her connecting office. "Are they here?"

"En route," he said. "They've had to be extra careful because of all the media coverage." He stared at his reflection in the window. Six feet tall, broad shoulders, and a military haircut. He was amazed his criminal activities weren't noticeable just by looking at him.

"I'm surprised to see you here. Where's your errand boy?"

"Running another errand. He'll be here soon."

"What about Brooke Adams?"

He turned. "She's the errand. Asher left the house a while ago headed toward Greenville. Buzz is on his way. He's working on taking care of her while her watchdog is gone—although he did say the security around the home was practically impenetrable."

"That's not good."

"Doesn't matter. I'm here now. I'll take care of her if it comes down to it—just like I'm going to have to take care of everything else related to this." He rubbed a hand over his jaw. "This is the last group. At least for a while. Things need to calm down before we can continue the work. *If* we even can. Dr. Madad is dead. Yusufi's been arrested. We don't have anyone in the orphanage anymore. The soldiers are still available for transporting the kids simply because they believe they're doing a good thing smuggling the orphans out of the country and into the loving homes awaiting them in the US—like Garcia thought he was doing." He couldn't help the smirk that lifted the right corner of his lip. "Of course, once the media publicizes the arrests and the fake adoptions— and what the children were being used for—those soldiers will disappear. But the ones who like the money will still be there." He raked a hand over his mouth. "For now, though, we're on hold."

The doctor's eyes bored into him. "Do you know how much money you're talking about walking away from?"

"Of course I know," he snapped. "But the fact remains, there are eyes all over the place looking for the two who escorted the kids here. And the kids. The news is running the footage relentlessly. We'll have to go through the whole process of setting everything back up. Finding people we can trust again."

"It can't be that hard, can it? Everyone in that godforsaken country will do just about anything for money. They'd sell their own mother. What's a couple of worthless orphans to them?"

She was a cold one. Colder than he was.

"Well, let's get this group taken care of and we can figure out the rest in the next few days. Are the recipients here?"

"Two. We'll be doing three today and two tomorrow. One heart transplant and two kidneys today. Two hearts tomorrow."

He shoved his hands into his pockets. "Right."

She sighed. "Look, we've been friends since childhood and I can read you like a book. Are you having second thoughts?"

"No, I bypassed those a long time ago." He waved his phone. "I'll text when they're here."

"And I'll get my team busy prepping the recipients."

As he walked out of the door, he could feel her eyes following him.

"Oh, I almost forgot."

He stopped and looked back over his shoulder.

"Condolences on the loss of your wife, Phillip. It's a great tragedy."

"Yes," he said. "Yes, it is. Unfortunately, it was the only way that I could get home quickly to patch up this mess of a mission. But sometimes it's necessary to sacrifice the one for the good of the many."

TWENTY-SEVEN

With the comfort of knowing Nicholas's security people were outside watching for anything out of the ordinary—like men with guns—Brooke sat on the sofa across from Monica and tried to see past the girl's defenses.

Even though she'd been the one to call Brooke, Monica was still wound as tight as a drum and having a hard time telling Brooke exactly what was going on with her. A deep sadness lay in her eyes, which was understandable. But it was more than that.

"Are you still blaming yourself for what happened to your mom?" Brooke asked.

"No. Not really. Not now that I know all the facts, but I just . . . ever since my surgery, I've really been questioning a lot of things. Dad said you were a shrink."

"Well, I prefer the term *psychiatrist*, but yes."

"So you help people work out their feelings and problems, right?"

"For the most part."

Monica bit her lip. "How much do you charge? I mean, I have a little bit of money, but . . ." She shrugged.

"Monica, I have no intention of charging you. I'm here to help if you want to talk to me."

"I do want to. I think."

"Excellent."

"I want to know—why me?" she asked, her voice low.

"Why you what, honey?"

Monica lifted her gaze and connected with Brooke's. "Why did I get sick? Why did I need a heart transplant? Why do I have to take anti-rejection medications for the rest of my life? Why was my mom killed? Why did my dad take a job that requires him to be gone all the time and the only way he gets to come home is if there's some family crisis? Just . . . why?"

Her voice cracked on the last word, tears cascaded down her cheeks, and all Brooke could do was stare. Heart transplant? *Heart transplant?*

Don't react. Deal with the issue first.

With effort, she found her voice. "That's a lot of whys," she said. "I'm sorry you're struggling so much." She drew in a breath and prayed for the right words. "When one goes through such a major ordeal, it causes you to reevaluate. Think things through a little deeper. Ask why." She smoothed the crease in her jeans while she considered what to say. "I can only share my experience with you and let you come to your own conclusions."

"Okay."

"I was burned in an explosion in Kabul. For a long time, I asked why. Why me? Sometimes I thought—and can still think on my low days—that it's punishment of some kind. Like I did something wrong and God's 'getting' me for doing whatever it was I did wrong."

Monica's eyes met hers. "I've thought that," she whispered. "That God was mad at me and punishing me."

"Is that why you didn't want to bring him into this conversation? Because you're kind of mad at him for letting this happen and you're thinking he's punishing you for something?"

The girl gave a slow nod. "That, and my mom's death and . . . just all of it."

"Well, the truth is, God doesn't work that way. Do you know anything about the Bible?"

"Sure. I go to church and I'm in the youth group."

"Okay, then do you believe the Bible and what it says about sin and corruption entering the world?"

"I guess."

"Well, that wasn't God's original plan when he created mankind. Once man sinned, things all of a sudden were out of sync with a perfect God. As a result, things started going very wrong."

"Like death and stuff?"

"Yeah. Unfortunately. Like death and stuff. And heart transplants and people who put bombs in restaurants that cause permanent scars, PTSD, nightmares, and all that. And sadly, things will continue to go wrong until Jesus returns to make things right again."

"No one has it easy, do they?"

"Not many people, no." Brooke spoke slowly, two words still weighing heavy on her mind ever since Monica had uttered them. "So you had a heart transplant?"

Monica nodded and sobs erupted from her. Brooke pulled the distraught girl into her arms, finally able to let her brain go to those two words. *Heart transplant.* Could it—no, it was a coincidence. Wasn't it? But maybe not? "Monica, where did you have your surgery? What facility?"

Monica sniffled, then sat back and wiped her eyes. "Um, at a private facility about an hour from here called the Frasier Center. It's near Lake Lure." She smiled. "It's not like a regular doctor's office, it looks like a fancy hotel. I think the only surgeries they do there are organ transplants. At least that's what I think I heard someone say."

"I've heard of it." Her blood pounded through her veins. No. She was crazy. It was just a coincidence. But still, crazy or not, she had to call Asher. Or Caden. Or someone.

"You know, Monica, there are a lot of people on the transplant list. The fact that you actually got one so quickly is amazing."

"Yes, I've thought about that."

"Do you know who your donor was?"

"No. My mom said it was someone my age and her parents wanted her to live on in me." She swallowed. "But the whole thing made them fight a lot."

"That's not your fault."

"Of course it is." She huffed and crossed her arms. "They were fighting about me. If I wasn't here, if I didn't exist, they wouldn't have been fighting." Before Brooke could protest, Monica twisted a strand of hair around her finger and said, "Before I got to the point that I couldn't walk, there was one night I couldn't sleep and I went downstairs to get some water and maybe watch TV. My mom and dad were in the kitchen arguing. I turned around to go back upstairs and she whisper-yelled, 'If you don't, she'll die!' I realized then how serious my heart issue was and that I could really die." She swallowed. "And I thought it might just be better for everyone if I did."

"I see." Brooke stilled to gather her thoughts. "You know why parents argue about their kids?"

"Why?"

"Well, there are a lot of reasons obviously, but in that situation, it's probably because they were both terribly afraid they were going to lose you. That kind of fear makes parents crazy—and they can resort to fighting to deal with the stress. But it's never the child's fault, and you can't take that responsibility on your shoulders." A pause. "I worded that wrong. You *can* take it on your shoulders, but you really shouldn't." She gave the girl a moment to answer, but she seemed to be thinking.

Finally, Monica sighed. "Maybe."

"What did your mom want your dad to do?" Brooke asked.

"I don't know."

A horrible thought popped into her head, but she had to ask. "How long after that argument did you get your heart?"

"A couple of months. I'd gotten a lot worse by then. Why?"

Two months? "That's pretty quick to get an organ," Brooke said. "You were very fortunate." She pulled out her phone and stood. "Will you excuse me just a minute? I hate to do this, and normally, I'd wait, but I need to make a quick call, okay?"

Monica frowned, but nodded. "Sure. Of course."

Brooke slipped into the half bath off the kitchen and dialed Asher's number.

He picked up on the first ring. "Brooke? Everything all right?"

"For now. But I've just discovered something interesting about Captain Newell's daughter."

"What?"

"Her illness that he was so private about? She had a heart transplant."

"What?"

"Yes, at—"

The door opened and she found herself staring at the weapon Captain Newell now held aimed at her head.

○ ○ ○

Asher frowned at the sudden disconnect and tried to call her back. It went straight to voice mail. He hung up and glanced at PJ. "Hey, I need to make a quick phone call. You mind if we pull over a minute?"

"Not if you pull into that McDonald's and let me grab a burger and some fries."

"Ouch. I didn't mean to starve you."

PJ shot him a grin. "You didn't."

Asher swung into the parking lot and handed PJ a twenty-dollar bill. "Get me some too. It's on me."

"Thanks, man. Be right back."

While PJ loped to the door, Asher dialed Brooke's number. Straight to voice mail. His gut started yelling at him that something was wrong. He tried again with the same result. Again, he hung up and stared out the window at the restaurant. A heart transplant? Monica? Newell had been so private about everything—he hadn't known. He forced his brain to think back. The captain didn't let himself joke around much with his unit. No one had really liked him all that much, but everyone respected him—and trusted him with their lives. And he came through every time he was needed. Eventually, they just chalked his personality up to the fact that he was who he was. And they accepted it.

Monica's illness came on suddenly. He remembered the captain mentioning a bad virus. Had that triggered the heart issue? Probably, because not long after that, he flew home without a word. He'd returned a few weeks later, tight-lipped and hard-eyed. More so than usual.

Asher's phone rang. He didn't recognize the number but answered anyway. "Hello?"

"Hello, little brother."

"Nicholas?" He made a mental note to put the number in his contacts so he could ignore it in the future. Then felt guilty for the thought. "What's going on?"

"I . . . uh . . . might have done something I shouldn't have."

It was so out of character for his brother to say something like that, that for a moment Asher was at a loss for words. He cleared his throat. "What do you mean?"

"Um . . . well, your lady friend, Brooke, asked me to drive her to Greenville. So I did."

"You what!"

"Well, she asked me to."

Asher slapped the steering wheel. "Do you not realize that her life is in danger? I can't believe she would go off like that after all the precautions we set up to keep her safe!"

"She . . . uh . . . well, you see, I discovered on the ride there that I rather like Brooke. I don't know what she sees in you, but I like her, and on the drive back to Charlotte, I started thinking about it and realized I might have well and truly put her in danger and that's why I'm calling you. Because while I might like to push your buttons, I wouldn't want to see her hurt."

"Where'd you take her?"

"To someone's house. I think she said it was your captain's house. The daughter called and insisted that she needed to talk to Brooke right away."

"What!" He pressed his fingers against his eyes. "I don't believe this. I can't believe she'd be so careless."

Nicholas cleared his throat. "Well, I might have let her believe that we had security around us—and . . . um . . . we didn't. So, technically, *she* wasn't careless. I was."

Asher had no words. He couldn't even make sounds.

"Asher?" The seriousness in Nicholas's voice caught his attention and slowed his racing pulse. Slightly.

"What!"

"Is she really in danger?"

"Yes, Nicholas, she's really in danger."

"Then how fast can you get to that house?"

o o o

Hands held out to her sides, Brooke stepped past the sofa where Monica had been only moments before. "Where is she? Did you hurt her?"

"Of course not. I sent her upstairs," Newell said. "Told her not to come back down until I asked her to."

"Can't have her see the gun, I guess?" Brooke was proud she was able to keep most of her terror from reflecting in her voice.

"Shut up."

"Is she the reason you got started in trafficking orphans for their organs?"

He scowled. "Yes. Now out the back door."

"You used the soldiers to transport them, didn't you?" It was starting to click now. "Isaiah kept saying he didn't know," she said. "But that's what he found out. He found out he wasn't transporting kids to great homes in America, he was sending them to their deaths."

"And he was going to blow the whole thing apart."

"So you set him up, framed him to be labeled a traitor."

"There was no evidence that he was a traitor, but he was supposed to be dead before that even became an issue. It was just something I had to use to get everyone in a hurry and to the café."

She swallowed. "You were hoping the bomb would take them out?"

"After the plan we originally put into place went south."

"Which was?"

"Michaels was supposed to be with his unit."

"The explosion that killed those soldiers and nearly killed Asher and the others?"

"Yes, only when Michaels didn't report with the others, we had to improvise."

"By sending them to the café to find him."

"Yeah. There was no way to call off the original attack once we learned Michaels wasn't with the unit, so we had to come up with a different plan, which was to bomb the café. And you better believe that took some finagling. But even that failed." He huffed a humorless laugh. "Seems like you and Asher have nine lives or something. You both should be dead several times over." He waved the gun at her and motioned her to the kitchen door. "Into the garage and then you're going to drive us."

"Drive where?"

"Where I say. Now, you might want to get a move on. If Monica comes back down, as much as I love my daughter, I won't let her live if she sees anything that she could pass on to the cops. Understand?"

Oh, she understood, all right. And she believed him. "At least tell me where you're taking me."

"To see if Dr. Frasier can use you."

"Excuse me?"

"Go!" His shout echoed and he sent a quick glance at the stairs.

Terror quivering through her, she stepped into the garage, worried Monica would come down to see what the shouting was about.

"There are people who know I'm here," she said as he shut the door behind him. "And there are cops watching the house."

"Really? I didn't see any. They must have left."

Brooke frowned, confused. "The man who brought me said there was a security detail with us."

"Beats me. They're not here now." He jabbed her lower back with the weapon. "Get in the passenger side and climb over to the driver's seat."

Brooke did as instructed, her mind racing. Okay, she'd thrown a monkey wrench into things by being at his home. She wasn't supposed to be there. He was improvising, trying to figure out what to do with her. Where to kill her? Most likely.

"Who's Dr. Frasier?" she asked.

"A friend."

Brooke clutched the steering wheel. He jammed the keys into the ignition and twisted. The engine purred to life.

"You're going to leave Monica here alone?" she asked.

"Her aunt's on the way. She'll be here in about ten minutes. Long enough for us to get out of here."

"Where am I going? 'To see Dr. Frasier' doesn't help much." Brooke bit down on the inside of her lip to keep from giving in to the panic crushing down on her.

"I'll give you directions." He pressed the button for the garage door. It rose and he pointed. "Go."

Brooke whispered a prayer, put the SUV in gear, and stepped

on the gas. With a sick feeling, she realized no one knew where she was except for Asher's brother. And even if he told Asher, all the captain had to say was that he wasn't there and didn't know where she'd gone. Of course, Monica could tell a different story, but Brooke doubted the captain would give the girl the opportunity. "How did you get involved in this?" she asked. "Monica?"

"Yeah. Give me your phone."

She didn't bother to argue, just pulled the device out of her pocket and handed it to him. He powered the phone down and tossed it out the window. "Michaels messed everything up," he muttered.

"How did he find out you were involved?"

"He didn't know I was, I don't think. All I knew was that he got stuff off Madad's computer."

"And you panicked."

"Something like that."

"Why set him up to be a traitor if you were just going to kill him—and all of the innocent people in there?"

"Wasn't going to kill him. Not at first. But then I couldn't take a chance someone would believe anything he said."

"Ruining his name would taint anything he said against anyone else. It would look like he was simply trying to get even with those who discovered he was a 'traitor.'"

"Turn here."

She did and continued to drive slightly under the speed limit, trying to figure out how she could alert someone while keeping her panic under control. Unfortunately, nothing came to mind. "What are you going to do with me?"

He shot her a sideways glance. "I'm still figuring that out."

"Right."

He was going to kill her. He had nothing to lose by killing her and everything to lose by letting her live. It was just a matter of when at this point—which was probably why he was so willing to answer her questions. "How did you convince Hamilton and Ricci to be your hired killers?"

"Their personalities never did fit with military life. I could tell that right off. They were always getting into scrapes with other soldiers. I noticed they would do pretty much anything for money and figured killing wouldn't bother them. It didn't."

"So, was that you at the hospital? Did you kill Hamilton?" Another sideways glance and this time no answer. "No, you couldn't have. You weren't here. How many killers do you have working for you?"

"Not enough, obviously, if I had to come home to take care of everything."

She frowned at the odd answer. "You came home because your wife was killed."

"Shut up and drive."

Brooke shot him a glance. "You had your wife killed, didn't you?" she asked, almost unable to wrap her mind around it.

"Oh, for the love of . . ." He sighed. "It was the only way I could leave Afghanistan immediately to take care of everything that was falling apart on this end."

"Did you love her?"

"Of course I loved her!" His throat worked. "But sometimes you have to sacrifice the one for the good of the many."

"For the good of the many?" She scoffed. "For the good of saving yourself, you mean."

His fingers closed into a fist, and for a moment she thought he'd hit her. He must have thought better about it and relaxed his hand. "And all of the other lives we've saved."

"While pocketing exorbitant amounts of money."

He laughed. "You think those families care about that? All they care about is getting an organ for their kid." He paused. "It's the kids that bring in the most money. Desperate parents. When I saw that look in my wife's eyes when Monica needed a heart, I knew. It's been very profitable."

"Until someone figured out what you were doing. Then it became cleanup time."

"Yes, but we won't be shut down for long."

"What about those kids? The orphans? What about their lives? Their hopes and dreams? Why is it okay to kill them like they're nothing?"

He shot her an odd look with his brow furrowed and eyes narrowed. "Because they *are* nothing. By taking their organs and letting someone else live—someone deserving who'll grow up to be something other than a terrorist—we're giving those children meaning and purpose."

Brooke swallowed. He was completely twisted, so caught in his evilness he was blinded by it. "Everyone was created for a purpose. Even those orphans—and it wasn't to be murdered. Cut up and used for parts. They weren't born to make you and others rich."

"Sacrifice. We all have to make sacrifices."

"You're not making sacrifices, you're leaving behind collateral damage. Innocent victims. People are dead because they were simply born in the wrong place at the wrong time—or married to the wrong man."

From the corner of her eye, she could see the muscle in his jaw flex.

"Like I said, shut up and drive."

TWENTY-EIGHT

Asher threw the gear into Park and opened the door. "Stay in the truck, PJ."

"But—"

"Just do it, please."

The teen jerked, surprise on his face. "Please? My dad would have ordered. Go. I'll stay here."

"Thank you." Asher raced up the front steps and knocked on the front door. "Captain Newell! Brooke!" Nothing. He knocked again with more force. "Brooke! Monica? It's Asher!"

He tried the door and found it unlocked. He shoved it open. "Monica?" The girl stood frozen on the steps, staring with wide, scared eyes.

A scream to his left sent his hand diving for his weapon. He curled his fingers around the grip and dropped into a crouch. A woman holding a dishtowel gaped at him from the kitchen entrance.

Asher held up a hand. "I'm sorry. I'm Asher James and I'm looking for Brooke Adams. I was told she might be in danger."

"I'm Ginny Howard, Yvonne's sister. Phillip called and asked me to come stay with Monica until he could get back."

"What about Brooke?"

"I don't know anything about her."

"She was here," Monica said, hugging herself with her arms, looking pale and frightened. "She came to talk to me, then Dad sent me upstairs and he—" She bit her lip.

"He what?"

"He pulled his gun and forced Brooke to leave with him," she whispered. "He told her he'd kill me if she didn't go."

Asher gasped. "What?"

His question echoed her aunt's.

Tears slid down Monica's cheeks. "I was wondering what had him so mad, so I spied on them." She let out a sob and dropped onto the step. "What's going on?"

Ginny ran to the girl and wrapped her arms around her. "Are you sure, honey?"

Monica nodded.

"PJ's in the truck," Asher said hoarsely, hardly recognizing his own voice. "I'm going to send him in here, then go after your dad and Brooke. Do you know where he's headed?"

The teen shook her head and sniffed. "No." Her head snapped up. "Wait. He said he was taking her to see if Dr. Frasier could use her. Dr. Frasier was the surgeon who did my heart transplant."

"Where?"

"At the Frasier Center."

Asher pulled his phone from his pocket and dialed Caden.

Monica's eyes met his once more. "She said he was involved in trafficking orphans for their organs. Is that true?" she whispered. "Please tell me it's not true."

Caden answered before Asher could figure out what to say. "This is Caden, what's up?"

"We know who's behind everything. It's Captain Newell. He's got Brooke and I think they're heading for the Frasier Center."

"The organ transplant place."

"Exactly."

"I'll get a team together immediately."

"See you there."

"No! Asher, you have to stay out of this."

"Brooke's there. I'm not staying out of anything." He hung up and turned to see PJ in the doorway, face pale, confusion written all over him. "I don't have time to explain right now, PJ, but I'll do my best later."

PJ gave a dazed nod and Asher darted out the door.

○ ○ ○

Brooke stumbled in front of Newell as he directed her via the muzzle of his pistol down a hallway. They'd slipped inside the medical facility through a back entrance, with him speaking on the phone in a low voice to someone named Buzz.

"Please think about this," she said. "You're going to kill me for nothing. The FBI and others have been working on this case, and they know what's going on."

"If that was true, they'd be beating down my door."

"Maybe, or maybe they're just biding their time, watching and waiting for the right moment to make their move."

"Right." He came to a door and pushed it open. "Get in."

"Please, sir, think about your kids. They need you."

"And if I let you live, they won't get me, will they?" He grabbed her bicep and shoved her into the room. "Besides, we can't let all of those healthy organs go to waste."

"Cap—"

He shut the door in her face. The low click of the dead bolt sliding into place chilled her. So that's why he'd kept her alive this long.

She let out a low scream and kicked the door. Her foot throbbed, but it made her feel slightly better. Then the shakes set in. She lowered herself to the floor with her back against the wall and dropped her forehead to her knees. What was she going to do?

She gave in to the despair for several minutes, then drew in a fortifying breath and looked around. "Think." Her only hope of survival was escape.

She rose, felt the wall for a light switch, and was rewarded. The space looked like any other storage closet. An old filing cabinet sat tucked away in the corner with one drawer half open. Cabinets lined the upper and lower portions of the wall to her left. A mop and water bucket rested near the coatrack on her right. Two rickety old chairs had been stacked and shoved into the far corner.

Brooke went to work pulling open drawers and cabinets, searching for anything she could use as a weapon until her eyes returned to the filing cabinet. She pulled the drawer open the rest of the way only to see a few paper clips, a rubber band, and a pair of fingernail clippers. Despair clawed at her. She stopped, panting, hands on her hips. *Think.* Could she pick the lock? That would be a no. MacGyver she wasn't.

Okay, then . . . no window, locked door, no weapon. No way out. She pressed her palms against her eyes. *Think, think, think.* She looked up. The air-conditioning vent was too small, but if she could remove one of the drop tiles . . .

Maybe. She closed her eyes and pictured the hallway. Yes, they'd passed patient rooms before reaching this one. She scooted the old chair next to the filing cabinet, hauled herself up onto the chair, then knelt on top of the filing cabinet. Working quickly, she pushed the tile nearest the edge of the wall up and slid it over on top of the one next to it. Rising to her feet, she pulled herself up until she was inside the ceiling to her shoulders. A quick glance revealed pipes and two-by-fours running above the drop tiles, which meant she could go over the wall into the connecting patient room and out the hopefully unlocked door.

Bracing her hands on the top of the wall and her feet on the portion below, she pushed herself up and scrambled onto the top of the wall, thanking God it didn't go any higher.

Resting for a moment, she listened. Heard nothing to indicate anyone was in the next room and reached for the ceiling tile nearest her. She managed to pull it up far enough to see the room was empty before she lost her grip and it dropped back into its rectangular resting place.

"Forget that."

Brooke sat up slowly, keeping her balance on the beam, and stomped her foot through the tile. It broke and fell to the floor in pieces. Thankfully, it wasn't as loud as she was afraid it might be. Without waiting to see if anyone was going to come bursting through the door, she edged off the beam and into the opening. Hanging halfway out of the ceiling, she looked down and found herself over the computer station.

With a grunt, she swung sideways and dropped.

The landing jolted her down to her bones, and for a moment, she simply sat there, breathing hard, her pulse racing. When she caught her breath, she scrambled to her feet and stepped over to the door. Gently, she pressed the handle and nearly gave a squeal of relief to find it unlocked. Hauling in a steadying breath, she cracked it and peered out into the hallway.

The empty hallway, thank goodness.

She needed to find the orphans—and a phone—but where to start? Since staying in the room wasn't an option, she slipped out and let the door shut behind her with a soft click. Brooke stepped to the next room and opened the door.

Empty.

The next three rooms turned up the same. No phone and no children.

Maybe she was searching the wrong floor? No. This was a busy facility overall, but this floor was practically a ghost town. Moving quickly, she continued her search room by empty room until low murmurs reached her. She stilled, then scuttled closer.

". . . ready in about fifteen minutes," a woman's voice said.

"Make sure they have enough of the drug to keep them out, then bring number zero four seven eight three to me."

"Of course, Doctor." Another woman's voice.

Footsteps hurried from the room and Brooke ducked into the nearest empty room she'd just checked. As soon as the woman was gone, Brooke peered around the doorjamb, only to pull back. Captain Newell was in the hallway.

"We've got a problem," he said to the doctor.

"What kind?"

"The kind that's not going to go away easily. We may be compromised. I think we should abort and walk away while we can."

"Meaning?"

"Get rid of the evidence while we can." Impatience tinged his tone. The stress must be wearing on him. Good.

"Are you insane?"

"No! I'm cautious."

"I'm not getting rid of already assigned organs. Now get out of here and go do what you do best. Make sure everything continues to run smoothly."

"Gerry, that's what I'm trying to do here."

"Excellent. Because I have surgeries to do."

Brooke held her breath and tried to control her rampant fear even while comforting herself with the knowledge that they didn't know she'd escaped yet.

After several nerve-racking minutes, more footsteps indicated the doctor and Newell were walking down the hall, away from her. Still, she waited. Was there anyone else in there? They'd talked pretty openly, so she was going to chance no one else was in there. Brooke scanned the hallway one more time, then slipped into the room adjacent to her hiding place.

Four beds. Four IV poles. And four dark-skinned, dark-haired, beautiful children. Her heart flipped and her stomach clenched. Two girls and two boys. The oldest girl looked to be fifteen or sixteen. The youngest, five or six. She had to be Paksima. The oldest boy appeared to be around ten and the other four. She'd found them. Now she had to figure out how to get them to safety.

The room was large, two rooms converted into one to give them the space to hold four beds, leaving room to work.

Hurried footsteps in the hallway shot adrenaline through her. She scurried over to the small closet, opened it, and squeezed inside, pulling the door almost shut, leaving a small crack to see through.

At first, all she heard were the footsteps, then a woman dressed in green and blue scrubs passed in front of her field of vision. A nurse. The sound of a bed unlocking and then rolling reached her. Heart pounding, Brooke watched it glide past and little Paksima's face blipped into view, then disappeared.

Brooke drew in a deep breath and blew it out slowly. She pushed open the door. The nurse screamed. Brooke grabbed her, shoved her against the wall, and threw a right cross that landed on the woman's cheek. Then a left jab to her stomach and a right uppercut to her face. She needed her unconscious. The nurse's eyes fluttered and she sank to the floor. Brooke's knuckles throbbed, but for the first time in her life, she was grateful for her father teaching her to box. She knelt and checked the nurse's pulse. She'd have a headache, but at least she'd wake up—unlike the children she helped murder.

Quickly, Brooke moved to each IV and shut off the drip. She figured it was a sedative to keep the children sleeping until they were taken into surgery to remove their organs. As soon as the drug wore off, they'd awaken.

She returned to the nurse and felt her pockets.

Bingo.

She pulled out the phone and tapped the screen. Password-protected, but she could still make an emergency call.

TWENTY-NINE

Asher had arrived at the Frasier Center seconds before the FBI pulled into the parking lot. Which meant he was able to slip into the building just in time. The foyer conveyed comfort, a feeling of peace and serenity. He let his eyes land on each person, watching as he hurried toward an interior exit door. Once inside, he stopped and thought. The first thing the FBI would do would be to start clearing the building. He had to make sure they didn't see him before he found Brooke.

He spotted a nurse heading down the stairs. "Excuse me, I was told there was some space to rent here. Where would that be?"

She frowned. "I haven't heard of any rental space."

"I don't think it's on the market yet."

"Well, the only area not used in this building is the basement."

"Of course. Thanks."

With a nod, she pushed open the door he'd just come through.

"On the floor! Everyone on the floor! Hands where we can see them!"

It had begun. Asher darted for the stairs leading down. If he'd calculated correctly, he'd entered on the second floor. He took the stairs as fast as he could move and found himself on the bottom floor. In front of a door with a key code.

Expecting that, he zipped under the stairs and waited.

And waited.

"Come on, come on."

Footsteps pounded above him.

The door shoved open and he heard a woman's voice. "I don't know what's going on!"

He darted from his hiding place and grabbed the person. She squealed and he gave the off-balance woman a push toward the stairs. "Go! Hurry!"

She did, racing up the stairs, and Asher slid through the door and found himself in the hallway of a busy area. An area that was supposed to be empty.

He didn't question how that could happen but instead went looking for Brooke.

"Hey!" A hard hand landed on his shoulder, spinning him around. "You can't be down here."

"Sorry—I think I can. Cops are here. You'd better run."

Wide blue eyes stared at him a moment before the man swallowed hard and took off for the stairwell.

Nurses and workers pushed past him, eyeing him, knowing he didn't belong there, but no one else said anything. He'd never find Brooke like this.

"FBI!" he yelled. "Everyone out of the building!"

For a moment, stillness. A piece of time frozen. Then, like ants, they scattered to the exits and doors.

"Brooke!"

He shoved open the next door. Empty. Then the next. Nothing.

A sign above the room to his right snagged his gaze. HOLDING AREA.

He pushed the door open to see Brooke kneeling over the body of a woman dressed as a nurse, phone pressed to her ear.

"Brooke!"

"Asher!" She threw herself at him and he caught her against him. "I'm so glad to see you!"

He lifted his phone even as his right arm trapped her. "Caden, in the basement, room labeled Holding Area."

"Put the phone down, James, and move toward the exit."

Newell. "You're done," Asher said without moving. "It's over."

"Maybe so, but I have enough money to disappear and live on it for the rest of my life. So I have no intention of giving up and going quietly. Now move."

Asher gazed down at Brooke, feeling her trembling. Shards of hate slashed at him and he drew in a breath. "No."

"So I shoot you and take someone else hostage?" He paused. "No, I shoot Brooke. Don't worry, I'll make sure it's a painful way to die."

Asher spun, keeping Brooke behind him. She gasped and stumbled. It was enough to knock him off balance and send him slamming into his former captain.

The man roared, lifted his weapon, and aimed it. At Brooke.

She ducked and Asher turned his back to the man, shielding her, expecting to feel the bullet burn a path through him.

Instead, the man pressed the muzzle against the back of his head. "Go."

Asher gritted his teeth and moved, following the directions he was given.

"FBI! Stop!"

Caden. Hope revived itself and Asher tried to stop, but Newell jabbed him with the weapon. "Move! Into that room!"

"Show your hands! Drop your weapon!"

Newell didn't bother to acknowledge the orders. Asher let Brooke go ahead of him into the room. Newell pulled something out of his pocket and held his thumb on . . . the kill switch.

A bomb.

"What are you doing?"

"Can't believe you risked your lives for a bunch of nothing kids. Kids who won't amount to anything and are nothing but a burden to those who have to take care of them. Worthless brats. They were just collateral damage in a stupid war until I gave them worth! I gave their lives meaning! And you've ruined it all!"

Newell pressed.

The building rocked and shook, and Asher's mind spun back for a brief moment to the explosion that had killed his unit members, his friends . . . his brothers.

Until Brooke's scream derailed his flashback. She knelt on the floor, hands over her ears.

"There's more where that came from!" Newell hollered. "Back off!"

Asher realized the man had always had an out—a plan—in case something like this happened. A plan that didn't include dying in an explosion he set. No, he wanted to live to spend his blood money. The bomb had been on the far side of the building. It was a warning. A scare tactic.

Newell tossed the kill switch and his hand aimed back for his pocket. Another kill switch?

Asher lunged. Shoved him back into the hall. He gripped Newell's hand and held on. The man roared, brought his weapon around.

The crack of a bullet echoed in the hallway and Newell's face exploded into a red mist.

Time slowed. Asher flinched and threw himself back. He fell to the floor and landed with a hard thud. "Brooke!"

She lay beside him but rolled at his shout. Relief shuddered through him. She wasn't hurt.

Her gaze went past him and her eyes stopped. Stared.

He turned to see Caden and his team rushing toward them, Caden's weapon still held on the dead man.

Time sped up once more and Asher rolled to his feet. Brooke scrambled up too. "The doctor," she gasped. "Geraldine Frasier."

"We've got her," Caden said. "She even gave up our mystery man too. Ever heard of Chester Howard?"

"Yeah," Asher said. "His nickname was Buzz. Only knew him for about four months."

"And he was one of my clients."

Asher turned to her and she met his gaze.

"I had him discharged as medically unstable. He was sent home the day of the bombing," she said.

"He and Phillip were in high school together," Caden said. "Got into a lot of trouble but managed to graduate and be model citizens for a while. He requested to be transferred to Newell's unit and finally got it."

"Was he suicidal or was he just playing me?" she asked.

"He shot himself when officers stopped him about a mile from here."

"Oh my . . ." Brooke drew in a deep breath. "Unbelievable."

"Anyway, we think we've gotten everyone involved. It's going to take some time to sort out, but it's over. The kids are safe." Caden shook Asher's hand. "And now you might want to go clean up a bit. Slasher movie isn't a good look for you."

"Right."

Brooke hurried back into the room. When she returned, she pressed a wet towel into his hand. He smelled alcohol. He rubbed his face until it was raw and the towel turned pink. She handed him another wet one, and he continued the process until he had himself as clean as he was going to get without a hot, steaming shower.

"We'll find you some scrubs to change into," she said.

Asher nodded. "It's over."

"Yes."

"They can't hurt anyone else."

"They can't."

For the next little while, he and Brooke stayed, watching the agents work. Finally, he blew out a breath. "I'm ready to go home."

"Home," she said. "That sounds amazing."

Epilogue

THREE MONTHS LATER

Brooke panted, sure she was going to die on the spot. "I . . . can't
. . . believe I let you . . . talk me into this."

Asher grinned back at her. "We're almost there. You can do it."

"I must be . . . insane," she gasped, "to have agreed . . . to this."

"You'll be glad when we get there."

"If I live that long . . . What happened to our normal jog around
your neighborhood?"

"You needed a challenge."

She sputtered. "I take it back. I'm"—gasp—"not the"—gasp—
"insane one . . . You are!"

"If you can survive being kidnapped by a skilled soldier, this
should be a walk in the park."

"Yes! Good idea. Walk." She stopped and planted both hands
on her knees. Truly, she could keep going but wanted to catch her
breath so she wasn't huffing and puffing like the big bad wolf. It
couldn't be that impressive to the man who looked like he could
go another hundred miles. "When I work out—or jog with you in
the neighborhood—the ground is level and smooth beneath my

feet. There's not an incline like this. What made you think this would be a good idea?"

"The view. Come on. Twenty more yards and we're there."

"No."

"I have trail mix. You can have some when we get there."

With a groan, she pushed forward. True to his word, twenty yards later, she pulled to a stop with surprised wonder. A waterfall cascaded to the rocks below, crashing and splashing in glorious splendor. "Oh my. What is this place?"

"Moonshine Falls."

"What?"

"People used to make moonshine here."

"Hence the name. Wow. It's gorgeous."

"Worth the hike?"

She offered him a small smile. "When you suggested going running, I had no idea it would lead here. No wonder you gave me a list of things to bring."

"You did great." He grabbed her hand. "Come on."

"Asher. Seriously? What now?"

"We go down."

"Down? We just came up! And where's my trail mix?"

With a laugh, he gave a gentle tug and she fell into step behind him.

And soon found herself on the back side of the waterfall. Every so often the spray would mist over them. She laughed. "Look. There are still moonshine drums here! Think there's anything left in them?"

"No. I'm pretty sure they were drained years ago."

Her smile faded and she watched him, her heart beating in her throat—and not from the exertion. "This is fabulous, Asher, thank you."

He pulled her into a hug and she decided she didn't mind that she was half frozen and getting damp. His embrace warmed her from the inside out.

"We've had a tough run of it," he said. "To tell you the truth, I can't believe we actually survived."

"I know. I feel the same. I just thank God we did." She swallowed. "And to see Kristin and Paksima together was a miracle. She's really going to get to stay in the US?"

"Because there's a price on her head back in Afghanistan, Caden said the request to offer her asylum was approved. Kristin is a certified foster mother and has been for a while." He gave her fingers a quick squeeze. "I think it's working out exceptionally well."

"Yes. Exceptionally."

"I still dream," he said out of the blue. "I still jump at unexpected loud noises. I still zone out sometimes. But . . . I'm better." He tilted her chin and placed a kiss on her lips. "That's thanks to you. I just wanted to tell you that."

"Thank you, but I didn't do anything. Running for our lives and stopping killers has kind of taken precedence over active counseling."

"Hmm. True, but you did do something. You *do* something. You just do it without realizing you're doing it."

"Okay, that's nice." A pause. "What? I'm confused."

He threw back his head and laughed. "Like that."

"Like what?" She gave him a light punch on the arm.

"You're funny and you don't know it. You make me laugh without trying. And when I look at you, I want to smile."

"Oh."

"Oh? That's it?"

"No, I'm trying to figure out how to tell you that I love you." He went still. "You do?"

"I really do." She pressed a kiss to his sweaty cheek. "I've been falling for you ever since you started following me around on base."

"What?" His cheeks went red.

"I noticed."

"I sure didn't notice you noticing." He grimaced.

She laughed. "Miranda called. She said Isaiah's being awarded a medal of honor. His full benefits have been reinstated. She said to tell you thank you."

He gave a slight shrug. "It was the least I could do."

"Hmm. But that's you, Asher. And it's simply one of the reasons I love you. You have a courageous heart, a passion for helping others, and a loyalty to those you love that most people have a hard time understanding. I find those traits very attractive."

He blinked, his jaw working. She could see how deeply her words had affected him. It took him a moment to gather himself and she let him do it. "I'll be honest. I never thought I'd find someone like you," he said. "Someone I can see myself spending the rest of my life with. But . . ."

"But what?" she whispered.

"My self-esteem has been in the toilet since I got back from Afghanistan. I try to act like my brother's words roll off—and most of the time they do—but sometimes, a few of them stick and I wonder if he's right. I wonder what my worth is and what I'm here for. And the fact that he put you in danger like he did makes me wonder if I'll ever forgive him."

"Asher . . ." She grasped his hands and squeezed. "Surely, you can see that God has big plans for you. And you saved my life several times, so I see lots of reasons you're here. As for Nicholas, I think he very much regrets his childish behavior."

"Possibly."

She could tell he wasn't really thinking about his brother, though. "What is it?"

"It hit home when the captain said those kids were nothing more than collateral damage. He said they were collateral damage due to the war, but I see it more about the money. The target was the money and they died because of the all-consuming greed to reach that target. He believed those kids had no worth except to save the lives of those who were worthy in his eyes, those who would grow up to make a difference in the world. He really believed that."

"I know. He was a sick man, but Monica and PJ are with their aunt now. She seems like a good woman who really loves them. They'll be okay in the end."

"I pray you're right." He glanced at her. "I promised PJ I'd still come see him and we'd hang out occasionally."

"I promised Monica the same," she said.

"Each of those children who were killed—and the soldier who tried to protect them—had a purpose for being here on this earth," he said. "Unfortunately, we'll never know what they would have grown up to be—or do—or the lives they would have impacted. But they had purpose. They had worth. They were created for a reason."

"Yes," she whispered. "Just like us."

"Just like us."

"And it's up to us to continue to impact lives," she said. "To make sure every person we meet realizes they have worth."

"How are we going to do that?"

"I don't know. We'll pray about it and see what God does, okay?"

"I'm good with that." He held her while the water rushed down. "Brooke?"

"Yes?"

"I love you too."

"I know."

His laughter rumbled under her cheek. She lifted her head and his lips closed over hers. For the first time in a long while, she couldn't wait to see what tomorrow held. Because even though they still suffered the effects of their experiences, they would face them together.

Asher pulled back and ran a hand over her cheek. "You ready to go?"

"Go where?" she asked, eyes still closed.

"Home."

"Does that entail walking?"

"Yes."

The amusement in his voice lifted her lids. "Then no." She sat on the nearest rock and held out her hand. "My trail mix, please. I'd like to enjoy it while I wait here for the medevac."

Asher gave another shout of laughter and kissed her again.

Yep, she decided. She might just stay here forever.

CHAPTER
ONE

Sarah Denning sat on the dirt floor of the Afghani prison cell and shivered in the ninety-degree heat, fighting the fear that had been her constant companion since the Taliban had attacked the school. One minute she'd been a guest teacher at the request of her friend Talia Davenport; the next, a prisoner of cruel men who would use her and kill her without blinking.

She tugged the piece of cloth covering her head lower and patted the bottom section that concealed her mouth and nose, while praying she could stay hidden until they were rescued. If rescue was even on the way. If their captors found out she was an American . . . or worse, who her father was—

The guard gave the barred door a violent tug and she jumped, her heart stumbling into overdrive. The door held fast. She doubted he was worried it wouldn't. He let out a satisfied grunt and turned to walk down the hallway, his boots pounding the dirt floor before he disappeared from sight. Sarah's pulse slowed a fraction. The longer he stayed gone, the better their chances of rescue. However, how long would that be?

"Sarah?"

The whisper reached her from the corner of the cell. "Fatima?"

"I'm coming over there." The teenager crawled on all fours, dodging her classmates, to curl against Sarah's side with a shiver. "What's going to happen to us?"

Sarah wrapped an arm around the fifteen-year-old. During her weekly guest teaching spots, she'd come to recognize Fatima as a bright, highly motivated young woman with the desire to be a pioneer in bringing change to her country. Sarah had treasured those days at the school and building relationships with the girls. "I don't know."

But she did. They all did.

"They're going to sell us," Samia said from the other side. "We're to be brides to the Taliban, aren't we?"

Brides? More like sex slaves. Punching bags. Assigned to a life of abuse and misery. And terror.

She, Talia, and the twelve students had been taken from the school and loaded into the back of a waiting van. No one had tried to stop them, and she hadn't dared resist. Approximately twelve hours later, they'd arrived here.

Wherever here was.

"I'm so sorry, Sarah," Talia whispered, her voice cracking, her fear tangible. "I've been there for three years, and while we've had a few minor scares, there's been nothing like this."

"It's not your fault, Talia, you couldn't know."

"I don't want to be a Taliban bride." Nahal, the youngest of the girls at thirteen years old, scooted closer to Sarah, as though Sarah could keep that from happening.

Sarah had been afraid before, but the images filtering through her mind sent the horror clawing inside her to a whole new level. She pulled in a steadying breath, desperate to find a way to remain calm and be strong for the other girls in the ten-by-twelve cell, because while she wanted to fight back, any sign of defiance would only get her—or one of the teens—killed.

She shuddered and let her gaze roam their prison. It consisted of four cement walls with a door on the one opposite from where she sat. A small barred window above her head streamed a thin ray of light, cigarette smoke, and low voices that sounded like they were arguing, although she couldn't make out the words.

Except for a brief stop at the outhouses lined up along the south wall that included lewd looks and a few comments she'd pretended not to hear, she and the other girls had been left alone by their captors.

Which was confusing, but welcome. However, she didn't expect that would last much longer. The one thing allowing her to keep her fear under control was the fact that they hadn't been searched. Knowing it would happen at some point, she'd seized the opportunity during a chaotic moment to snag the satellite phone from the pocket of her burqa. Using the bodies crammed against her as a shield, she'd pressed the SOS button and sent out her distress signal.

Minutes passed, the only sounds the hushed whispers and terrified weeping of her cellmates mixed with the low voices of the guards outside the window. Sarah leaned her head against the wall and watched the hallway while her hand searched through the folds of the cloth. Fatima looked up at her as Sarah's fingers closed around the sat phone. Did she dare take a chance to see if anyone had called? If there was a message? If help was on the way? All she had to do was sneak a peek.

"Don't ask why," she whispered to Fatima, "but can you sit slightly in front of me?"

"Yes." The girl moved enough to shield her from the guard's gaze, should he return.

With shaky fingers, she pulled the phone from her pocket.

"What are you doing?" Talia asked. Her eyes widened at the sight of the phone. "If they know you have that, it won't be good."

"I know. I need to find a place to hide it."

She glanced at the screen. Nothing. No response that her plea for help had been seen. Cold dread sent a wave of nausea through her. The SOS should have gone out to her brother, FBI Special Agent Caden Denning, and to their father, Lieutenant General Lewis Denning. Even if her father ignored the message, Caden should have been able to track the phone and have help on the way before these monsters could blink. He might be in the United States, but he had a long-range reach. As did their father. She'd thought carefully about adding him to the SOS list, then decided to do so "just in case."

This situation was about as "just in case" as one could get, and for once, she was glad her father was who he was—although she'd bite her tongue in half before admitting it. Then again, if admitting it would get them out of here, she'd shout it from the rooftops.

Surely, the message had gone through. She pressed the SOS button once more and slipped the phone back into her pocket. Caden would do something. Her father? The last time she'd talked to him had been when he'd told her he disinherited her for going into the Army. She'd laughed. "I don't need or want your money." She needed and wanted his love, but that had never been within her grasp.

Because of her ongoing conflict with her father, Sarah had kept a low profile, never acknowledging her relationship to the powerful man. Just before she'd joined the Army, she'd dyed her blonde hair a dark brown and decided to go by a different first name, insisting her family get used to calling her by it. Her only feature that might draw attention to her was her green eyes. Otherwise, with her flawless Pashto, she should be able to pass as a native. At least, that's what she told herself.

The guard's heavy footfalls sounded in the hallway once more, and her adrenaline spiked. Another guard joined him. They stood at the door grinning and pointing, talking openly about the girls' futures. Bile rose in the back of her throat, even as the comforting presence of the phone pressed into her hip.

Please, Lord, send help.

o o o

Former Army Ranger and Special Ops soldier turned private contractor Gavin Black monitored the situation. From his position just outside the compound, protected only by a hill of sand, he could hear the faint hum of the plane's engine fifteen thousand feet above him. "It's a go," Gavin said into the headset. "Once you're down, wait for my signal." He'd gone ahead, on the ground and at great risk to himself, to make sure the others could breach the compound in a way that would catch the occupants off guard—and give him and his team the advantage. Mere seconds would make the difference between life and death.

When the lieutenant general had called Gavin and requested his services, he hadn't been able to refuse—and not just because of the man's rank.

"My daughter's been kidnapped," he said, "taken by the Taliban from a school where she was a guest instructor. She, another teacher, and twelve female students are being held at a compound in the middle of the Registan Desert. The only way in without detection is to drop in at night."

Registan Desert? There was more than one compound in that suffocating place. "Which compound, sir?"

"Hibatullah Omar's. And they're saying he's behind the kidnapping."

Gavin stilled. Of course it would be *his*. "That's not possible. Omar's dead." Gavin had been a part of the raid that led to his death. But another terrorist organization could have taken over the compound.

"Somehow he's risen from the grave. We've received satellite footage that he's up and running again. You know that compound. You lived there for over a year. I need you to put together a team and get Sarah and the others out of there."

Yes, he'd lived there. Working undercover as a terrorist, gaining the trust of one of the most horrific murderers in the Middle East. And Gavin had set him up to die. If Omar was truly alive, then he'd know about Gavin's betrayal.

Already on the ground in Kabul for another reason, Gavin had dropped what he was doing and quickly navigated his team onto this assignment.

Rochelle Denning. Also known as Sarah. He'd met her in Kabul when they'd been deployed at the same time. Met her and found her fascinating. They'd gone out for three dates, shared an amazing kiss, and then she'd quit answering his calls and texts. Not one to tread where he wasn't wanted, Gavin had let it go in spite of his confusion over her sudden cold shoulder.

The general had shared that Caden had already called his resources with the FBI, but they wouldn't be much help in the Registan Desert.

The men in the plane would parachute far enough away to remain undetected, then make their way across the open fields of sand to the compound and to the north wall, where Gavin would meet them and lead them inside. With the night vision goggles and binoculars, he could make out the entrance he'd used to come and go undetected when he was living at the compound.

"There's no way that's Omar," Cole Lawton said, his voice clear in Gavin's ear.

"I wouldn't have thought so either," Gavin said, keeping his voice low, "but the pictures don't lie."

"I saw his body, Black. He was burned to a crisp. We've got pictures of that as well, remember?"

"Yeah." And before they could extract that body for DNA testing, they'd come under fire and had to fight for their lives to make it to the waiting bird.

He blinked against the memories. Unlike many of the people he served with, he didn't suffer nightmares often, but that didn't mean he wanted to dwell on the stuff nightmares were made of.

"You think they know who they snatched?" Lawton asked. "That she's Denning's daughter?"

"I sure hope not." Because if those killers knew they had the daughter of one of the highest-ranking men in the US Army, there would be no saving her. He checked his watch, then the altitude of the plane. Just a few more seconds, then . . .

"It's go time," he said. "You know what to do."

"You sure this is going to work?"

"I'm sure." Mostly.

"What's Plan B?"

"There is no Plan B. I don't believe in them."

With the pack on his back and night vision goggles over his eyes, he watched the plane. His adrenaline pumped at an all-time high. "Three seconds," he said, mentally counting down.

On cue, the men propelled themselves out one at a time. Gavin could almost imagine he was with them, spreading his arms, feeling the wind pressing against him. He shuddered and focused back on the compound. He had to time it just right, which was why he was going in on the ground and not coming down through the sky. Among other reasons. But the most important was that he have the door open when his team arrived.

"I'm coming, Sarah," he whispered. "Hang on, I'm coming."

CHAPTER

TWO

Sarah had buried the satellite phone in the corner of the cell's dirt floor only minutes before the guard had returned. Since then, he'd stayed just outside the door, and one hour turned into two.

"What are they waiting on?" Fatima whispered.

"I don't know." Every so often another guard would come and the two men would exchange whispers. Then he'd turn and hurry down the hallway, only to return a half hour later to repeat the whole thing. "I'm going to move to the door and see if I can hear what they're saying," she whispered to Fatima. "Stay put."

Eyes wide, Fatima nodded.

On hands and knees, so as not to draw attention by standing, Sarah moved through the group, pressing a comforting hand on a shivering teen's shoulder or squeezing the ice-cold fingers of another as she passed. Talia's terrified gaze met hers, and she pressed her lips together, her displeasure at Sarah's movement clear.

But if the phone hadn't worked like it was supposed to, they were going to have to know what was going on. At the door, she slid against the wall. The other guard should be returning any moment. As though he'd read her mind, footsteps pounded down the hallway to stop in front of the door. His radio crackled and

Sarah thought she caught the words, "Search them one by one. Bring her to the conference room. We will make the video there."

Bring who?

"Get up! All of you!"

Sarah jerked at the order and slowly stood. The other girls followed her lead.

The guard who spoke was in his early thirties with a long beard and body odor strong enough to knock her out.

And a rifle gripped in his right hand.

When all of them were standing, huddling together, the guard threw open the door and lifted the rifle. He pointed it at Fatima. "You. Come with me."

Fatima stepped through an opening in the group. When she reached Sarah, she grabbed Sarah's hand in a death grip. The teen shook like she'd splinter apart any second.

The guard jabbed Fatima with the rifle. "What is your name?"

"Fatima."

"Remove your head covering."

Slowly, Fatima pushed the cloth away, her eyes downcast.

"It's not her," the other man said. "But I will take her for a little while." He jabbed his weapon at Fatima. "Come with me."

The teen shuddered but didn't move to obey the order.

The guard's eyes gleamed. "Come, I said. Obey or die. Which will you choose?"

Still gripping Sarah's fingers, Fatima lifted her chin. "I choose to die."

A multitude of gasps sounded behind her.

He pulled the trigger. Fatima jerked and fell, her hand sliding from Sarah's grip.

Screams echoed.

"Fatima!" Heart pounding, ears ringing, Sarah dropped to her knees and pressed hard against the wound, barely able to control the rage she wanted to unleash on the guard. But the girl . . .

"Fatima," she whispered.

"It hurts," Fatima whimpered.

The rifle jabbed Rashida, the girl next to Sarah. "You. Get up."

"Kinaaz," Sarah said, "come press on her wound."

Without hesitation, Kinaaz, the gentle soul who loved poetry, nature, and puppies, darted to her friend's side and replaced Sarah's hands with her own.

"Hold on, Fatima," Sarah whispered, "help's coming."

"I said get up!"

Rashida wailed and covered her head with her arms. The guard adjusted the rifle.

"Stop! Don't shoot her!" Sarah stood and stepped between the rifle and the other girls, ignoring the nausea curling in her gut. "What do you want?" she asked, keeping her head lowered but watching him through her lashes.

His eyes glinted and raked her up and down. "I didn't tell you to interfere."

Sarah waited for the bullet. It didn't come, but she thought he considered it.

"Remove your head covering."

Sarah reached to do so, and the smile that split his lips turned her stomach once more. He jerked the rifle, indicating she was to hurry up.

The guard behind him chuckled and muttered something under his breath.

Gunfire erupted from the hallway, and the terrorist flinched, his rifle wavering for a fraction of a second. She lunged at the man, slamming her elbow into his throat. He went down, and she clamped a hand around the barrel of the rifle and rolled, jammed the stock into her shoulder, and aimed it at his face.

He charged at her and she pulled the trigger. Felt the kick against her shoulder. His face exploded into a red mist.

Bullets spit into his partner behind him. Footsteps pounded on the dirt floor. Another spray of gunfire above her head brought screams from the girls still in the cell. Fire exploded in her side and then her arm.

Just as quickly, the shooting stopped.

Ears still ringing, Sarah ignored the burning pain just under her rib cage and swung the rifle toward the hallway that opened into the area where she and the teens were being held. When she spotted US Army uniforms, she dropped the weapon and lifted her hands above her head. One hand. She couldn't lift the other without massive agony racing through her arm.

"Move away from the weapon!"

"Hands! Show me your hands!"

The commands rolled over her and she let out a sob of relief. "Don't shoot!" she screamed. "Don't shoot! I'm an American!"

"Sarah!"

The voice came from behind the first soldier. Even in her terrified, semiparalyzed state, she recognized the voice. "Gavin!"

He rushed to her and snagged the rifle from the dirt.

She refrained from launching herself into his arms. Instead she yanked the burqa covering from her head and drew in a ragged breath. "Thank God."

o o o

Gavin lowered his weapon, helped her remove the rest of her burqa, and stared into green eyes he'd recognize anywhere. "Sarah."

"About time you guys showed up," she said.

"Had to stop for a burger. Knew you could take care of yourself until we got here." His words came out gruff, filled with emotion he had no right feeling at the moment. Surprised, he cleared his throat.

She huffed a short laugh that ended on a hiccuped sob. "Right." She didn't take her eyes from the man on the floor. "I killed him."

"No, you didn't." He listened to the voice in his ear. "The threat has been neutralized." They were safe for now. Plan A had worked.

She swiveled her gaze to him. "What?"

"You missed."

"Not even. I don't miss."

"Whatever the case. We need to get out of here."

She stepped forward and hugged him. "I'm so very glad to see you."

"Same here." He gave her a quick squeeze and she gasped. He frowned but was intent on their next move. "Come on, we've got to go before their reinforcements arrive. You ready?"

"As long as there's room for the other girls. Fatima is injured and needs a doctor."

"There's room and we have a medic with us." He turned to the girls in the cell and, in Pashto, said, "All of you, follow those two soldiers and we'll get you to safety."

His Pashto must have been good enough, because the girls hurried from the cell. He stepped over to the fallen teen and her friend, who still knelt beside her, hands covered in blood but still pressing hard. "Don't take your hands away yet, okay?"

She nodded.

"Gavin?"

He turned.

Sarah's hands clasped her side. She swayed, then sank to her knees.

"Sarah!" He strode back to her. "You've been hit."

"Thank you, Captain Obvious. I hadn't noticed."

He slung the rifle over his shoulder and caught her just as she passed out.

Acknowledgments

I'm so very grateful for those who were willing to answer my questions! ANY mistakes can be laid at the author's feet, not these fabulous resources.

Many thanks to the following people:

My family! I love you all bunches. Thanks for always encouraging and supporting me!

My Greenville, SC, brainstorming group—Edie Melson, Emme Gannon, Linda Gilden, Erynn Newman, Lynn Blackburn, Tammy Karasak, Michelle Cox, Alycia Morales, and Molly Jo Realy. I love you ladies!

My suspense brainstorming group—Lynn Blackburn, Colleen Coble, Robin (Miller) Carroll, Voni Harris, Carrie Stuart Parks, Pam Hillman. I couldn't do this without you guys. Thanks for all the fantabulous ideas!

Tim and Melanie Rose—wonderful fans who offered insight into the world of the army. Thank you!

Corporal William Ryan Tinsley—stationed in Afghanistan. Thank you for answering my many texts and for your service, Ryan! Stay safe!

Brian and Ronie Kendig—Thank you so much for reading and providing feedback on the first draft of the initial scenes in the book. You guys are awesome. And readers, if you don't know about Ronie's books, you're missing out. Check out her website at www.rapidfirefiction.com.

Judy Melinek, MD, Forensic Pathologist, Alameda County Sheriff-Coroner's Office CEO, PathologyExpert Inc.—thank you so much for putting me in touch with the fabulous Grace Dukes.

Grace Dukes, MD, Forensic Pathologist, Pathology Associates, Greenville, SC—thank you so much for answering all of my questions! I can only hope I did justice to your answers! If not, readers know that's on me, not you. :)

Thank you always to the incredible team at Revell. I love working with you guys!

Thanks to my agent, Tamela Hancock-Murray. Thank you for always having my back. I love you, my friend!

And most especially, thank you to this incredible guy:

Vincent Davis—SPC (Specialist) Davis, 489th Civil Affairs Battalion—thanks aren't enough. You are amazing. I so appreciate all the time and effort you put into making the opening of this book just perfect. And if y'all like historical reads, look him up on Amazon. He's an awesome writer. AND, if you need any marketing help, Vincent is your guy. Check out his Warrior Book Marketing Group at: http://warriorbookmarketing.com/.

Again, thanks to you all!

And last, but the One who is ALWAYS first—thank you to my Lord and Savior, Jesus Christ, who allows me to do what I do. Please bless these words and allow them to touch someone's life.

Lynette Eason is the bestselling author of *Oath of Honor*, *Called to Protect*, *Code of Valor*, and *Vow of Justice*, as well as the Women of Justice, Deadly Reunions, Hidden Identity, and Elite Guardians series. She is the winner of three ACFW Carol Awards, the Selah Award, and the Inspirational Reader's Choice Award, among others. She is a graduate of the University of South Carolina and has a master's degree in education from Converse College. Eason lives in South Carolina with her husband and two children. Learn more at www.lynetteeason.com.

Connect with
LYNETTE

Sign up for Lynette Eason's newsletter to stay in touch on new books, giveaways, and writing conferences.

LYNETTEEASON.COM

 Lynette Eason | LynetteEason

Printed in the United States
By Bookmasters